HIDDEN
VALLEY
ROAD

HIDDEN VALLEY ROAD

A NOVEL

PAULETTE ALDEN

Published in the United States of America

Library of Congress Cataloging in Publication Data:
Alden, Paulette, author
Hidden Valley Road: a Novel / Paulette Alden
Greenville, S.C.: Radiator Press
Identifiers: Library of Congress Control Number: 2024918939
ISBN: 978-0-9885189-4-0 (pbk.)
978-0-9885189-5-7 (ebook)
Subjects: South Carolina—Fiction. / Greenville, S.C.—Fiction. /
Racism—Southern State—Fiction.

Cover photograph: Paulette Alden
Cover Design: *the*BookDesigners
Interior Design: *the*BookDesigners

For Jeff

CHAPTER ONE

LEE TRAMMELL JR. and Smoky, his fifty-pound, mixed-breed black dog, stepped out of his trailer in Blue Ridge, South Carolina, into the rising heat of late May for their morning constitutional. He carried a leash, but Smoky ran free, dashing into the empty field next door, his doggie heart wild with anticipation: maybe there would be an exciting forest critter in the high weeds there—a coon or possum, or possibly a black or king snake. Smoky didn't actually want to catch anything, being nonviolent at heart, though Lee figured if the right circumstances presented, he could go for a kill. After a futile search, Smoky came running back, pink tongue hanging out, and Lee leashed him, at least until they cleared the scattering of modular homes, one-story red-brick houses, and double-wides that lined Hidden Valley Road.

He was meeting the Lunch Bunch at noon at the Golden Corral. He wondered if they knew it was his seventy-fifth birthday. He hoped not. They'd met on the fourth Saturday of every month for the last fifteen years, except in August when it was too damn hot to go out. They'd had two attritions this year: Jonny Williams succumbed to lung cancer, and Erskin

Meadows' daughter finally stabled him in a home. Erskin had gone down fast, a series of strokes. Now when Lee visited him, which, granted, was not that often, about the most he could do was wipe the drool off Erskin's chin. In high school he'd been their star basketball player; a tower of strength.

He had come to the last house before the forest reclaimed the land, a concrete block structure, painted white once-up-on-a-time, with a crumbling red-brick chimney and cement steps, also crumbling. Time and the elements had won the battle. Lee stood looking at it. The McBees were there one day and gone the next. McBee was a prominent name over in Greenville, Vardry McBee having been one of the city found-ers in the 1800s. But these McBees weren't prominent; they were Black and kept to themselves. The neighbors down the road, the Dunlaps, whose place was littered with wrecked cars and rusted farm equipment, had recently hung a large Confederate flag on a flagpole tall enough to be at the state capitol in Columbia. The McBees had gotten the message.

Lee unleashed Smoky, and he was off into the woods. The McBees had identical twin boys, shy, nine or ten years old. They were afraid of Smoky; Lee had always kept him leashed when he walked by their place. One day a week or two ago, when the boys were out front, he'd asked if they wanted to pet him. They hung back on the far side of the ditch, pushing each other to go first, giggling with fear and mounting bravado. Lee told Smoky to sit, and he waited, patient and calm, until the boys found their courage. Finally they jumped the ditch and approached. After a few false starts, reaching forward then pulling back, first one boy and then the other gently stroked the silky black fur on Smoky's back. Identically, like mirror im-ages, they looked up at Lee, their faces glazed with glee.

Now their house was abandoned.

He'd had only a nodding acquaintance with the parents. He regretted that. He could have been a better neighbor. He'd met the father once, when he came knocking on Lee's door, wanting to borrow a crescent wrench. Introduced himself, polite and friendly: Marcus McBee. A tall, strong, friendly-seeming man on the jet-black end of the spectrum. Lee hesitated; he didn't like to loan his tools. But he went to his toolbox, leaving the man standing at the door, and handed the wrench over without asking him in or what the problem was. The man returned it the next day, along with a loaf of banana bread wrapped in foil. Even then Lee hadn't introduced himself, offered his hand.

Now they were gone. It chewed at him. He wasn't much of a Christian, had stopped going to church decades ago. But he'd imbibed the teachings: love your neighbor. Do unto others. And he of all people should have extended a neighborly welcome. Would they have felt they had an ally, that not everyone on the road was sending a not-so-subtle message? But maybe it was as simple as they'd found better housing or decided to change school districts. A million reasons. But they had to pass that big Confederate flag every day to get to the county road.

He'd reached the point beyond the McBees' house where the land turned to woods, mostly scrub pine and second-growth hardwood—sugar maples, sassafras, sweetgum, tulip poplars, briars. Part of the road ahead was so dark from the dense canopy of trees that cars turned on their headlights in the middle of the day. There was a deep mysterious ravine at the end of the road, not an official dump like the county ran, but a place where sorry people threw out their old mattresses, microwaves, tires, black garbage bags full of dead bodies for all he knew. Sometimes they didn't even bother to make it as far as the ravine, just left their shit on the side of the road. The ravine was deep and hungry, a big wide mouth that gobbled up everything that came its way; you couldn't even see or hear when things hit the bottom, if there was one. Voracious green leaves of kudzu blanketed the ravine, nature fighting back against what man discarded.

Smoky, off leash, renewed his search for forest creatures—chipmunks and squirrels, mostly, though an occasional box turtle would stump him by not coming out of its shell. If he barked in alarm, he'd come upon a snake, hopefully not a rattler. Lee would call him back, and usually he'd come for the Milk Bones he carried in his pocket. One time Smoky had scared up a skunk, and Lee had to wash him in buttermilk in the big metal washtub out back. It was weeks before the stink dissipated.

The day was heating up, the sky a resonant blue, the sun asserting command. Crows cawed down at the ravine. He wiped his forehead with a white handkerchief. Seventy-five years old today, he marveled, and his thoughts ran to his mother. She had passed at fifty-seven in 1981, when he was forty. A breeze stirred in the tall loblolly pines around him, like a hand passing over them. When he was little, her breasts were a safe place to nestle, her soft bulbous stomach a pillow where he laid his head. Her smell, always sour and sweet. At the end she was skin and bones. Breast cancer. The contradiction in that.

Growing up, he didn't know what had happened to his father. He was there one day and gone the next, just like the McBees. Lee was six, his brother Earl three, when their father stopped coming home. Lee didn't ask any questions: theirs wasn't a family that talked. Sometimes he'd miss his father, a feeling as deep and inconceivable as if he'd lost an arm or leg. Other times he'd *feel* his father. The feeling was different from a memory. Was it fear, was it hatred, was it love, was it longing? There was no name for it.

NOW, calling Smoky to come, he started home. He needed to call his grandson Lyle, check on him. He hadn't spoken to or seen him in weeks—a bad sign. Lyle's father Buddy, Lee's only child, had been killed in a flaming car wreck at 4 a.m. on the Asheville Highway. He was twenty-two years old. When he was nineteen, he'd knocked up an eighteen-year-old girl from Simpsonville. She had the child but wanted nothing more to do with Buddy or the baby. The girl's parents had raised Lyle with some financial help from Lee, and a rare, awkward visit. When Lyle was fourteen and running wild, they told Lee they'd had enough, it was his turn. He was sixty-five then, working full-time at the Greenville County Library and looking forward to a quiet retirement. But there was no one else to take Lyle.

Lyle was twenty-four now. He'd managed to finish high school, mainly because Lee kept on him, but he had no occupation to speak of, mainly working on junk cars as far as Lee could tell, though there was plenty he didn't know. Sometimes he'd see him with the Dunlap lads down the road, sitting around a cable spool that served as a table, drinking beer and smoking marijuana, no doubt.

He'd come to the McBee house again. No one was ever likely to move in. It would either weather and age like a decomposing body in the woods or be demolished. He thought of the two little boys who'd petted Smoky. Where were they now? How were they faring? Smoky was barking at the back of the house, and when Lee went around to find him, he saw a car parked back there, almost out of sight. The McBees' brown Dodge sedan. He was surprised they were back.

The two little McBee boys were standing on the top cement step of the back door. Smoky was wagging his tail, doing his "Come on! Let's play" bow, barking in invitation, while the boys stared at him wide-eyed. Lee caught him by the collar and leashed him, told him to sit. He fussed at him a little, mostly for show. "Bad boy. You scared the boys. It's okay," he reassured them. "He won't hurt you. He just wants to play."

"He didn't scare us none," one of them said defiantly.

"Okay," Lee said. "Well, that's fine, then. Would you like to pet him?"

"No," the other boy said.

"He's part retriever," he told the two boys, who had ventured down to the bottom step. "He loves to retrieve."

He looked around for a good stick. There were plenty of downed trees and old limbs beyond where the yard met the forest in back. He found a nice sturdy stick, bare of bark. Letting Smoky loose, he threw it to the edge of the yard. Smoky was after it in a flash and came prancing up to drop it at his feet, looking up at him expectantly: *Again*!

"Do you want to throw the stick?" he said to the boys.

Simultaneously they shook their heads, no.

"Maybell don't like sticks," one of them said.

"Is Maybell your dog?"

They shook their heads in tandem, yes.

Lee tossed the stick, and again Smoky retrieved it, dropped it, and sat expectantly.

"Are your folks here?" Lee asked, realizing it was a ridiculous question. The twins hadn't driven themselves there.

At this one of them—they were impossible to tell apart—called "Mama!" The back screen door opened, and a tall Black woman stood scowling in the doorframe, statuesque, her arms long, thin, and muscular in her sleeveless yellow dress. An unreadable expression passed over her angular face. He'd seen her occasionally hanging laundry on a line in the side yard, or when she drove by, she'd wave politely if he was out front. That was all.

"Mrs. McBee?" he said, standing up, leashing Smoky, who had taken to chewing on the stick. "I apologize for disturbing you. My dog was off leash. I didn't realize anyone was here. He ran around back here and barked at the boys. He just wants them to play with him. To chase a stick," he added.

"Can we throw the stick, Mama?" the one on the left asked.

"I'm Lee Trammell," Lee said to the woman. "I live down the road. The trailer on the right."

The woman nodded but said nothing.

"Can we throw the stick?" the other twin begged. "Just once, Mama?"

"Y'all shush and go on in the house," the woman said sharply.

Without a word, they squeezed past her through the screen door.

"I'm really sorry for the trouble," Lee said. "Smoky wouldn't . . ."

"I don't want trouble!"

Lee's eyes widened, and his eyebrows shot up in surprise. Maybe this was not just a quick trip to pick up something they'd left.

"I kept a key," the woman said. "In case we needed it."

"I see," Lee said. "That makes sense," even though it didn't.

She came out the door and sat down on the top step. The day was heating up, no breeze, and there were large sweat circles under her arms. She tucked her skirt around her legs. Her skin was walnut brown, and her shins had a chalky tint. She was wearing pink flipflops. It was no cooler on the steps, but at least it was in the shade. She stared out into the woods. Lee knelt down next to Smoky on one knee, even though that knee protested. "Do you want to throw the stick?"

The woman looked at him in surprise. After a long moment she stood up. "Yes," she said. "I most definitely do."

LATER, after she had heaved that stick as far as she could into the woods five or six times, she called the boys outside. "Now you take turns," she said. "Nice like." Smoky had been searching for the stick in the woods, and now he came and dropped it in front of the woman. *Again?*

"Jackson first," she said to the boys. "Then James. Then Jackson gets another turn. Then James. Take turns nice or I'll stop the game." She handed the stick to the boy named Jackson and sat back down on the top step. Jackson threw it tentatively into the yard. Lee could read Smoky's mind: *Aww, that was no fun!* He brought it back to Lee, and he handed it to James. James hurled it as hard as he could, and when Smoky brought it back, Lee handed it to Jackson. After a few more rounds, they began taking turns, petting Smoky, growing braver, forgetting their fear, turning it into a contest: Who could throw it farther?

"How do you tell them apart?" Lee ventured.

"What do you mean?" the woman said, but her attempt at humor fell flat. She patted the top step next to her, an invitation. "I wouldn't mind," he said. "I'm a little stiff. And my balance is not the best. I just hope I can get up without assistance." At that, she stepped down to the scrubby grass to give him a hand. He hoped he wouldn't pull her over but she was strong. They sat on the top step and watched the boys in silence for several long minutes. "Is there some trouble, Mrs. McBee?" Lee asked after a while.

"You mean why are we hiding out in an empty house?"

Lee, watching the boys and Smoky, took this under consideration. "I met your husband once," he said. "He borrowed a crescent wrench from me."

"Marcus." She paused. "He can be a mean drunk."

They sat again in silence. "I'm sorry. Does he know you're here?"

"It will pass," she said, standing up. "Okay, that's enough, boys," she called.

"I'm thirsty, Mama," James said, coming up to where they sat. "Me too," Jackson echoed. Smoky was panting, finally having had enough.

"Is the water still on in the house?" Lee asked.

"We have what we need." She paused at the screen door. "I forgot my manners, Mr. Trammell. My name is Delila. Don't start up that business about Samson. I heard that one a million times." She gave him a weak smile. "Call me Del. Okay, boys, let's go."

"Bye, Smoky," they said in unison and followed their mother into the house.

BACK at the trailer, he turned on the TV for background noise while he shaved, put out Smoky's kibbles, fried up two Jimmy Dean pork link sausages and two eggs. Made a pot of grits. He always woke up hungry for a hot breakfast. He didn't see how people could eat cold cereal for breakfast, though he often ate it for supper. He took his best pair of khakis out of the closet, inspected the crotch to make sure there were no pee stains. Seventy-five years old today, and a dribbler. Had to sit down like a girl. "Like a girl!" he informed Smoky, who lifted his alert face off his paws where he was lying on the hook rug. He gave Lee an inquisitive look.

It wouldn't take much for Marcus McBee to find Del and the boys if he wanted to. But the McBees were none of his business. He had his own fish to fry. He dialed Lyle's cell phone. Lyle lived—off and on—with his girlfriend in Greenville. Sarabeth. She had a nice three-bedroom red-brick ranch house in the Chick Springs neighborhood. Her parents had bought the house as an investment, letting Sarabeth live in it while she worked as a paralegal in one of the downtown law firms. The phone rang and rang but no answer. Lee frowned. He'd go by Sarabeth's after lunch, then, see if Lyle was there. Sarabeth was too good for Lyle, in Lee's opinion. He'd probably gotten her into marijuana for sure, but he prayed not those opioids he'd heard about on the news. Supposedly a doctor had to prescribe them. For pain. As far as he knew, Lyle had no pain—physical pain, that is. But from personal experience, Lee knew there were all kinds of pain: dark o'night pain; crazy-making pain; kill-yourself pain.

NOT sure when he'd be back, he let Smoky out back one more time. Smoky wouldn't mind the chance to sleep on the couch all day, as long as Lee returned by supper. He double-locked the trailer and backed his Camry out the red dirt driveway, avoiding the potholes. He passed the Pooles' double-wide, same vintage as his own, but gone to wreck and ruin, and farther down the road on the left, the Dunlaps' decrepit two-story farmhouse. He slowed to see if he could spot Lyle. The three Dunlap lads, as he thought of them, were sitting, per usual, around their wooden spool table. No sign of Lyle. He gave a short toot, enough to pass as friendly, but he couldn't forgive the Confederate flag. The ignorance of it. But of course it wasn't ignorance. They knew exactly what it meant, what they meant it to mean. Even they couldn't have missed how the state finally took down the flag—that big middle finger to South Carolina Blacks —at the capitol last year after Dylann Roof shot nine Black church members who had invited him into their Bible study group.

AS he drove the fifteen miles to the Golden Corral on the outskirts of Greenville, he wondered if Margo Williamson would remember today was his birthday. Unlikely. Her birthday was November 5, a date as unforgettable to him as December 25. When Lee first met her, she and her husband—husband!—had bought an old Victorian mansion a few blocks off Main Street in Travelers Rest, just north of Greenville. That was ten years ago. They'd moved to South Carolina from Minneapolis; her husband planned to make the old house into a bed-and-breakfast. Folly. Lee could have told them that from the start, not that they asked. Margo had been hired at the Greenville library, where Lee worked, as a children's librarian. She would be the breadwinner while her husband renovated the house.

They'd taken to each other from the start—not something Lee had experienced before. When Margo was introduced at an endless staff meeting, as she surveyed the room, her gaze landed on Lee and held. She was medium height and weight, looked fit, probably a walker, in her late fifties he guessed, her coloring pale, her hair auburn, naturally curly. Probably Irish extract. She had a perspicacious look, and he suspected a sardonic sense of humor. He was too shy to introduce himself that day while others crowded around to welcome her. But a few days later he ran into her in the staff room. "I've been wanting to meet you," she said, offering her hand, shaking his with a firm, dry grip while smiling into his eyes with her sage-colored ones. "I expect us to become very good friends," she said, surprising him.

Later, after they had gotten to be those very good friends, he asked her why she had chosen him. She said she didn't know. She just did. "When I first saw you, I could tell you're a person of substance. And you have a kind and ironic face."

"I'm funny looking, huh."

"Fishing for compliments," she admonished, and flounced away, dismissing him with a little wave over her shoulder.

He looked forward to seeing her every day at work; that was all; he took what he could get. He didn't really know if romantic love was what he felt, never having experienced it before. He just felt a pressure to be with her when she was absent, a need to see her. She was the only person he could have asked about such a feeling. But he couldn't imagine bringing it up, not to mention she was married. Married!

Three years after they arrived, Margo told him she and her husband were moving back to Minnesota. The bed-and-breakfast idea was not working out, to say the least, and her husband was buying a fried chicken franchise back in St. Paul. Lee felt almost felled by the news.

They corresponded frequently, letters in his mailbox, her perfect penmanship in blue-black ink on cream-colored envelopes. They were both great letter writers; none of that email stuff for them. He studied her address in Minneapolis: as foreign and remote as if it were the moon. At some point, her letters began to taper off. After weeks had passed since her last one, he wrote three more times, hoping maybe she had just been busy or . . . he didn't know. Finally, he understood she wouldn't be writing back.

It took him a long time to relinquish hope of seeing a cream-colored envelope in his mailbox—though occasionally he still did. Hope.

CHAPTER TWO

HE PULLED INTO the gravel parking lot of the Golden Corral All-You-Can-Eat-Buffet. A lot of cars and pickups were already in the lot and some he recognized: Sammy's bright red Corvette ZR1, the pride of his life; Buster's Pontiac Grand Prix; Bobby's practical pickup truck, the wheels coated in red mud from his long, unpaved dirt road; and Joey's "Cool Comfort" van with a white polar bear lounging with a cold tropical drink under a palm tree painted on the side. Air conditioning and refrigeration was a good business in South Carolina.

He didn't see his brother Earl's black Mustang, a new car every year, a perk from the Ford dealership. He'd hoped he'd be at lunch today. He wasn't officially part of the Lunch Bunch, but with their dwindling numbers, Lee had recruited him and occasionally he made an appearance. It would mean something if he remembered today was Lee's birthday. Earl was the opposite of Lee: glass not just half full but overflowing. He'd been married for fifty years to the same pleasant woman and had two successful sons, in that they were educated and employed. When Lee thought of Earl, he thought of an untroubled mind. It was refreshing, in a way, though it meant that they weren't close. They were friendly, if not friends, and that was enough. He admired how Earl had been able to plow through life, apparently no doubts, no worries slowing him down. He'd worked as a salesman at the Ford dealership in town for forty-five years, and in his heyday had made a six-figure salary, which he'd reminded Lee of several times a year. Well, why not? He deserved it.

The aromas from the noon buffet hit his nose as soon as he pushed open the heavy wood door: collard greens cooked with ham hocks, sweet potatoes in syrup, fried okra, canned green beans, meat loaf, ham slices floating in liquid, fried flounder, and baked and fried chicken. Always corn bread and bake-and-serve rolls. There was a cacophony of voices and clanking silverware, waitresses laying on Southern charm as they teased their customers, white and Black, urging them to *Go back, go back, plenty more where that come from.* Honey-colored sweet tea flowed like waterfalls from plastic pitchers. It still amazed him to see Blacks and whites together in a restaurant. For the first three decades of his life, no Blacks would have been welcomed here; might even have been arrested.

He spotted Sammy, his best friend since third grade, forty pounds overweight, thick bushy white eyebrows overhanging his blue eyes, and a white bandage on a shaved area of his scalp, surrounded by untamed white hair; he'd been to a dermatologist. His familiar laugh echoed across the room from the table where the Lunch Bunch was sitting. Buster and Joey pushed their chairs back to stand and shake Lee's hand, and the others, already digging into their lunches, waved their forks in greeting.

"Go get yourself a plate, man," Buster directed. "We waited on you like one dog waits on another!"

There in the middle of the table was a grocery-store bouquet of flowers with a balloon floating above: *Happy Birthday!* It had to be Sammy; he knew Sammy's birthday as well as he knew his own: June 27. One month apart. He knew Sammy's life as well as he knew his own. They'd been in each other's weddings, marrying a week apart. Big church weddings, as if that guaranteed a successful marriage; a successful life. Both marriages were on the rocks within five years. Sammy couldn't hold a job because of his drinking, and when he was loaded, he was aggressive and mean, totally against character. His lovely wife, Mary Lou, who had graduated top in their class, divorced him and promptly married a lawyer over in Spartanburg and moved away.

As for Lee, he too had married when he was twenty-five. Fifty years ago now; he could hardly believe it. Like they say, another life. Just a kid himself, and a lost one at that—just like Lyle, it pained him to think. Elaine had thought having a baby might fix whatever was wrong with the marriage; whatever was wrong with Lee. Buddy had been born premature and was in an incubator in the hospital for almost twelve weeks. Lee would look at his skinny wrinkled limbs, the tiny monkey face. He knew the words for what he should be feeling. But he felt nothing. Elaine did the feeling for both of them, and when she divorced him within the year, he didn't blame her; he wanted her to save herself. No one could stand under the dark cloud that was him back then.

"'Bout time you joined the club," Joey was raising his ice tea glass to toast him. "The Seventy-fivers."

"It's not as bad as it sounds," Buster deadpanned. "It's worse. If it's not your hip, it's your knees. If it's not your knees, it's your ticker. Not to mention you can't remember your own damn name!"

"Have you considered the alternative?" Sammy said, raising his bushy white eyebrows.

Just then Lee felt someone grab him around the middle from behind, lifting him a few inches off the floor. It could only be brother Earl. He'd been a wrestling champ in high school, while Lee had avoided sports as much as he could. How two boys from the same parents could be so unalike was just another mystery of life he'd never solve. He struggled out of Earl's body lock, and mock-punched him on the jaw. "Happy birthday to you-u," Earl began singing, "Happy birthday to you-uuuu-uuuu," he drew out comically, waving his arms for people to join in until some of the other diners began singing along with him. "Okay, okay," Lee said, motioning like a choir director for the singing to stop. "Glad you could make it, Earl. When did they start letting you off your chain? I thought you were always too busy to get away for lunch."

"It's not every day my big bro turns seventy-five. Let's go load up," Earl said, slapping Lee on the back and starting toward the steam table. "I got to be back in a jiff. Wonder if they got any liver and onions today."

Earl had been three when their father left; he couldn't even remember him. It was as if the family stock of worry, depression and anxiety, and light-hearted devil-may-care confidence and happiness had been divided between them—with Earl getting all the latter and Lee the former. But Lee had recovered. Just like Sammy had recovered from alcoholism. It had taken Sammy a lot of counseling, setbacks, struggle, and weekly AA meetings. But drink was no longer a part of his life. And Lee had made his own recovery. That was not to say that he'd changed character completely. He was no Earl. And it had taken almost half his life to start the upward climb. That had started when he was forty, and his mother, Emylyn, was dying of breast cancer.

H E was visiting her for Sunday lunch that cold, drizzly winter day in 1981. He'd driven over from the apartment he rented near the Depot in Greenville to her house in Berea, as he always did on Sundays. The temperature was hovering right around thirty degrees, and if it dipped lower, as it was forecasted to do, the rain would freeze. His drive home would be treacherous. They'd run out of conversation, and there were stretches of silence as they ate pot roast and mashed potatoes. Lee felt flat, unable to summon any words, but that was not unusual.

His mother, Emylyn, was fifty-seven years old then; she'd had Lee Jr.—named after his father, Lee Trammell—when she was seventeen, Earl when she was twenty. That winter of 1947, when Lee was six years old, he found his father's shotgun leaning against the dresser in his folks' bedroom. Usually it was mounted above the door out of reach, but his father got it down sometimes to go squirrel hunting on Paris Mountain. Lee knew better than to touch it, but he sat on the floor, cradling it across his lap so he could examine it. When his father came home, he screamed at Lee not to never touch his gun! He took off his belt and told Lee he'd teach him a lesson he'd never forget. And Lee never did. Before then, he had loved his father unconditionally and thought his father loved him the same. No more.

And there was more. His father stopped coming home for days, and when he did, Lee's mother said hardly a word to him. Lee shrank away when his father tried to hug him the way he used to do, the way he'd call him a sack of potatoes and throw him over his shoulder to make him laugh. Then came the day that spring when their mother took Lee and Earl to the big building with so many high steps on Main Street. That day floated in his memory in bits and pieces, fragments of a nightmare. The place was swarming with excited people, pushing and shoving to get in. He clung to his mother's hand, terrified he'd get lost or crushed in the crowd. Up in the balcony were the colored people, their faces expressionless. He saw his father sitting with a lot of other men up front on benches. He wanted to run to him, but he knew he couldn't. His mother put her arm around him and pulled him in close on the hard seat. He buried his face in her big soft breast. His mind closed down, no more sounds, no more sights, just the sweet-sour smell of his mother's sweating flesh.

After that, his father only came around on rare occasions, and at some point, he stopped coming. That summer his mother moved them to a cabin five miles outside of Slater, a tiny country town. Lee didn't know why one day they lived in the four-room house that was home and the next they were living in a cabin with bare pine walls. Granny and Papa stopped coming around and so did his father's folks; his dad's friends disappeared. His mother didn't explain. That was the way adults were; nothing was ever explained. He worried that his father wouldn't be able to find them if he returned one day, but something kept him from asking his mother about it.

His mother, who had always been at home, went to work at the Slater-Marietta mill, twelve-hour shifts. Aint Mary, who was not really an aunt but an elderly colored woman whom their mother paid $2.00 a week, kept Lee and Earl during their mother's shifts. Aint Mary earned her pay by listening to the radio and dozing off in the tiny front room while Earl and Lee played outside. The piney woods came right up to the cabin. There were prickly pine needles and pine cones everywhere, and golden resin that stuck to their fingers. Aint Mary would fix Earl and Lee peanut butter sandwiches when they were hungry. They'd eat in the shade under a big white pine and sleep off the afternoon heat on a scratchy wool blanket Lee had found in a cedar chest. He loved Aint Mary, who was motherly and kind and arthritic, missing all her teeth.

THAT cold winter Sunday in 1981, before his mother had served dessert, banana pudding, his favorite, Lee said he'd better start home. He went to the front window, which was covered in a sheer lace curtain, and pulled it aside to look out. The long needles of the pine out front were sheathed in ice. The weather was as good an excuse to leave as any. He felt a strong desire to go home and lie in bed. It would be a relief to be alone. He had to recharge, as he thought of it, before getting up the next day to be at the library by eight. He was reasonably good at his job—reliable, accurate, helpful. His work was mostly behind the scenes, cataloguing and in collections management and reference. He didn't enjoy his work, but at that time in his life, any enjoyment was above his pay grade.

He rose to clear the table, but his mother didn't rise to help. It was so unlike her, he looked at her. Her hair was thin and flat on top, something he hadn't noticed before. She was close to a redhead, but with more brown, and now he noticed, gray. A thin veneer of freckles covered her face; her arms in an old familiar sweater were folded on the crocheted table-cloth in front of her. She had her head down, as if in prayer, which was not like her. She wasn't religious, but more than that, she was a doer, not one to sit when there was work to be done, dishes to be cleared and washed. He paused, holding the mashed potato bowl with its chipped gold rim in one hand and his plate in the other.

"Sit down," she said without looking up. "I have something to tell you."

He set the dishes back on the table and pulled out his chair. It*'s bad*, he thought. *Something bad.*

She looked right at him, held his eyes. He saw her. He hardly ever looked at her she was so familiar. But he saw her face as it was now, not as it had always been: Mama. When had she aged? He hadn't noticed. She looked as if she'd been dusted with white powder. Deep wrinkles creased the sides of her mouth, and furrows were carved across her forehead. Puffy purple pouches under her eyes. When had all this happened?

"There's something in my right breast," she said matter-of-factly. "It's been there for some time. About the size of a peach pit."

He sat completely still, trying to understand the words, what they meant. Would mean. He could no longer feel his hands, so he spread them on the table and opened and closed his fingers to bring some life back to them.

"Have you been to the doctor?"

She shrugged.

"You have to go see Dr. Hawkins. Right away!"

"Of course I've been," she shook her head, half-laughing. "I'm not an idiot, Lee."

"What did he say?"

"There are treatments." She sighed, as if this were not good news. "Of course they'll take my breast. Then radiation and probably chemo." She didn't look at him.

He tried not to whimper. "But you'll live, right?"

She looked at him in that direct way she had. "Of course I'll live," she said. Then added, almost as an afterthought, "Until I die—just like everybody else."

THEY removed her right breast, leaving that side of her chest scarred and fiery red. She developed lymphedema in her arm, a painful swelling that landed her back in St. Francis Hospital. But the cancer spread to her bones. By summer she was down to seventy-six pounds. The nuns in their black and white habits, who reminded Lee of angels, gave her ice chips, morphine. Food was a distant memory. He could hardly believe he was going to lose her; it didn't seem possible. But to deny it was to deny his eyes. He and Earl took turns staying with her, and one August night, figuring the end was near, he sat by her bed in the semi-darkness, holding her good left hand, stunned into a stupor by the enormity of what he couldn't stop.

There was so much he wanted to ask her, so much he didn't know. *Theirs was not a family that talked.* But then suddenly, deep in the night, when he wondered if he had dropped off and was dreaming, she said clearly, "Do you remember?"

He couldn't believe she'd spoken; she'd seemed too far gone. He had prepared himself never to hear her voice again.

"Mama," he leaned close. She had a pungent medicinal smell. "Remember what? Do you need something? Is there something I can get you?"

This time her voice was stronger, strangely insistent. "I never told you. But you have to know."

He wondered if she was hallucinating. What was she talking about? He felt afraid, of what he wasn't sure.

"I didn't know how to tell you. You was so young." She began coughing, and he pushed the button that would elevate the head of the hospital bed.

"Do you remember any of it?"

"Any of what?"

"You was only six. You was there."

And now a memory began to rise up, indistinct, clouded by time. The room, the big room, the high balcony, so many excited people. Tall windows, dark wood. Cigarette smoke, so many people smoking, it hurt his lungs. Rain pouring down outside the open windows. The May heat. Wanting to climb in his mother's lap, bury himself there. Feeling so little, so afraid. Something big going on, something serious, something scary.

"What?" he said to his mother.

She turned her head to him in the dim light of the hospital room machines. Her face was gaunt, her eyes huge above the flesh stretched almost translucent over her cheekbones.

New images surfaced: God in a black robe, sitting above them behind a huge desk. Reading slips of paper, saying over and over in an angry voice, "Not guilty, not guilty, not guilty . . ." The room erupting in shouts.

"Your daddy was on trial. Along with all 'em others. Twenty-eight of 'em. For killing that colored man."

Lee's mind reeled. What was she talking about? She was out of her mind. Hallucinating.

"They snatched him from the Pickens jail. Beat 'em,

stabbed 'em. To get 'em to confess. Then they finished the fella off with a shotgun. In them woods off old Bramlett Road."

He knew the jail well, a red-brick building on Johnson Street. It looked like a homemade castle, red-brick, two-stories, rounded turrets. What was she saying? His father had been part of a lynch mob? "I don't understand."

"That colored fella kilt one of 'em cabbies. Like your dad was. Like 'em all was." Her voice was stronger, more urgent. "They got off," she said. "Ever last one of 'em. It weren't right. But that's the way it was back then."

"Daddy was one of them?"

She nodded, silent again for a long time. "I thought it was best not to tell you. I thought I was doing the right thing. You never asked about 'em. I thought maybe you knew. But I seen what you been like, Lee. All these years. How somethin' always weighing you down. Maybe that weight's your daddy." She was silent again. Then, she said, "A man's got a right to know his own history."

He laid her frail hand, which he had been gripping too hard, on her concave stomach. He put his head in his hands, resting his elbows on the bed. She reached out and stroked his hair, just as she had done when he was a child.

"Your daddy weren't a bad man, Lee. He done a bad thing. Pulled in by that lynching crowd. But he were there, he were part of it. And it weighed on him. Just like it's weighing on you. He hung hisself. On top of Pinnacle Mountain. Couldn't live with the guilt no more." She paused. "I give 'em credit for that."

Lee sat in stunned silence for a long time. Strange, nightmarish images raced through him: the gleeful faces of the defendants he had seen as a child; the judge repeating "not guilty" over and over; his father producing a new yo-yo with a diamond on it out of his pocket; his father hooking a slippery, squirming worm on his hook; shaking Dots gumdrops into Lee's open palm; a whupping, his father's face unrecognizable, grim and determined.

He lifted his head to look at his mother. Her head was tilted back, her mouth wide open, her eyes unseeing. He ran his hand over the thin hair on her head.

A cadaver now.

C H A P T E R   T H R E E

AFTER LUNCH WITH the Lunch Bunch, he headed over to Sarabeth's. He wondered if there would be good news: Lyle had a job. He had to work to have money (didn't he?); he couldn't just live off Sarabeth (could he?). She had fallen for Lyle two years ago, but it'd been a rocky relationship from the get-go. With broad shoulders on his six-foot frame and a movie-star face, Lyle was a looker, Lee would give him that. But he hadn't settled down at twenty-four, and Lee feared he might never. Always chasing some impractical dream, like opening his own repair shop (without a garage or tools) or going salmon fishing in Alaska to make enough in one summer to live on for a year. It was high time—past time, in fact—for Lyle to grow up and get a grip. That's how it came to Lee.

Today he wanted to talk to Lyle about an idea he'd been thinking about for the last couple of weeks: enrolling at Greenville Tech in automotive technology. What Lyle needed was a real trade. Not just pickup jobs, but a real skill, a certificate or degree of some sort, credentials. Today's cars were sophisticated machines; you had to know about electronics and computerized systems. And with brother Earl being an institution at the Ford dealership, Lee felt sure that if Lyle had a degree from Greenville Tech, Earl could land him a good job, a *real* job, in the Ford Service Center. He was excited about the idea but cautioned himself not to get his hopes up.

Lee himself had always worked. His first job was as a page at the Greenville County Library, all through high school and summers. His mother had finished eighth grade, and his father, she'd told him, had a fourth-grade education. It was his mother's dream that Lee attend college. His high school English teacher suggested North Greenville Junior College, in Tigerville, up near Travelers Rest. He'd never heard of it. When he received his letter of acceptance, his legs gave up, and he sat down on the linoleum floor in the kitchen. "Lee!" his mother rushed to kneel beside him. "What . . ." He handed her the letter. Her tears wet it so much that he had to take it outside and lay it on the spring grass to dry in the sun.

SARABETH'S red Fiat 500, another contribution from her parents, and part of her appeal to Lyle no doubt, was in the carport. When he rang the bell, she opened the door and smiled at him ruefully, shaking her head: "Not here. Haven't seen him in weeks. We broke up. Or I should say I did. Finally. Come on in, but don't put your foot in that bucket there." She'd been mopping the faux-marble floor of the foyer. She was wearing pedal pushers, her gingham top tied in a knot under her breasts. Her long brown hair, normally nicely coiffed for work, was tied up high in a straggly ponytail, if ponies had tails on top of their heads. In the two years she'd been with Lyle, Lee had grown fond of her. She'd tried to have a normal relationship with Lyle; what she most desired was a partner, a mate. A husband eventually; a child or two. She'd invited Lee to Sunday dinner a couple of times, but Lyle was mostly monosyllabic. Lee and she had wrestled together over the problem of Lyle. She was a good person, a straight shooter, six years older than Lyle, and it was too bad, he thought, that she had wasted two years on him.

"I told him not to come here anymore." Sarabeth grimaced. "I was tired of being used." A pause. "I know it's the right thing but it's still hard."

They were standing in the foyer with its gold gilt mirror and a large urn of dried grasses; he was unsure if he should stay or go. But she ushered him down the hall to the pine-paneled den and offered him a Coke or ice tea. He declined, explaining he'd just come from the Golden Corral, and he didn't want to interrupt her Saturday.

"You're not interrupting," she said. "I'm glad to see you. You're about the only good thing that came out of that fiasco." Now her eyes did brim. She was the kind of daughter anyone would like to have. "But enough about me," she said, forcing a smile. "How you doing, Lee?"

"Oh, me? I'm okay. For an old man. The usual aches and pains." He paused. "Listen, I'm really sorry, Sarabeth. You did the right thing. I don't know what's wrong with Lyle. Why he couldn't do right by a wonderful girl like you." Old man tears filled his eyes. Age had brought on this condition, where his emotions were too near the surface, too ready to choke him up, flood his eyes.

"Oh I've left the 'girl stage,'" she said. "I turned thirty last month. I'm officially an old maid." She laughed a phony laugh.

"Some good man is going to be lucky to have you,

Sarabeth," he said, knowing it was lame. "My ex-wife, Elaine. After things didn't work out for us, she went on to find a better man than me. A veterinarian. Just give yourself some time. It hurts now, but it won't hurt forever."

"He got me into dope. Did you know that?" She sank down on the faux-leather couch, resting her head on a needlepoint kitten pillow. "And I liked it. You'd be surprised how well I can roll a joint." She sat up and raised her eyebrows at him, assessing his reaction.

He didn't know what to say. He didn't know anything about marijuana, except that it was bad, not to mention illegal. Before he could come up with something, she said, "The thing is, Lyle hangs with those Dunlap nitwits. Sometimes he didn't come home for three or four days. He just wants to smoke weed all the time. It was way past time to give him the boot. Life has been a lot more peaceful, I'll tell you that."

"I'm sorry, Sarabeth. I mean for . . . You're a wonderful young woman! You deserve the best!" His eyes teared again. What an old fool he was.

"Not wonderful enough, apparently," she said dryly. "I don't know where he is. And I don't care. You can try those idiots that live right down the road from you."

DRIVING back to Blue Ridge, Lee considered his options. He could stop at the Dunlaps' place, see if Lyle was there or where to find him. Or he could go straight home and take Smoky out for his afternoon walk. The first option had all the appeal of walking on a bed of nails. Though they had lived on the same road for twenty years, Lee hadn't had much contact with the Dunlaps, and he'd like to keep it that way. As far as he could tell, no female had ever lived there, and he could imagine why. The father, H.C. Dunlap, must work some-where, but he was never around. The lads, three of them, who ranged in age from about eighteen to maybe mid-thirties, apparently didn't work at all. But maybe their business was the junkyard of wrecked cars that filled the yard and drugs. Dogs who were always having puppies napped on the warm asphalt of the road in front. Over the years, several had been hit by cars, their black-and-white spotted bodies stiff with rigor mortis on the shoulder. It infuriated Lee that they treated their animals with such disregard.

No, he would stop another day, when he felt stronger, fresher. For a seventy-five-year-old geezer, he told himself, he'd had a big enough day. He had plenty to reflect on, to review, though his short-term memory had holes in it. Did Sammy say the dermatologist had gotten all the cancer on his head? He tried to recall what Joey had said about his granddaughter . . . or was it grandson, and was it leukemia or asthma? Buster was moving into a retirement place—or was it in with his daughter? Well never mind. It had been good to see his brother. Earl had showed up, broken bread with him. That bread was cornbread, he chuckled to himself. And Sarabeth. Now that Lyle was out of her life, he would miss seeing her. There would be no reason to stop by. Although maybe he could. He didn't know.

He stopped the car when he got to his driveway to check the mailbox. He already knew there wouldn't be anything from Margo; she wasn't the birthday card type. Just a bill from Duke Power and a bunch of grocery fliers. Well, never mind. He hardly thought about her at all anymore.

When he entered the cool sanctuary of the trailer, Smoky was waiting at the door. He was the best boy in the world, joyful, polite, obedient, calm. His heart was pure love. When he was just a young dog, some asshole had put him out on Hidden Valley Road. Lee had first seen him in the woods behind his house, skittish, starving. After his first dog, Mutt, had died twenty years ago, he swore he'd never get another one. It was just like that song, *Mr. Bojangles: His dog up and died, he up and died; after twenty years he still grieved.*

But this stray dog watched Lee from the woods. He began leaving scraps in a metal pie pan near the picnic table out back. The dog would approach and eat but run if Lee so much as opened the back door. He had retired the previous month, five years ago, and having a lot of time on his hands, he began to sit at the picnic table, waiting. If the dog wanted to eat, it had to come for the food while he sat there. And gradually Smoky— for that seemed to Lee to be his name—began to come near. Lee offered him Milk Bones, but the dog had to come to him to get them. Finally, he let Lee stroke him. He looked at Lee as if to say, "It has taken me so long to find you!"

He filled Smoky's bowl with fresh water and drank a glass of water himself from the plastic pitcher in the icebox. He gave Smoky a couple of Milk Bones from the top of the icebox, Smoky sitting before he could give the command. "Good boy," he praised, stroking his head which had a bony point at the top. His brown eyes were liquid and deep, and he lifted a paw, making Lee laugh. "I didn't say 'shake,'" he chastised him. "Now that's the last," but he gave him another Milk Bone. Who had trained whom?

He was a little tired, he realized. "That's because you're seventy-five," a voice inside scolded him. But another voice defended, "But you weren't tired yesterday when you were seventy-four!"

He leashed Smoky, and they started down the road to the left. To go right meant he'd have to pass the Dunlaps, and their pack of barking spotted dogs would come racing out to challenge Smoky. He hoped the McBees' brown Dodge would be gone, but no, it was still tucked around back. He looked to see if the window air conditioner was hanging out the side window on the house, but it was gone. They must have taken it with them when they moved. But what could he do? He had no business getting involved with colored people, not that they were looking for his help. People didn't use that term anymore, though that was the word when he was growing up, and it still lived somewhere in his head. Well, it was a better word than what some people used to use; the word his father had used. His mother had told him to say "Negro" because that was a polite designation. Now "Black" was the word.

He remembered the day when his eyes were first opened to race. Not that it wasn't all around him growing up—race—but it was so much the fabric of life, he didn't notice it exactly; or maybe it was that he ignored it. There were colored people and there were white people, and everyone knew it, and everyone accepted it. That was the way it was.

Then one afternoon in May of 1960, when he was at his job as a page at the library, six or eight young people—high school students, close to his age, nicely dressed—the girls wore pastel summer dresses and carried pocketbooks, the boys slacks and cotton shirts the same as he wore—came into the library and took seats at the reading tables. A couple of them opened school books, and some took magazines from the racks. He was loading his cart of returned books to restack, and at first he didn't realize anything was wrong. But Mrs. Walker, his supervisor, and Mr. Stow, the head librarian, suddenly huddled together behind the main desk, whispering in an excited way. It was then he realized he had never seen any colored people in the library because it had never happened. They were not allowed. He knew that. It might even be against the law.

In a short while several police officers in their blue-gray uniforms with guns in their holsters arrived. All the library patrons stared in silence as the young people rose from their chairs, gathered their school books, and were quietly escorted out of the library. Watching in fear and shock, Lee saw that the students were prepared, that they knew what they were doing. They were not afraid. They were breaking the rules as if they were glass.

In the *Greenville News* the next day, it was big news, how Negroes had tried to integrate the library. After that, there were more sit-ins on Main Street, at Woolworth and Kress. The library was closed to prevent Blacks from using it. He was out of a job. He knew, vaguely, about *Brown v. Board of Education*. But the schools in Greenville weren't going to integrate. Hell no! There was unrest in the air, that was for sure, but it was remote from his own mostly-unconscious white life. But as if a door had been kicked open, the glass wall shattered, he became aware of Black people, their lives, their grievances.

HE had cleared the McBee house with no sightings of Del and the boys. The house itself seemed to be asleep; maybe they were napping after being up most of the night. But with no beds? The whole situation was disturbing. Maybe Del had called someone who had come and picked them up.

It was late afternoon now, and patches of sun and deep shadows dappled the asphalt; the wind stirred the tall pines, and his mind, freed, roamed to Elaine. He wondered how she was doing; he hadn't seen her in a couple of years. Their marriage had lasted five years, but it hadn't been much of a marriage, given the way he was. Back then, it was as if he had stepped into lake mud and couldn't pull his feet out. He went to work every day at the library, passing for normal, but joy was a distant green shore he could see but had no way to get to. Elaine tried to understand, to help. But the mud swallowed him up to his legs, his hips, his chest, until all he could think about was the pistol he kept in a shoebox in the closet.

A few days before his mother went back to the hospital for the last time, she'd told Lee she had something she wanted him to have. After Lee wiggled open the top drawer of her old wood bureau, which always stuck, she directed him to get a scuzzy-looking blue fuzzy-wuzzy bedroom slipper out. It had some heft, surprisingly, and when he looked, inside was a pistol. He jerked back, as if it were a snake.

"It was dangerous business driving cab," his mother told him, sitting down on her bed, a frail version of her former self. "Your dad always carried this pistol. He'd want you to have it."

Lee was appalled. He wanted nothing of his father's, let alone a gun. But he took it, not wanting to cross his mother at this late stage. But as the mud of depression swallowed more and more of him, this pistol began to dominate his thoughts.

HE and Elaine had remained friends through the divorce, her second marriage, Buddy's death, and the death of his mother. She came to his mother's funeral, one of the few in attendance, and after the small reception at the church, she sat him down and insisted he see a therapist. He had never thought of depression as a thing.

The therapist's name was Beverly Proctor, MSW, and she worked for a counseling outfit he'd been referred to by the library's insurance company. She was post-middle-aged, overweight, and empathetic, with a round earnest face and thin brown hair that didn't cover her scalp. The whole thing felt unbelievably awkward: her small suffocating office in the basement of an old church; the lumpy pillows on the hard pew recycled from the sanctuary upstairs; Beverly in her secondhand desk chair, her swollen feet reminding him of yeast bread rising in her shoes; the leggy vine in a jar of water, striving for life on the dim recessed window well. He understood he was there to talk and that he might cry, which he didn't want to do. Therapy as he understood it was about telling things you wanted to keep to yourself. When she asked him to tell her something about himself, the pistol floated into his mind, falling slowly through the air, and he started with that.

He shed a lot of tears in that office over many months. He was amazed at himself. He had always been self-contained, private, guarded. Now he was a gusher! And when he left after each session, he felt lighter. As if his tears were drying up the mud. Finally—he had been building up to it—he told her how his father disappeared that spring of 1947 when he was six, how it was only when his mother was dying of breast cancer that she told him the whole story. Beverly encouraged him to read about the lynching and trial in the *Greenville News* at the library. There was his father in the mug shots the paper had published of the cab drivers. His father was twenty-four years old. It was the first time Lee had seen his face since he was six.

CHAPTER FOUR

BACK AT THE trailer, he opened the freezer: two packages of hot dogs as well as a partial freezer-burned one that had been opened and not sealed properly; twelve frozen buns. In the cabinet there were three large cans of Bush's baked beans as well as an assortment of Campbell's soups and canned vegetables: corn, green beans, mustard greens, German potato salad, beets, which he never ate but felt he should. It was six o'clock. He always ate early and then watched TV or read before going to bed by ten.

He looked around the trailer. It was two-years-new when he bought it twenty years ago in 1996. He was living in a six-hundred-square-foot apartment in an old brick building built in 1916 in downtown Greenville when he happened upon an ad in the newspaper: "Must sell; like new double-wide; two acres in Blue Ridge; no neighbors nearby."

He knew Blue Ridge from when he'd attended North Greenville Junior College in Tigerville. He'd loved driving around that sparsely inhabited rural area with its rolling hills and forests; at least it was sparsely inhabited twenty years ago. On a whim, he called the number, drove out, and entered his dream home. Not that he had ever dreamed of living in a mobile home. The trailer had a cathedral ceiling, albeit a low one, an open floorplan with a handy counter that divided the kitchen and living room, one large bedroom, one smaller one, two baths. Lots of closets, a washer and dryer. It was roomy, maybe three times the size of his apartment. Everything newish and nice.

But what sold him, immediately and completely, were the woods out back. Beyond a good-sized grassy backyard lay a dense forest of Southern hardwoods, interspersed with tall straight loblolly pines, saplings struggling for light, and tangled vines. Trees not huge and majestic like redwoods or graceful, like the Spanish moss-draped live oaks in the Lowcountry, or austere like white birch on a snow-covered bank of a cold blue lake (he'd done all his traveling via books). But looking into those trees—the intricate interplay of bark and limb, the multitudinous shades of green, the leaves dancing free yet bound, shadows and sun, he wanted to live where he could look into those woods forever.

H E got the pistol—the one he used to think about too much before he went into therapy— from the shoebox on his bedroom closet shelf where he'd put it when he first moved to the trailer. Sammy, who had helped him move, couldn't believe he had such a "fabulous" pistol; he himself had a number of guns, was something of an aficionado he announced modestly. He took the pistol to clean and oil it, showed Lee how to load and unload it, and took him to a firing range where they practiced slaying cardboard men. After that adventure, Lee put it back in the shoebox and back on the closet shelf; he hadn't thought about it since. But now he got his safe deposit box from the floor of Lyle's closet and unlocked it with the key he hid in a solo red sock in his underwear drawer, deposited the gun and box of bullets inside, and locked the box. He didn't want any inquisitive twins to find it.

HE put away the clean dishes in the drain rack, punched up the pillows on the couch, emptied a cereal bowl of old peanut shells. He checked the two bedrooms; he always made his queen bed. Had made his bed every single morning since he was seven—he marveled at how many times that would add up to. The other smaller bedroom with the double bed was Lyle's. He couldn't remember when he'd last spent the night. He sponged out some toothpaste in his bathroom sink.

"You wait here, Boy," he said to Smoky, who was stretched out on the round rag rug in the living room. "I'll be right back." He barely lifted his head, tuckered out. "Too much stick," Lee chuckled. He stepped outside, taking in the early evening. He wondered about Lyle. Maybe he was right down the road at the Dunlaps' place. Well, that would have to wait. He locked the door, started the Camry, and drove the short distance down to the McBee house.

THE brown Dodge hadn't moved. He went to the backdoor and knocked. Silence. He knocked again and called through the door, "It's me, Del. Lee." Another long wait, and then Jackson—or was it James—slowly opened the screen door. Soon enough, Del appeared, with the other twin peering from behind her. "What?"

"Can I come in for a moment?"

Just then a car passed slowly in front of the house. Del and Lee locked eyes, listening to tires rolling over the asphalt.

"Probably unloading some old junk on the side of the road, too lazy to take it all the way to the ravine," Lee said, but adrenaline was making his ticker do a gig inside his chest. "I was wondering. Have you made any plans for where to go tonight? Unless you're going home, I mean." He was watching her intently, trying to get a read.

Del was staring at him. She gave an almost imperceptible shake of her head.

"A relative or a friend's, maybe?"

The same no.

Lee nodded, digesting this. "Well, if I'm not out of line, maybe you and the boys would like to sleep at my place tonight. And well . . . you know what I'm talking about."

This was met with more silence.

"Hey," Lee said to the boys, who were watching him from either side of their mother. "How'd you like to come sleep in my trailer tonight?"

"A trailer is not a house," Jackson said.

"We can have hot dogs. And baked beans. Do you like baked beans?"

"Yuck," James said and screwed up his face.

"You can sleep in my bedroom," Lee said to Del. "The boys can have my grandson's room. I'll sleep on the couch. It'll be good." He paused. "Then tomorrow . . . well, like they say, that's another day."

LEE and Del were sitting at the drop-leaf table in the dining area adjacent to the living room, mugs of ice water in their hands. The boys were in bed in Lyle's bedroom with the door half-shut; Smoky lay on the floor at Lee's feet, snoring softly. All the blinds were pulled, and they sat in the dark except for the dim glow from the light over the stove. Earlier, during supper, a car sped down the road past the trailer. "That's him," Del said. *He needs a new muffler*, Lee thought. They had left her car at the empty house. Lee didn't want it at his place for Marcus to see.

About ten minutes later, the car sped back toward the county road. Then the night was quiet again, except the molecules of air that had been set astir.

"Did he hit you?"

He saw Del's jaw tighten. "Yes sir," she said, avoiding his eyes. She tilted her head and pushed back her black hair. Her cheekbone was swollen, and beneath her brown skin, there was a darker bruise.

"Would some ice help that?"

When she didn't answer, he got a dish towel, wrapped some ice cubes in it, and handed it to her. "I'll check on the boys."

He pushed the door open enough to look in. It took his eyes a minute to adjust to the dark. From what he could tell, they were asleep. Soft, steady breathing, in unison. Jackson and James. They were nice boys, mostly well-mannered, bright, caught now in a bad situation. He hoped Marcus McBee knew what he was risking.

The things Del had brought from the empty house were scattered on the floor in the living room: an open suitcase with some clothes crammed into it, a couple of plastic bags with food, bottled water, and games and books for the boys.

"You're worn out," he said to Del now. "And I'm pretty done in myself. You use the bathroom first. Take a shower. There's some clean towels on the shelf. If you need anything, ask."

She raised her eyes to him where he stood by the counter. "Thank you," she said. "I don't know why you're helping us.

But thank you."

"It's nice to have you and the boys here. Company. I'm alone so much, you know. And tomorrow, we'll talk. Figure out the next thing."

When she'd used the bathroom and gone into his bedroom, shutting the door behind her, he got up from the couch. He let Smoky out the kitchen door, where he made his rounds, doing his business and patrolling the backyard. When he came back in, he didn't know what to make of the two shut bedroom doors, looking at Lee for an explanation. When Lee offered none, Smoky lay down next to the couch to await further developments.

Lee ran a wet washcloth over his face and what was left of his hair, short gray on top, white sidewalls. He brushed his teeth, peed, not for the last time that night. The doc called it "geriatric dribbling," three or four times a night. His blue broadcloth pajamas were hanging on a hook in the bathroom, and though he would have loved a shower himself, he was dying to get to bed—even if it was the purple couch. He pulled a blue sheet from the hall closet. He could use the throw pillows for his head and the crocheted afghan his mother had made for cover. When he lay down on the couch, Smoky looked at him in a beseeching way, putting one paw up on his arm: *Me too.* "There's no room at the inn," he said, patting Smoky's head. "Be a dog and sleep on the floor for a change."

He squirmed, trying to get comfortable. He was 5'8", having lost an inch or two (or three) to age, but straightening out meant his feet rested on the armrest. He turned on his side, curling, but his knees were precariously close to the edge. He felt the old bones in his back protesting. Well, he didn't think he could sleep anyway. If he were an owl—and if owls had ears—his would be turned toward the road, listening for the sound of that Pontiac's bad muffler. But all was quiet. There was no reason in the world that Marcus might suspect Del and the boys were in his trailer.

Del and the boys in his trailer . . . It was such a strange turn of events, he needed to get his mind around it. But if you come upon people in trouble, you try to do something. Del was afraid, he could tell that. At least here she was safe for the night. He would ask her first thing in the morning where they could go. Surely they had a relative or friend they could stay with, or maybe they could go home. Maybe Marcus would be ready to have them back, contrite, apologetic. But what kind of man would strike his wife. Or a small boy.

So much had happened so quickly. When the twins first arrived at the trailer, they had been subdued, sitting silently next to each other on the couch. He started bustling around in the kitchen, getting out a pan to boil the hot dogs, wrapping the frozen buns in foil to heat them in the oven. He put Del in charge of opening the baked beans and heating them, and he said to the boys, "Who's hungry? Who wants to help?" At this they came to life. He told them where to find the National Parks placemats, handed them silverware to set the table, gave Jackson the ketchup and James the mustard for the table, and enlisted their help on either side to pull the table out from the wall to make room. He gave James the bag of potato chips to fill a bowl, and Jackson forked dill pickles onto a saucer.

When they sat down for dinner, he was about to charge into a hot dog when Del stopped them all to say a blessing. It had been forever since he'd blessed his food, but it was familiar to him. His mother had said a blessing at every meal.

Then the boys ate two hot dogs each, and when James refused the baked beans, Jackson ate his. They ate like hungry dogs, sneaking bits of hot dog under the table for another hungry dog. Prompted by Lee, they told him about school, how they'd be going into fourth grade in the fall, giggling and excited by the attention. Del was quiet, but she and Lee smiled at one another, Del shaking her head at the boys' animation and at moments, foolishness. After dinner they played one of their games, Chutes and Ladders, until Del told them it was time for bed. Lee heard them talking quietly to each other in Lyle's bedroom for a while, and then they were silent.

Now, lying on the couch, Lee thought of how he'd eaten so many meals alone in this trailer. He couldn't remember the last time he'd had anyone in. It had been so enjoyable—so fun to have the boys, to serve them hot dogs (thank goodness he'd gotten two packages—BOGO), to hear their stories, see them laugh and punch each other. They reminded him of race cars that went from zero to eighty out of the blocks.

He had missed his own son's childhood. After the divorce, Elaine had raised Buddy, with Lee basically an absentee father, sunk in the mud of depression. His therapist Beverly Proctor called it functional depression: he went to work, he appeared sufficiently normal to his co-workers, he carried on, but he could find no joy in life. Elaine, who if anything was a high-functioning optimist, had tried to help, but being Elaine, she had finally opted to save herself and Buddy. And then, at twenty-two, Buddy was gone, taking with him any chance for Lee to make amends. Lee had driven up the Asheville highway to where Buddy's car had collided with the transport truck. A large section of pavement was burned black, the surrounding trees and shrub brush off the side of the road charred into ash. And Buddy left behind a child whose teenage mother wanted nothing to do with him.

Lyle was an angry, sulking, miserable teenager when his maternal grandparents, who had raised him from shortly after his birth, handed him over to Lee. He didn't know how to relate to him then, and he didn't know now. He needed to get in touch with him, see how he was doing, talk to him about Greenville Tech. Sarabeth had said he was smoking weed all the time. He was sure the Dunlap boys were responsible. He would go to their place tomorrow, talk to Lyle if he was there, or find out where he was staying.

But first he had to get Del and the boys on their way, wherever that was.

CHAPTER FIVE

ALL FOUR TIRES were flat.

The four of them stood behind the empty house, looking at the Dodge. He expected one of the boys—Jackson—to ask what had happened, but neither twin spoke.

"Okay," Lee said. "That's okay. I was planning to take you in my car anyway."

But where? He hadn't figured that out yet. All he knew was she couldn't stay here. Over cornflakes at the trailer, while the boys slept in, he had tried to talk to Del about whether she thought she could go home this morning.

"I'm not going home," she said flatly, angrily. "I don't want to lay eyes on him. I'm not going to pretend what he did is okay."

Lee took this in with a sinking feeling. "Well, what about your folks?"

She shook her head. Her father had died when she was a teenager; her mother had remarried and lived in Montgomery. "She didn't approve of me marrying Marcus. She didn't think he was good enough for me." There was a long pause. "We aren't too close."

Lee felt his stomach churn.

"What about a sibling? A relative?" He stopped himself from saying "no matter how distant."

The head shake, no.

"Members of your church?"

She shook her head again. "I fell away from the church." Another long pause. "I don't want anyone to know."

Lee excused himself and went in the bathroom to take some Tums. Del was painting herself into a prideful corner.

"Look, there are shelters for domestic violence victims…" he tried when he returned, but then he trailed off. He was vaguely aware—very vaguely—that there were such places, at least he thought so, but such a resource didn't spring to mind. He couldn't see Del and the twins in a shelter. Del didn't look like someone down and out, though apparently at least at the moment she was. She struck him as dignified, full of presence, and definitely stubborn.

"I'd rather stay in the empty house." She didn't look at him.

Lee nodded again, though he felt flummoxed. "How did y'all come to live way out here in the boondocks?" he asked, partly to buy time while he tried to think of what next. It wasn't the customary thing for Blacks to be living in Blue Ridge. There were a few, but it wasn't the norm.

"You might well ask. Marcus thought it would get the boys away from bad influences in town—though he's the bad influence when he drinks." She snorted, shaking her head. "The owner sold the house we were renting in Southernside out from under us to a developer who wants to put up condos for rich white people." She didn't try to disguise her disgust at this, and why should she?

"But why Blue Ridge?"

"One of the guys where Marcus works owns that piece of . . . Well, anyway, he rented it to us cheap. As if he was doing us a favor. But when those rednecks down the road started flying that fucking flag . . ." She glanced at Lee. "Sorry, Mr. Chastain. It's just . . ."

"It's okay. You're fucking forgiven," Lee said. "And it's Lee. Okay, go on."

"Sorry. I don't usually talk like that. I'm losing my mind. And certainly my manners."

"I think you're doing pretty well under the circumstances."

"Well, anyway, Marcus found us another piece of . . ."

"Shit," Lee finished for her.

It was the first time Lee had seen the hint of a smile.

"In Nicholtown."

"What does Marcus do?"

"He's the lead man in his department. Fisher's. That big car parts warehouse on 85." She paused a moment and added, "His boss, Mr. Snoddy, thinks the world of him. Says he wishes he had ten more like him. His own son can't hold down a job himself."

"What does Marcus do there?"

"Oh. Marcus gets the computer printouts when car dealers send in orders. When the guys bring the parts to him, he checks them off to make sure the order is right before it goes out. They do a lot of business with BMW."

Lee nodded. "And you?"

"I'm a teacher. Or I was. Now I take care of the boys."

"Well, you can't stay here. It's not safe. The boys can't go outside—he might drive by again and see them. When is school out?"

"They finished up last Friday."

"Do you have any money? Maybe a motel for a few days. Or I could pay…"

She shook her head.

They sat in silence again.

"What's he like?"

Del searched for the answer on the ceiling. "Dr. Jekyll and Mr. Hyde," she said at last. "When he's not drinking, sweet as sugar cane."

"How often does he drink?"

"He never drinks during the week. He works regular hours Monday through Friday. It's a good job, with good pay. He likes it, and he makes the rent every month on time. I won't say he's a perfect husband, but he's a good man. But on some Saturday nights, his demons catch up with him. Or I should say one demon in particular. His dad. He was mostly absent when Marcus was growing up. But when he did come around, he was a terror. To Marcus and his mother. On those Saturday nights when Marcus isn't in by midnight, I know to expect trouble. That's what happened this time."

"And?"

She clenched her jaw. "I was mad that he'd come home stumbling drunk. I told him I was fed up. That's when he smacked me. In the face. It knocked me off my feet. I fell against the kitchen table and bruised my hip. At least the boys were in bed, asleep. I hope."

"Was that the first time he hit you?"

"No sir. As long as he keeps drinking, it won't be the last." Her hand went up to her swollen cheek.

"And then?"

"He passed out. That's when I decided to get away, just like that, no plan, no nothing. I didn't want to lay eyes on him when he woke up. To hear his excuses." She stopped again. "I threw some things together, got the boys in the car. Middle of the night. My mind was just scrambled, frantic, and I didn't know where to go. I thought of the house on Hidden Valley Road. I had that key. It was totally empty, no furniture, beds, nothing. I didn't think he'd come looking there. Then you showed up. An angel sent by God."

Lee stood up, went to rest his eyes on the deep woods out the window over the sink. "No angel," he said. "It was just an accident that I found you. Have you called him?"

"He keeps calling and calling. I'm not answering."

He stood there studying the forest for several silent minutes. *The woods are lovely, dark and deep . . . But I have promises to keep . . . And I have miles to go before I sleep.* Obligations. Duty.

"What if I go see Marcus?"

He turned to see what Del thought of this.

Her eyebrows shot up in surprise. She met his eyes with her brown ones.

"Okay," she finally said, holding his eyes. "And good luck." Not in the way some people say it, sarcastically, but genuinely: *Good luck.*

"Okay, then."

He picked up his cell phone and dialed.

"Sarabeth," he said. "I have a favor to ask. A really big favor . . ."

CHAPTER SIX

DRIVING OVER TO Sarabeth's, his mind was awhirl. It was eleven o'clock on Sunday morning. He could hardly believe that about this time yesterday, he had been on his way to the Golden Corral. So this is what being seventy-five is like! He'd wondered when he left Sarabeth's yesterday if he'd ever see her again. But he hadn't hesitated to call her. He knew Sarabeth in some kind of gut way; he *knew* her. And she had that three-bedroom house. He'd told her he'd be right over. He didn't even feel nervous about asking such a favor. He had a sense of rightness, of knowing what was needed in this situation and how to get it. Though he also knew he might be sorely surprised. He was going to ask a lot.

If things went well at Sarabeth's, he'd drive back to the trailer and gather Del and the boys and take them there. It made his mind spin to think of it. He refused to entertain the impossibility of it. It was rare in his life to feel so certain, as if all anxiety and hand-wringing had fallen off him. He would work this problem out, he would do what needed to be done, he would manage it, and all would be well. He refused to listen to the small voice that told him he was a fool. He had heard that voice all his life, but now he told it to shut the fuck up.

He'd told Del not to let the boys leave the trailer under any circumstances. He didn't tell her his plan—nor did she ask. And all he'd told Sarabeth on the phone was he had a big favor to ask. He had to speak to her in person. He parked in the driveway behind her Fiat. He went to the kitchen door, and she opened it before he could knock.

"Has something happened to Lyle?"

"No, no," Lee said. "Not that I know of, at least. Can I come in for a minute?"

"Of course, Lee," she said. "Sorry. I just . . ."

She'd gotten a scare. She wasn't really over Lyle. Maybe she never would be. She stepped aside and he went in the kitchen. It smelled of bacon. She was still in her bathrobe, pink seersucker, so Sarabeth.

"Coffee? I've almost drained the pot, but I can make more." She looked at him in a questioning way. "What's this about a big favor? You know I'd do anything I can for you, Lee. Let's sit down. Are you in some kind of trouble?"

They sat in the breakfast nook, and Lee folded his hands, which were shaking a little, on the tabletop. "In a manner of speaking," he said, and then he told her the story of how he had found Del and the boys hiding out in the empty house down the road, how Del's husband had hit her, how he'd let them spend the night at his trailer, how Marcus, the husband, had punctured the tires on Del's car. He was afraid Marcus might figure out they were at the trailer. And then what, he didn't know. "And by the way," he said. "They're Black. Del and the twins."

Sarabeth scoffed. "This is the New South, Lee. I have

Black friends. My supervisor is Black. I don't care if they're purple. Are you asking what I think you're asking?"

"Just for a night. Maybe two."

"I see. Well, I'm not sure about taking strangers into my house, Lee. You were good to take them in." She paused. "I'm not sure I'm that good."

They sat there in silence; he waited.

"What's that Bible verse about strangers?"

"I was a stranger . . ." he said.

"And you took me in," she answered.

"I was thirsty . . ."

"And you gave me drink."

"I was hungry . . ."

"I didn't know you were religious, Lee. I've never heard you quote the Bible."

"Not really," he said. "Just that verse, and a few others. For some reason it stuck with me. 'I was a stranger . . .'"

"And you took me in," she answered. "Is that the favor?" She had a little half-smile on her face, like she was indulging a naughty but beloved child. "Only you, Lee," she said. "Only you."

He didn't know if she meant only he would come up with such a cockamamie ask, or if she'd only do it for him.

"But only for a night, Lee," she said. "Or two if necessary."

"I understand. Thanks. I'm grateful. I'm going to go talk to her husband, assess the situation." Where did this language come from?

"Right," Sarabeth said. "'Assess the situation.' But let me get this straight. You don't really know this woman, right?"

"Not . . ." he searched for a word. "Not literally. But she's a good woman. Like you."

"Oh for Pete's sake, Lee." Again she had that little teasing smile on her face. She made him wait it out for several seconds. "Okay," she said at last. "But only for a day or two. And you owe me, Lee Trammell. You owe me."

WHEN he got back in his car, he made a fist and pounded it on the steering wheel: *Ouch!* Well, now all he had to do was go back to the trailer, get the address from Del where he could find Marcus, then transport her and the kids to Sarabeth's, then go have a word of prayer with Marcus . . .

Wait a bloody minute! Maybe Marcus McBee wouldn't be too keen on having a "word of prayer" with a crazy old white guy who was messing with his family. He thought about the time when Marcus came to the door to borrow the wrench. He was very big, very dark, his slave ancestors' blood evident in his complexion and build. He had also seemed polite, friendly. Lee could still kick himself for acting like an ass: not inviting him in. His neighbor. Would he have invited a white stranger in? Probably not. But was he less inclined to ask Marcus in because he was Black? In 2016? He hoped not.

He felt like a fool for telling Sarabeth that Del and the kids were Black. But for so much of his life, his generation, that distinction *did* matter. Did anyone raised in the Jim Crow South ever achieve total color blindness? Maybe that would always exist: not racism—that could be eradicated, consciously, purposefully, whole-heartedly—but just registering color. Race. On both sides. Unfortunately, there were too many, especially in the South, who were still hanging on to the racist past under the guise of heritage.

He thought about that Confederate banner flying high above the Dunlaps' junkyard. It represented Southern heritage, all right, but that heritage was slavery, and all that had come afterward to hold Blacks down and back. And then there was his own little bit of personal history. Did his father have that same look of insane fury when he joined a lynching party that he had when he whipped Lee?

But surely Marcus would want to have his wife and kids back. Surely whatever his drinking problem was, it could be solved. Surely. Marcus would be remorseful and maybe even thank Lee for trying to help. Probably not. Anyway, he didn't know what else to do.

"Screw your courage to the sticking place," he coached himself.

Wow, that sounded painful.

HE stopped at McDonald's and got a sack of hamburgers, French fries and Cokes. At the trailer, he found Del on the couch watching a televised sermon on TV. Jackson and James were lying on the round rug, coloring in coloring books; Smoky leapt up in ecstatic joy at the sight of him. "Who'd like a hamburger?" he asked, and the boys leapt up with their own version of ecstatic joy, shouting "Me, me!" Del was watching him, her face impassive, waiting to learn her fate, it seemed to Lee. "Come eat," he said to her, and she was silent while the boys chattered away happily, eating their burgers and telling Lee about school mates: who was popular, who was a dork.

When they'd all eaten, including Smoky, who had gotten a patty without the bun, and the boys had helped gather the paper wrappers and napkins, Lee told them he needed to talk to their mother for a few minutes. "You two go on in the bedroom and finish coloring a picture to show me."

"Can Smoky go with us?" James asked.

"Can he get on the bed with us?" This time, Jackson.

"You go on in with the boys," Lee urged a somewhat reluctant Smoky. He wanted to stay with the adults, being one of them. But he obeyed, and Lee shut the door.

"I've made arrangements," he said awkwardly, "for you and the boys to spend the night with a lady friend of mine. Her name is Sarabeth, she's single, and has a three-bedroom house. She's a good person. You'll be okay there for the time being. Until I can see what the situation is with Marcus. Is he usually remorseful after an episode? Do you think he'll be home this afternoon?"

Del stared at him for a few seconds in that way she had, then nodded her head. "He should be. He has to be at work tomorrow morning at 7:00 a.m., so he'll be straightening himself out today." She stepped to the counter and took a pencil from the jar where Lee kept them, scribbled on a pad nearby, and handed the piece of paper to Lee.

Lee read the address, not that he recognized the street. But Del had said it was in Nicholtown, an old Black neighborhood on the far side of Cleveland Park in Greenville. He had never had any business in Nicholtown. All the elation he'd felt when Sarabeth said she would take Del and the boys was replaced by anxiety. What if Marcus was hostile or even furious that Lee—a stranger and a honky at that—had interfered in his family's affairs? And what kind of man would puncture the tires of his wife's car just to spite her?

He opened the door to the bedroom. Jackson and James were lying on the bed, stroking Smoky, who was stretched out on his side between them. He barely lifted his head to acknowledge Lee. "I call him Smoke," James said, his small hand caressing the black fur. "He likes me."

"I can see that," Lee said.

"Are we going to live here?" Jackson asked. "'Cause if we are I gotta go get some things." He looked up at Lee with a worried face.

"Well," Lee said. "Here's the situation. You boys and your mom are going to spend a night or two with a friend of mine. She's a really nice lady. You'll like her." He paused. How much to say? How confusing all this must be to them. It certainly was to him.

"Because Daddy hit Mama," James pronounced.

"Your father didn't mean it," Lee said. "He has a drinking problem."

"He's a mean drunk," Jackson said authoritatively.

"My father had a drinking problem," Lee said and felt a stab in his gut.

They stared at him.

"He was only mean when he drank. Like your father. It's the liquor that makes them mean." He had to stop. After a moment he said, "Now we're going over to Miss Sarabeth's. Get your games and books. I'll give you a grocery bag to put them in."

CHAPTER SEVEN

SARABETH GREETED THEM as if it were the most natural thing in the world that a stranger and twins were showing up on Sunday afternoon to spend "a night or two."

"I've been needing some folks in this empty house," she said, smiling. "Welcome."

"It's a beautiful house," Del said, all manners and reserve; this couldn't be easy for her. It must be intimidating and painful for her to be landing in this unknown woman's nice suburban house, when her own house was, in her own words, a rental piece of shit, and she had an alcoholic husband who had struck her.

The boys were standing silently on either side of their mother, subdued by the situation.

"What's your name?" Sarabeth asked one of them.

James looked up at his mother. "Go on, tell her."

"James Brown McBee."

"And I bet you're Michael Jackson McBee," she said to Jackson, who looked surprised but then broke into a little moonwalk. Sarabeth laughed. "Will you teach me how to do that?"

"I can't," Jackson said. "You gotta be Black."

"And young," Sarabeth added.

"And limber," Lee said.

"His name actually is Jackson," Del said. "It's a family name though."

The boys, having recovered from their initial shyness, were looking around. They gravitated to the urn with dried grass intermingled with large cattails.

"What are those things?" James asked, pointing at the long brown stems.

"Cattails."

Both boys stared at her.

"They ain't from cats!"

"They aren't from cats," Del corrected.

"They'd have to be mighty fat cats, wouldn't they?" Sarabeth pulled two of the cattails out of the vase. "Whew, dusty! Here's one for you and one for you. I'll show you your room and then you can take them out back and have a sword fight."

"Can we, Mama?"

"It's okay," Lee said to Del, "It's fenced. They'll be fine."

They all followed as Sarabeth led them down a carpeted hall to a room with yellow floral wallpaper and twin beds with yellow bedspreads. "This will be your room," she said to Jackson and James.

"This is a girls' room," Jackson said.

"No, it's a guest room," Sarabeth corrected. "And you're my guests."

James went to the far bed and patted it. "This is my bed," he announced.

WHILE the boys ran out the kitchen door to the backyard with their cattails, Sarabeth showed Del her room, painted a pale blue with a white matelassé spread on a high four-poster bed. "This is definitely a girl's room," Del said. "Climb aboard," Sarabeth invited, and Del hesitated a moment, then threw herself across the bed dramatically, heaving a huge sigh. Both women laughed. "Let's finish the tour," Sarabeth encouraged, and Del got to her feet. Sarabeth showed her the adjacent bathroom, with a white waffle-weave bathrobe hanging behind the door. "Please use it," Sarabeth insisted. "I bought it for company but I never have any. 'Til now! Just tell me what you need. There's shampoo in the shower and fresh towels on the rack. Make yourself at home."

"I can't thank you enough," Del started, ". . . for taking us in like this. I'm sorry . . ."

"Pshaw!" Sarabeth said. "I'm happy to have you."

AFTER he got in the Camry, Lee pulled the address Del had written down where he could find Marcus. On this Sunday afternoon, the last thing Lee wanted was to be driving into Nicholtown to confront an alcoholic wife abuser—and a Black one at that.

Nicholtown was not a large neighborhood, and it was built on a hill, with winding streets. It was near downtown, which was bursting with prosperity and rising home prices, but Nicholtown was still mostly Black, with modest wood-frame or brick houses. Greenville might be the New South, but there were still pockets of the Old South like this one. The neighborhood was a mix of nicely-maintained homes, rundown shotgun houses, and rental places that shouted poverty and neglect.

It was a bright hot day, and Black folks were back from church, some still in their Sunday best, fanning on their cement porches, men working on their cars, visiting with neighbors, eyeing Lee either suspiciously or with curiosity. He wound around up and down, until he found the address Del had given him. A Pontiac with its muffler hanging down was parked in front of a one-story house with a chain-link fence enclosing the small front yard. Parking behind the Pontiac, Lee thought how Marcus better get that muffler replaced soon before it fell off completely.

He opened the metal gate, climbed the four concrete steps with peeling red paint, and knocked on the front door. A ferocious barking erupted from inside the house. Afraid he'd fall, Lee backed down the stairs as quickly as he dared; there was no rail to hang on to. His heart was pounding such that he could feel his pulse throbbing in his neck. He looked around for a stick or anything with which to defend himself, but the yard was bare except for a deflated basketball.

The door opened slightly, and all Lee could see was the teeth-bared mug of a pit bull restrained by a dark hand on a collar that looked medieval with its metal spikes. A drowsy-looking Marcus cracked the door enough to look out. "What you want?" Lee could tell that he'd woken him up. In fact, he wasn't sure he was actually awake. Lee couldn't take his eyes off the hand on that collar.

"Aww, she won't hurt you none," the man said. "She might kiss you to death is all. Stop that now, Maybell! Enough!" he addressed the dog sharply. But he didn't let go of the collar, and the dog continued to bark furiously. "What you want?" in the same sharp tone.

"I'm Lee Trammell. We met once. When you borrowed my wrench."

Marcus focused on him. "You that old dude live in that trailer."

He was waking up. "Just let her smell the back of your hand," he ordered, and he let go of the dog, which rushed out at Lee. Terrified, Lee held out his hand, which he expected to lose momentarily, and the dog, all sixty pounds of it, in its rush to get to Lee, almost knocked him off the last step, but she stopped just short and began to sniff the hand. The animal had a scrunched-up face, fierce little eyes, and someone had cropped her ears too short; she sniffed all over Lee's hand for what felt like an eternity. "She's smelling my dog," he said weakly to Marcus.

"Okay, Maybell, enough!" Marcus said sharply. "Get your butt back in here!" The dog trotted up the steps and through the door that Marcus held open for it. "Never could get that drip under the sink to stop. What you want? I'm pretty busy right now, man."

"I never thanked you and your wife for the banana bread. I wasn't a very good neighbor, and I regret that. Could I come in for a minute?" Lee didn't see how they could discuss the situation on the front steps. The neighbor lady twenty feet away next door had pulled her rocker over on her porch the better to hear, and three little Black boys of various ages had their fingers entwined in the chain-link fence, watching.

"Like I said, I'm real busy, man."

"Too busy to talk about Del and the boys?"

Marcus eyed Lee for a long uncomfortable moment. "Okay," he said at last, and Lee cautiously mounted the steps again. "Are you sure the dog is . . ."

"She won't hurt you none. Just a big baby. Come mere, Maybell," and the dog came up to Marcus and got her boxy flat head rubbed.

Lee stepped into the living room, which was darkened on this bright Sunday afternoon. "We just renting this place," Marcus apologized. "This isn't our furniture. Our stuff's in storage 'til we find permanent housing." A sheet wadded on the worn sofa looked as if someone had kicked it all night. Empty Coke cans, a pizza box, and an ashtray overflowing with cigarette butts were on a low, scarred faux-wood coffee table. The room smelled of body odor, stale smoke, and Maybell, who was now occupying herself with licking her crotch. Marcus, in boxer shorts, didn't ask Lee to sit down, but he sat down anyway on one of the armchairs.

"What you know about Del?" Marcus asked.

"Why don't you sit down?" Lee said. "So we can talk."

"They at your place?" Marcus towered over him.

Lee shook his head. "They're fine. But I don't think Del wants to come home until she feels safe." His heart was racing. How did he get in this situation, talking to this hostile man about something that was none of his business?

Marcus shook his head. "It was an accident. She provoked me. I wouldn't hurt her on purpose. She knows that. I don't know why she's acting a fool!"

Lee sighed. "Would you please sit down? This might be a lot easier."

"What's with you, busting in here on a Sunday afternoon? This is our business, not yours!"

"Do you have any ice tea?"

Marcus stared at Lee. He ran his hand over his closely cropped hair. "What you say, ice tea?"

"That would be nice," Lee said. "I'm feeling a little—like I need a pick-me-up."

Marcus eyed him warily. "Crazy old man," he muttered and left the room.

Lee heard water running in the kitchen. He eyed Maybell. He considered seeing if she would come for a head rub but decided against that. In a few minutes, Marcus brought him some instant ice tea in a beer mug.

"Pre-sweetened," he said, pushing the tangled sheet aside and sitting down on the sofa. He set his own glass of tea on the coffee table. "I gotta clean this place up 'fore Del gets home," he said.

They sat for a long time in silence. The tea was terrible, too chemical, too sweet. Lee himself made sun tea, setting a gallon jar of water with tea bags in the hot sun until the color was a golden hue.

"It won't happen again," Marcus said at last. "Tell her I'm sorry, and it won't happen again. I miss her and the boys. Tell her." He raised his eyes to Lee. "I need my wife and boys. I made a mistake. I was drunk."

"But it's happened before."

"What business is this of yours, old man?" Marcus jumped up, frightening Lee, arousing Maybell, who barked excitedly.

"Shut up!" Marcus said to the dog. "You tell Del to come home! She's my wife. She belongs here."

Lee was silent. He sipped his tea, the taste bitter. "My father was an alcoholic," he said. "He hit me with his belt when I was six. I never forgave him. I didn't understand how he could love me one minute and hurt me the next. I hated him after that. Do you understand what I'm saying?"

Marcus rubbed his big hand over his face.

"Del left because she's afraid of what you might do to her when you're drunk. She doesn't want the boys to be around that. And she was mad. She doesn't want to hate you. But that's not up to her, Marcus. It's up to you."

Marcus was silent.

"I want my wife and boys back," he said finally. He paused again. "Tell her it won't happen again."

"I'm not sure that will be enough," Lee said, standing up. "Thanks for the tea. And Marcus. You have to get those tires fixed. If you can't get them repaired, you have to replace them."

"What you talking about?"

"You know what I'm talking about. The four tires on your Dodge. The ones you punctured with nails. They're flat as a flitter."

Marcus stared at him. "You think I'd do that to my own car?" he snorted. "Crazy old white guy."

C H A P T E R   E I G H T

WELL THEN, LEE mused to himself as he wound his way out of Nicholtown, since Marcus hadn't punctured those tires, maybe it was time for a little neighborly visit with the Dunlap lads.

But while he was in town, he'd better swing by Sarabeth's and see how things were going there. He needed to tell Del about his visit with Marcus. But what? The predictable things: Marcus was defensive, angry, hurt, and afraid that he'd finally blown it, that Del wouldn't be coming back. But Lee thought there was more to Marcus than the obvious and the predictable. You could tell a lot about a man if you spent half an hour with him. Like the way Marcus had gone in the kitchen and brought Lee the ice tea. He could have thrown Lee out, but instead, he served him tea. Behind that facade of toughness was a good man, Lee reckoned. One he'd like to get to know better.

Of course, Marcus would have no interest in getting to know Lee, a crazy old white guy. It was a complete fantasy that they could get to know each other, tell about their lives, become friends. They had nothing in common. And Marcus had hit Del, more than once. Could he be rehabilitated? That remained to be seen. Maybe if he could stop all the drinking, since once he started, apparently he couldn't stop. It was in his favor that he held down a good job, paid the rent, married a fine woman. And there were the twins. He had a lot to lose. And so did they.

He pulled in behind Sarabeth's Fiat. It seemed days ago since he'd dropped off Del and the twins that morning. He felt tired and wired at the same time. He wasn't sure what to do if Sarabeth told him they had to leave on Monday when she went back to work. Back to the trailer with him, he guessed. Having met Marcus, he didn't feel he was dangerous—unless he went on a bender. But taking them in himself was no solution.

He opened the kitchen door and heard voices in the den. "Anybody home?" he called and Smoky came running, all wiggles and smiles. "Hi, boy," he said, rubbing his pointy head. "Were you a good boy? I missed you! Maybell," he explained to him when Smoky began sniffing him suspiciously. "I wasn't cheating on you."

Jackson came into the hall. "Did you see Dad?" he asked. "Is he coming to get us?"

James followed and put both hands on Smoky's back, claiming him. "I want to stay here," he said. "It's fun, and I have my own bed."

"Come on in," Sarabeth called, and Lee found the two women with their legs curled under them sitting at either end of the couch, a bowl of popcorn between them. A big jigsaw puzzle was spread out on the carpet. James came running in and plopped down on his apparently double-jointed knees next to it, holding up a puzzle piece. "It's Mount Everest," he indicated the half-formed picture on the floor. "And this here is a piece of snow!"

Del was looking at Lee with a mixture of hope and worry.

"Want some popcorn?" Sarabeth held up the bowl. "Cokes in the frig. We're engaged in a deep conversation here," she grinned at Del. Her hair was in pink curlers.

"We're competing for who had the most embarrassing clothes in junior high."

"You cannot…you absolutely cannot…" Sarabeth said, "…top my baby blue velour track suit. The pants legs were long enough for a six-foot guy. I was always tripping over them."

In the background a guy was rapping, "I need a one dance, one dance, I need a one dance…"

"Okay, you score pretty high with that," Del said. "But I bet you didn't have a popcorn shirt. Bright green, itchy as hell."

"Speaking of popcorn," Lee said, and he took a handful and sat down in the recliner. "What does he mean he needs a one dance?" he asked.

"I'm Drake," Jackson began chanting and dancing along with the record. "I need a one dance, one…"

"Enough of that," Del said. "Help James with that puzzle."

"No!" James wailed. "I want to do it myself!"

Jackson dropped to his knees and grabbed a handful of puzzle pieces.

"I spy two little boys who are about to go to their room," Del said, and the boys quieted down.

"Sarabeth, let's take Smoky for a little walk," Lee said. "Del, I'll fill you in in a minute."

THEY walked with Smoky down the street toward the corner. It was a nice subdivision of red-brick ranch-style houses built mostly in the '80s. On this sunny Sunday afternoon, people were out watering their azaleas and camellia bushes, and children were playing touch football in the street unless a car came slowly by. Lee complimented Sarabeth on such a nice neighborhood. When they got to the corner, they turned onto another street of similar houses. Lee couldn't tell one street from another; unless you knew the neighborhood, it all looked the same. He asked Sarabeth how things were going.

"I really like Del," Sarabeth said. "But she's in a fix. Did you talk to Marcus?"

"He wasn't exactly happy to see me," Lee said. "But I don't think he's a bad guy. He has a drinking problem."

Sarabeth explained that Del had told her all about that while the boys played in the backyard with two badminton rackets and a birdie. "She wondered if his hitting her was her fault. I disabused her of that notion PDQ. Do you know she used to teach school? At Eastside High. English and civics. But Marcus wanted her to stay home when the twins were born."

"She mentioned she'd been a teacher. I don't really know her."

"Do you think they'll be able to go home?"

"That's the sixty-four-thousand-dollar question. Does she want to?"

"Not if she's going to get smacked again. They can stay with me for a while, Lee. It's no problem."

"Sarabeth," he moaned. "I didn't mean to put all this on you!"

"It's actually nice for me. Having them in the house. It's been pretty empty since Lyle left."

"He's next on my list."

"We talked about a lot of girl things. Men! I told her about Lyle. She's going to cook me some soul food while she's here. But the boys need something to do, somewhere to go during the day until school starts. Will she have a car?"

"Ah," Lee murmured. "A car." He paused. "Yes, she will have a car."

"Okay, good," Sarabeth said. "I want them to stay."

NEXT Lee sat with Del in the backyard in aluminum folding chairs in the shade of the house. Sarabeth kept the boys inside, doing the jigsaw puzzle with them.

"She's so great," Del said.

"She likes you too," Lee said. "I didn't really know, but I figured you two would get along."

Del had had a shower and washed her hair, and the yellow cotton dress she was wearing yesterday had been washed and ironed. Now he could see the schoolteacher in her: someone competent, mature, no nonsense.

"So. Did you see Marcus?"

"I went to the house. Marcus was . . . Well, first there was Maybell to contend with."

"That dog! She's actually sweet. But she comes on strong."

"Well, once I got past Maybell, we talked for a bit. At first Marcus was angry that I was there—interfering."

"I figured he'd react that way."

"I think he's very remorseful. He just doesn't know what to do about what he did. And it's not the first time. That's a bad sign, Del."

She nodded in agreement but was silent.

"I don't think there's any guarantee that it won't happen again. Not until he gets some help."

"What kind of help?"

"Maybe some anger management counseling. AA for sure. Would he go to meetings?"

"Probably not."

"He might if he knew you weren't coming back until he did. Sarabeth said you could stay here for a while. How would you feel about that?"

"It's unbelievable," Del said. "That she would do that for us."

"Well, that's what she said. Let's just take it a day at a time. You need to look into a summer program for Jackson and James. Let's start with that."

"I don't want you to think Marcus is a bad person," Del said. "He's not. He hasn't had it easy. When he was growing up, it was just him and his mom. Except when his father would show up asking for money and beat the bejesus out of his mother if she didn't have any. She worked as a maid and had to be available whenever the white folks needed her. Various relatives and neighbors looked after Marcus. He had to drop out of school to work when his mother's health began to fail."

"That's rough," Lee said. He put his elbows on his knees, leaning forward, stretching his old-man back, which was whining. There was a small, satisfying pop. "You said he handles the computer program for the parts at the warehouse?"

"He keeps track of the inventory, handles the ordering when things are running low. He's very reliable and capable. But one of the guys he supervises is always badmouthing him to Mr. Snoddy. Wants his job. Assumes he can handle it better than Marcus. Just 'cause he's white!"

Lee nodded. "The past is not dead."

"It's not even past. Faulkner. I taught twelfth grade English."

Lee nodded. "I don't need to tell you the past is not past."

"I live it." They sat in silence a moment, contemplating this. "You seem like an educated man, Lee. What did you do?"

"Librarian."

They were quiet again.

"How did you and Marcus meet?"

"I was home from Benedict College one summer. I had a job in Woolworth's downtown. He was so good looking! Tall, handsome, charismatic. Flirty. Those long eyelashes! Sweet, I could tell. He bought some Skittles, and then the next day he was back for more." She smiled at the memory.

"And more the day after that," Lee grinned. "He really likes Skittles apparently."

Del laughed. "We were so young then! I was twenty; he was eighteen. I was getting a college degree, and he was working construction—which is why he wasn't good enough for Mama. But there was no stopping us. He wanted me to quit my teaching job after the twins were born, so I did. I didn't mind. Twins are a lot for a new mother. I've been thinking of going back to teaching now that the boys are older." She paused. "I can't believe how kind you're being to me." Del looked him in the eye. "Thank you, Mr. Trammell."

"It's Lee. And I have an idea. Someone who might help Marcus. I don't know. I'd have to ask. He's an old friend. All the way back to grammar school. He was a raging alcoholic for years. Finally, after he had pretty much messed up his life, he began going to A.A. Still does. I think he might be willing to help Marcus. Get his ass to meetings, someone to call if he's tempted."

"White, I assume."

"Would that be a problem?"

"Not that I know of. Marcus is not what you'd call a reverse racist. But he probably feels more comfortable with Black folk."

Lee took this in. "Let me ask Sammy. I'll see what he thinks. But right now I need to get going. I still have another stop to make," Lee said. "Some business to take care of."

CHAPTER NINE

HE HAD A pretty good idea who had driven nails into those tires. That Confederate flag wasn't enough for them. No, they had to make a statement: *No niggers welcome here.* He would have to go talk to them. Confront them, if it came to that. That was not a pleasant prospect, to say the least. But it was another one of those situations (the second today!) where you look around, and there is no one else. You have to do it yourself.

He knew the way back to Blue Ridge so well, his mind could float free while his eyes minded the traffic. How he wished he could talk all this over with Margo! She would give him wise counsel. On their many walks during their lunch hours, she had advised him on Lyle, who was proving to be a teenage handful, and she had her own parenting trials; her daughter Jane was involved in what Margo thought was a disastrous marriage. Now, clearing town and picking up speed on the Poinsett highway, he wondered not for the first time what might have happened if her husband hadn't flopped in the Victorian B&B biz and taken her back to Minneapolis, aka the moon? But she went willingly. Didn't she?

The last time he saw her, in the library parking lot, when they said goodbye the day before she and her husband left town, she'd said, rather shyly, "I want a hug." They'd never touched before. He's gone over this moment again and again, how she put her arms around him with care and deliberation, and he, shaken, had put his around her and pulled her tight against him, as if he'd never let go. He didn't know who instigated the kiss. Was it Margo, or had he been the one who put his lips against hers? They kissed for a long moment there in the library parking lot, not caring who saw. He breathed her in, hoping for enough to last a lifetime. Then she was gone.

He drove down the county road and turned onto Hidden Valley Road. If there was a valley, it was so well hidden that no one had ever found it. It was well named, he thought; so much in life is hidden. He swung by the trailer to check the mail and to let Smoky pee and put him back in, telling him to guard the house. Smoky looked a little miffed, but Lee didn't want him waiting in the hot car or getting embroiled with the Dunlaps' dogs. Before he had even locked the front door, he knew Smoky was heading toward the couch. He wouldn't mind a little peace and quiet, given the commotion of the last night and day; Lee wouldn't mind a little of that himself.

HE drove the short distance back toward the Dunlaps' and parked in the shade on the side of the road, carefully avoiding the deep ditch. Their yard was a graveyard of wrecked cars, kind of fascinating if you were interested in crashes. Some of them made Lee wince. No one could have survived the smashed front end on that Toyota, and the shattered windshield on a sports car had a head-size hole in it. Another small car, the make undetectable because it had gotten it from the front and back, was compressed to half its size. He walked a path through the derelicts of hoods, tires, a couple of old refrigerators, and assorted unidentifiable rusted junk. A gaggle of six or seven black-and-white spotted mongrels came running toward him, barking but thankfully wagging their tails. The biggest one, a female with a swollen belly, some kind of hound mix, sniffed his crotch good until he shooed her away.

No one was around. It was four o'clock now on this Sunday afternoon. Usually the "boys" were hanging out under an oak tree at the spool table, with weathered wood chairs picked up at the Pickens flea market, no doubt, scattered about. A pile of empty Bud Lite beer cans and cigarette butts littered the rough wood top and the bare ground around it. His mother's word for these kind of people came to mind: *no-count*. His pulse quickened. For all he knew, someone would answer the door with a sawed-off shotgun! Blue Ridge wasn't that far from the Dark Corner, that dangerous mountainous enclave of bootleggers, stills, and shotguns, mainly during Reconstruction but afterward too. Today, rich retirees and escapees from Florida summers built McMansions in its hills and hollows.

He climbed the wood steps, which must be original to the hundred-year-old farmhouse. The land on this country road had been farmland back then, and now except for a scattering of brick houses, modular homes, and trailers, it had been reclaimed by second-growth forest and scrub brush. A useless doorbell hung from the door frame, so he knocked and waited. He waited some more, then knocked again, pounding his fist on the door to try to rouse someone. He pictured those four flat tires. Pure meanness. That and racism. Birds of a feather.

To his surprise, Lyle opened the door. His lank, unwashed hair was disheveled, and he wasn't wearing a shirt, just blue jeans that hung too low on his muscular body, his belly button bulging. It had bothered Lee when Lyle was born that his umbilical cord had been botched. His chest, hairless, looked very white. They stared at each other.

"You living here now?" Lee asked. "Sarabeth told me she kicked you out."

Lyle just shrugged.

"Can I come in?"

Lyle shrugged again but held the door open.

The house was showing its age, and more. It had never been kept up, had a musty odor, and another organic smell that Lee assumed was marijuana. On the scarred glass coffee table were several stubby pipes, a bag of what looked like crushed brown weeds, a lighter, a pack of Lucky cigarettes, an empty package of Cheez-Its, and a Coke bottle almost full of ash and butts.

"Can we sit down?" Lee asked. "And please don't shrug again." He took a seat on the threadbare brown sofa. He wondered if it had fleas. Lyle sat across the coffee table from him. "Maybe you'd like to try a toke," he said and began stuffing a pipe. "Maybe it would loosen you up, Lee." He had always called his grandfather by his name—never Pop or Granddad. It was too late for that when he came to live with Lee at fourteen.

"Put that away," Lee said. "I want to talk to you about something important. Greenville Tech. How you could get a degree in automotive technology. Then maybe Earl could get you on at the Ford Service Department."

Lyle had finished lighting the pipe. He held the smoke in,

and when he released it toward the ceiling, he said, "I'll think about." He held the pipe out to Lee.

Lee held up his open palms to decline. "Okay, you do that." He shook his head, feeling hopeless. "Do you need some money?"

"I always need some money."

Lee handed him a fifty.

"You could come live with me," Lee said. "There's your room in the trailer. Go to school at Greenville Tech . . ."

"Like I said, I'll think about it." Lyle blew smoke circles into the stale air.

Lee nodded. "In that case, are the lads home?" He didn't know their names, had never had anything to do with them. "I need to talk to them about a little matter of some flat tires." His heart pounded, and he wondered if he could get through this without having a heart attack. Wouldn't that be perfect!

"They won't know anything about that," Lyle said. "They're upstairs. Sleeping."

"Then go wake them up and tell 'em I'd like to talk to them," Lee said. "I'll wait outside."

His legs felt shaky as he went down the front steps. The dogs circled around him again, yapping and getting in his way; he felt like kicking them. He wondered if any of the Dunlap boys would come out. He doubted it. But he would rest a moment in the shade, and then . . . he didn't know.

A half hour later, all three of them came out of the house. They all wore worn jeans permanently stained with motor oil and red dirt. The oldest, biggest brother had a big bushy beard where a squirrel could live, Lee thought. He had never understood why a man would want massive face hair like that. The smallest brother, probably the youngest, had on a faded gray T-shirt with the name Alice Cooper in spooky script and an image faded almost into extinction of what appeared to be a guy licking a snake. The other fellow, who must be the middle one, was shirtless, his chest well-developed, as if he worked out. Lyle was nowhere to be seen. They don't seem happy to see me, Lee thought, and this struck him as humorous. He stood up and offered his hand, which hung in the air, untaken. "I'm Lee Trammell—your neighbor down the road. The trailer on the left. And your names are . . ."

No response. They stared at him. There was something both quizzical and menacing in their faces. They probably had those same expressions the day they were born, Lee thought tiredly to himself. "Why don't we all sit down," he said, taking a ladderback chair with two missing back rails. "I don't suppose you'd offer me a cold one?" he indicated the pyramid of empty beer cans on the round table. "Maybe you'd join me." Sweat was running down his neck.

The oldest bearded one tilted his head slightly, and the youngest one, who could apparently read head language, disappeared into the house and returned clutching four beers against his "Alice Cooper" chest. He dumped them on the table, and each brother reached for one, so Lee took the last one.

"Ah, thank you," he said, popping the top. He was not normally a beer drinker—or any kind of drinker. His stomach was getting quite a ride today: instant ice tea with a Bud Lite chaser.

The three boys—grown men of course, but when you're seventy-five, all younger men are boys—pulled out their own mishmash of chairs, sat down, and guzzled their beers.

Lee lifted his can and said, "To neighbors." To this, the boys raised their cans in his direction. It was a start.

"I knew your grandfather," Lee reminisced. "I moved out here in 1996. He still did a little farming back then. I bought the trailer from a fellow who got a divorce and had to sell. I love the countryside around here. Course now it's getting more populated. People moving in."

"Why you here, old man?" asked the middle, shirtless one.

"Oh, sorry," Lee said. "I didn't catch your name."

"Mark," he said, and he stood and actually offered his hand, which had quite a grip. "Mark Dunlap."

Lee gave it as firm a shake as he could. "And you?"

"Matthew Dunlap," the oldest, bearded one nodded. "Pleased to meet you," and he extended his hand across the table.

"And I suppose you're Luke?"

"How'd you know?" the younger boy said. Lee couldn't tell if he was joking or serious. He had a sullen, dull look about him.

"All good biblical names," Lee mused. "Well, let me ask you this. Is my grandson living here now?"

"That's his business," Matthew said. His lips were very pink inside the squirrel's nest.

"Is he on drugs?"

"We don't do drugs here," he said.

"Well, that's good to hear," Lee said. "I guess you know there's an opioid epidemic going on around these parts. At least that's what they're telling us on the six o'clock news."

They all stared at him. He had never met folks who just stared in place of conversation.

Finally Mark spoke. "We don't have time to sit around jawin' about the news…"

". . . with a crazy old man," Lee finished for him. "Well, in that case, let me ask you this. Are you aware that there's a Dodge Charger behind that empty house down the road? Last night someone punctured all four tires. With nails. Pure meanness, wouldn't you say? To mess with someone's car like that." He took a swig of his beer, bitter in his mouth. "I suppose . . ." he swept his arm toward the wrecked cars, "that you boys know a lot about cars. And tires. You're probably professionals, I'm guessing."

"That car's none of our business," Matthew said.

"It isn't?" Lee said. "Well, I kinda thought it was."

"Why would you think that?" Mark, the buff one, said. "We got a crazy old man here," he said to his brothers. "Thinks we had something to do with flat tires!"

"That's the second time today I've been called a crazy old man," Lee said.

"Then you must be one!" Luke snorted and looked to his brothers for approval, but they were stone-faced.

"True enough, Luke," Lee said. "But I bet you boys know how to fix tires like that. Maybe pulling the nails out, patches—I don't know myself, but I'm sure you boys know all about fixing flat tires."

They stared at him. "And why would we do that?" Mark said at last. The oldest, bearded one—Matthew—was watching Lee with a silent intensity.

"Oh, I don't know," Lee said. "I just thought you might take an interest. As a kindness. Well, anyway, I'm afraid the police will be coming around to investigate that kind of vandalism in the neighborhood. We can't have it, I'm sure you'd agree. Might even be a felony, I don't know. And given what they're calling an epidemic hereabouts, they'll probably snoop around to see if anyone down this stretch of road is selling drugs. Opioids. Cooking crack even. Is that the right verb? Did you know they have these dogs that can sniff out drugs? They're trained to do that. Amazing, the noses they have. Especially marijuana. K-9s, they call them." He shook his head in wonder. "K-9 dogs, get it?"

Silence.

He stood up. "Now if you'll excuse me. Thank you for your hospitality. My K-9's waiting at home, and I feel a nap coming on. Must be the beer. By the way, that Dodge—the one with four flat tires— belongs to a Black family. I don't suppose you knew that." Lee raised his eyes to the big Confederate flag.

The Dunlap lads were silent. Cat got your tongue, Lee thought to himself. Feeling a little tipsy, he wove his way through the spotted dogs to his car, opened the driver's door, and got in. For a moment, he felt overcome, as if he couldn't drive home: Lyle! His grandson, whose life he'd been mostly absent from; son of Buddy, dead at twenty-two in a violent car wreck; great-grandson of Lee Trammell, who lynched a Black man and then hung himself, leaving his own sons fatherless and adrift. Quite a legacy.

No wonder Lyle was into drugs.

CHAPTER TEN

OH GOD! WHAT a welcome sanctuary his trailer was! Peace! Solitude! What a night and day it had been! He didn't bother to preheat the oven, just shoved a frozen chicken pot pie in. When he turned it to 400, the oven sent out noxious fumes, but luckily he had disconnected the smoke alarm. He intended to clean the oven someday but that day mysteriously never came. Sarabeth and Del had invited him to stay for supper. Sarabeth had bought a cut-up chicken at Winn Dixie which Del was going to fry; there would be potato salad and watermelon, they cajoled him. But he'd passed, saying he had one more stop out in the country and would just go on home. And what a stop that was! The sight of Lyle when he opened the door! What was the word they used? Wasted. Lyle had looked wasted.

And the Dunlap lads. What to make of them? They were like mongrels themselves. It was hard to see what lay beneath their facade of muted hostility, if anything. They were like lost boys—not the ones in Peter Pan but boys who looked as if they'd never had much, who had grown up part feral. Manners, education, civility—all missing. Of course, they weren't boys. They were grown men, except for the young-est. Luke. Lee guessed his age at about eighteen, maybe nine-teen. There was something empty about him; no one home. Matthew, the oldest, hadn't said much, but he had a flicker of amity, a glimmer of intelligence, watching from behind that beard, taking everything in but keeping his own counsel.

Smoky was stretched out on the floor, his head on his paws. He looked up at Lee with his brown eyes where Lee stood pondering at the kitchen counter. He wished Smoky could speak. He would offer good counsel. Del, Marcus, Lyle, the Dunlap lads . . . A day ago Lee had a quiet life. A boring life, granted. Since he retired, he'd had trouble filling his days. He'd read the paper in twenty minutes max and could only justify going to Ingles for groceries once a week; of course there was Walgreens for his prescriptions, always a treat, and walks with Smoky. Then there were books, which he got at the Travelers Rest library once a week; but how many hours a day could anyone read? He wasn't that good at puttering around the yard or upkeep on the trailer, especially all the things that needed attention but could wait. He didn't go to church, appreciating the irony that he was put off by the very thing he needed: fellowship. At least there were naps.

He regretted now that he hadn't stayed for supper at Sarabeth's. How good that fried chicken would have been! He set the timer on the stove for forty minutes and lay down on the couch. He longed to drop off for a nap, but his mind was too agitated by that Dodge sitting out there behind the empty house on four flat tires. In all likelihood, the lads would strip it tonight like wolves scavenging a deer carcass.

And there was Lyle. Another lost boy, only this one was his. He'd been well-cared for by his maternal grandparents, who were modest, well-meaning evangelicals but strict and old-fashioned. They had been shocked and bewildered when their all-of-eighteen-year-old daughter Rebecca—Becca— got pregnant by Buddy. Out-of-wedlock pregnancies were supposedly no longer a source of shame; somehow Sam and Olive had missed that update. But the real problem was Becca wanted nothing more to do with Buddy, her parents, or even baby Lyle, in no particular order. She just didn't, and she proved it by moving to—the last Lee heard—Colorado. Olive and Sam had taken over raising Lyle, with infrequent visits from Lee.

"Your turn," they said when they delivered fourteen-year-old Lyle to Lee, turning over a sulky, angry, acting-out young teenager with pimples. Lyle had run away and been gone for an agonizing week for Olive and Sam; he crept home like an outside cat that had gone stray but found the wider world inhospitable. Lee was sixty-five then, ten years ago, still working full-time at the library, ill-equipped to take on a teenage boy. He hardly knew his grandson, not having been involved in his life except for an obligatory visit a few times a year and presents on his birthdays and Christmas, mostly ones Lyle had no interest in. He didn't know how to talk to Lyle. No one had ever talked to him when he was growing up.

They got through the four years Lyle lived with him somehow. By then Lee's depression had abated to a large extent, not that he became the life of the party. And while he would always be an introvert, he enjoyed getting together with his friends in the Lunch Bunch, especially Sammy, whom Lee had seen through his struggles with alcoholism and adventures in AA. And there was brother Earl, whose family always included Lee and Lyle for holiday dinners.

When Lyle graduated from Blue Ridge High School, he moved in with boys unknown to Lee and then later showed up at the Dunlap lads'. He and Lee were neither estranged nor close. Lee understood he had failed Lyle. But Lyle was by nature equanimous, dropping by unexpectedly and disappearing for periods of time like that outside cat, leaving Lee with no idea where he was or what he was up to. But he always came around sooner or later.

HE didn't bother to put the pot pie on a plate—just ate it out of the aluminum container while he stood at the kitchen counter. He washed his fork and rinsed out the glass he'd used for milk, which didn't sit well with beer. He had to go check on the Dodge. He leashed Smoky. Usually a walk was good therapy for a troubled mind. It might help just to see that all was well at what had been the McBees' house. The McBees. He wondered what demons egged Marcus on to drink just one more, and then another and another. He'd read that alcoholism wasn't a simple matter of willpower. There were biological factors, what exactly he couldn't remember. Genetics? Also situational problems. Troubled childhoods. It was a complicated matter. Same for drug addiction. He'd only walked in his own moccasins, not Marcus's or Lyle's. It still seemed a miracle to him that he'd been delivered from his own affliction.

He and Smoky walked along slowly in the early evening light. On these balmy late May nights, it wouldn't get dark until around 8:30. He saw the first flickers of lightning bugs flashing in the woods, bringing back memories of catching them as a child and putting them in a Mason jar that flickered in the dark. The loblolly pines, second growth—the old trees having been logged decades ago—were like friends. He prayed this stretch of road would never be developed. He'd hate to see lots cleared for new houses, his friends cut down, slaughtered really. This was still rural country, far enough from town that not many people wanted to live out here. But that was changing fast.

He came around the side of the empty house. Thank God the Dodge was still intact. At least there was that. He examined the flat tires, which had lost even more air, if that was possible. The car now sat solidly on the ground. He didn't see how those tires could be repaired or how the car could be driven on them enough to get to the nearest repair shop in Travelers Rest. Del needed that car. But of course that was Marcus's problem, not his. Marcus had better get to the car before the lads did. They would love to lift if not the entire car, then any and all usable parts.

He sat down on the back steps and let Smoky off leash. He went poking around the backyard, where he found the stick the McBee boys had thrown for him. He pranced around with it, making a game of tossing it in the air, then pouncing on it. Lee thought of those skinny little McBee boys, Jackson and James. They were darn cute. They had deeply black skin, and their hair buzz-cut so close to their scalps, they looked bald. At first he couldn't tell them apart. Now he saw how distinct they were, Jackson a pinch stockier, more extroverted, bracing into the world while James was more sensitive, thoughtful, hesitant. They probably knew a lot more about their parents' troubles than they let on.

As he was musing about all this, he heard a distinctive sound: a car with a bad muffler coming down the road. He knew that car, and he stood up. The car pulled in the drive, a door opened, and all at once an explosion of pit bull came racing around the house. Maybell zeroed in on Smoky, running up to him aggressively, putting on the brakes at the last moment. Smoky, stiff-legged, hackles raised, held his ground. "Yo Mama!" Lee imagined them yelling. He called frantically for Smoky to come, knowing it would do no good. He knew better than to try to break up a dog fight once it started, especially with a pit bull involved. Marcus came running around the house, yelling "Maybell, get your butt over here!" He jammed on his own brakes at the sight of Lee. "What you doing here?"

Together they stood at the edge of the yard, watching the two dogs work it out. They had now advanced to some serious butt-sniffing, circling each other round and round. "Quite a way to make a new acquaintance," Marcus observed. Lee was still holding his breath. Suddenly Smoky took off, running in wide circles around the yard, and Maybell accepted the invitation, giving chase. Then they reversed, with Maybell in front. They'd pause occasionally to mock-box, up on their hind legs, mouthing each other with open jaws but no teeth. Then Maybell picked up the stick and took off with it, Smoky giving chase.

"Apparently they're friends now," Lee observed.

Marcus snorted. "All it took was a good snoutful of ass."

Lee laughed, and they sat down on the top step. "I didn't expect to see you here," he said.

"Well, here I am," Marcus said. "Had to check on Del's car. But what you doing here?"

"Same thing. I was worried about it." He shook his head. "But I suppose if someone is looking to strip it, they'll do it in the dead of night."

"I don't intend to let that happen," Marcus said. "I'm

spending the night."

Lee looked at him in surprise. "What do you propose to do if someone comes?"

"I'm prepared."

"What? A gun?"

Marcus nodded, his eyes on the dogs, who had had enough play, and were now lying in the grass. Smoky had reclaimed the stick and was chewing on it. Maybell was turtle up, her belly splotched with pale pink and gray, kicking her four legs in the air to scratch her back.

"I always pack when I'm coming to redneck country."

"Oh for Pete's sake. Listen, Marcus, I'm not sure 'packing' is such a great idea. And where is the thing? In your car?"

Marcus snorted. "A lot of good it would do me there." He pulled his white T-shirt tight against his right side at his waist. Lee saw the outline of what looked like a large pager. But of course it was no pager.

Before he could respond, they heard what sounded like a pickup truck approaching. Both men were silent as they listened. Lee prayed it would just go on by to the ravine, but he knew it wouldn't. They're here, he thought, and again his heart beat hard. In a few moments, the pickup parked behind Marcus's Pontiac in the driveway. He heard the doors open and two voices speculating on the car. "That muffler's about to fall off." He knew that voice: Lyle's. And of course, predictably, a dog came loping around the side of the house: the black-and-white spotted bitch, the leader of the pack and mother of all mutts at the Dunlaps'. Smoky and Maybell leapt up and commenced furious barking.

Marcus and Lee leapt to their feet too. "Okay, you guys!" Marcus yelled with impressive authority at the dogs. "Get the hell out of here," he yelled at the new dog, who cowered like it expected to be hit. Maybell got busy smelling the bitch's butt, while Smoky looked on with what Lee thought was a smile on his face: *This is so much fun!*

Matthew and Lyle came around the house, stopping short at the sight of Lee and Marcus. "What's going on?" Matthew said after a few beats. His beard looked even bushier than it had that afternoon. "I didn't know there was a party."

"I hope you remembered to bring the beer," Marcus said.

"I thought you were bringing it."

"Marcus," Lee said, trying to take some control of the situation, "this is my grandson Lyle. And this is Matthew Dunlap. A neighbor down the road."

"At the house with the Confederate flag?" Marcus lifted his eyebrows.

Dear God, Lee thought, are we about to have another fight—the human kind? He tried to defuse.

"This is Marcus McBee, Matthew. He used to rent this house. He owns that Dodge."

There was a long moment of silence. Then Matthew stepped forward and offered Marcus his hand. Marcus paused a moment and then shook it briefly.

"You're about to lose your muffler," Lyle observed to Marcus.

"That's the least of my worries." Marcus nodded toward the flat tires.

Matthew walked over to the Dodge and slowly circled it, examining each tire. Marcus watched him as everyone went silent. "What you propose to do about it?" he said at last.

"Well, I suspect the car will need to be towed," Matthew opined.

Lyle came over to the car to take a look himself. "We could tow it to the house," he said to Matthew. "Use two of those used tires in the shed for the front tires. Enough to get it down the road. The Dunlaps got a big ol' tow truck," he said to no one in particular.

"I'd be wary about leaving it here," Matthew said to Marcus. "You don't know who might be going by. People cruising down to the dump. Undesirables. All hours of the night. We hear their trucks go by."

Jesus, Lee thought. He's offering to tow the car to their place so they can scavenge it at their leisure!

Matthew sat down on the top step. "Join me?" he gestured to Marcus. "Take a load off."

Marcus was silent. Matthew got out a pack of cigarettes and selected one, tapped it lightly on his knee, and lit it with a disposable lighter. He inhaled, and when he blew the smoke out, Lee smelled the same skunky smell of Lyle's pipe smoke. Matthew handed the joint to Lyle, who inhaled, held the smoke, and then handed it to Marcus. Marcus studied the joint for a moment and then took a drag. He handed it to Lee. "Come on, Lee," Lyle said, grinning. "Have a hit. It won't kill you. Maybe it'll loosen you up."

Lee had never smoked, not even a cigarette. The idea of smoke in his lungs appalled him. But now he took the joint and tentatively inhaled, immediately choking and coughing, struggling for breath. All three men laughed.

"Takes a little practice," Matthew said, not unkindly.

Lee felt his face flush. He passed the joint back to Matthew, where it started around again.

Finally Matthew put out what was left of the joint on the bottom step.

"Can you tow it with your truck?" Marcus asked. Was he offering his car up to the Dunlap lads, a lamb to slaughter? This whole scene felt surreal to Lee; could he be stoned without even one—what was the word Lyle used—hit? He had worried about leaving the car here all night. But if the Dunlaps stripped the car in their own yard, at least they'd know who to call the cops on.

Lyle walked over to the Dodge again, lifting the hood to inspect the engine. He looked better than he had at the house—maybe he'd taken a shower. His long brown hair was slicked back, and there was color in his face, not pallid white; he was still a good-looking guy. "The Dunlaps are mechanics," Lyle called over to Marcus. "They know all about cars. They're in the wreckage business. They sure as hell can tow it."

Again Marcus was silent. They all waited.

"Let's get started," Marcus said, "while we still got some light."

LEE sat down on the top step, feeling old, tired, and out of it. This situation was totally out of control—at least his control; all he could do was sit back and watch. Lyle took the pickup and went down the road to get the tow truck. Marcus and Matthew stood in the backyard.

"What kinda job you got?" Matthew asked Marcus. He took out a pack of Lucky's, offered one to Marcus, took one himself, and lit both with his Bic lighter.

"Warehouse. Car parts. I manage the orders."

Matthew nodded. "You like it?"

"The pay's okay, and they hire big black niggers—as you might put it."

Matthew took a drag on his cigarette. "I get what you're referring to. But personally, that Confederate flag doesn't mean a rat's ass to me. My baby bro had to have it." He blew out a smoke ring. "I have to pick my battles with Luke, if you know what I mean."

"I don't. And why he'd want a flag advertising the South getting its butt kicked, I don't know."

Matthew gave a half-laugh. He took another drag on his cigarette. "Luke says it's about heritage. Honoring those who fought in the Civil War. Or as he refers to it, the War of Northern Aggression."

"I see," Marcus snorted. "Honoring those who fought to keep my ancestors enslaved."

"'Fraid so," Matthew said. "But just for the record, my people didn't own any slaves. My great-grandfather farmed the land behind the house—with a mule and plow." He waved his hand in the direction of the farmhouse down the road. "He was an upstanding citizen, from what my grandmother told me, but his grandson, my dad, was a whole other story. Liquor was his occupation. That and cruelty. The sins of the father were visited on the sons. We were a different kind of slave, I guess you could say."

Marcus drew on his cigarette, staring out into the woods behind the house. "It's nowhere near the same," he said heatedly. "I'm sorry your upbringing was rough. I'll tell you about mine sometime. But at least y'all were white!"

Lee stood up on the top step. "Cut it out, you dogs!" he yelled, and the two men standing in the yard turned to stare at him. The three dogs jumped up and came running up to him, barking. "Not you dogs," he said. "You human dogs—getting your hackles all up! Cut it out before someone gets hurt!" He paused a moment. "Maybe you should try sniffing each other's butts!"

Matthew and Marcus stared at him. Then Marcus burst out laughing. "I'm gonna pass on that."

"Old man getting feisty," Matthew observed.

"Yeah," Marcus said. "I see that."

An ancient mud-coated tow truck was rumbling into the yard. Mark was driving with Lyle in the passenger seat. They hoisted two worn tires out of the truck bed, and Lyle got busy with a jack taking off the Dodge's flat front tires, replacing them with slightly less-flat used tires. Lee watched Lyle work, surprised at his proficiency. He must have learned how to change a tire at one of the garages where he'd worked or maybe from the Dunlaps. Matthew supervised as Mark backed the truck up to the Dodge, and Lyle crawled under the back end, attaching a large hook with a thick cable that Mark cranked from the tow truck to lift the rear of the car. Matthew tossed the butt of his cigarette in the grass, carefully grinding it out with his boot.

"Nice to meet you, bro," he said to Marcus. "See you around, Lee."

"What about the tires?" Marcus said.

"We'll have to see about that," Matthew said. He opened the passenger door of the truck and climbed up next to Lyle with Mark in the driver's seat.

Lee and Marcus stood watching the tow truck slowly leave the yard, the Dodge hoisted on its wobbly front tires. It started back down the road, the Dunlaps' black-and-white hound trotting after it.

CHAPTER ELEVEN

FIRST THING MONDAY morning Lee was on the phone, calling his little brother Earl. All night long, tow trucks had rumbled through his sleep, and Lyle's thin face, a combination of innocence and debauchery, had swirled in and out of focus. He had turned on his side, then his back, then the other side, back and forth, trying to find that sweet spot on the mattress where he could drift into oblivion. At some point Smoky had bailed off Lee's bed and crept into the living room and onto the couch. "Hope you got your beauty rest," Lee admonished him in the morning. Smoky managed to look, at least to Lee, both remorseful and rested.

During one of the many turns during the night, Lee had a brilliant thought: Earl! At seventy-two, Earl was an institution at the Ford dealership, a "brand" so to speak of Davis Ford. For decades during his heyday, he'd been the most productive salesman. Now, when a former customer came in (and he had many of those) and asked for him, he sprang into action, clapping him on the back (and, if a couple came in together, he'd give "the missus" a peck on the cheek), pretending he remembered their children, promising an amazing deal. But after warm greetings, he'd turn them over to one of the younger salespeople up to date on interest rates, loan matters, credit checks, and the technical specs of the increasingly complicated automobiles that Detroit was turning out. He still loved surveilling the two large lots of new and used cars, taking spins in new models, and trading off-color jokes with the salespeople. Earl was untroubled water, and he might be able to help with the riptide of Lyle.

Lee had never asked a favor of Earl. But now he was going to see if he might find Lyle a job at the dealership. Didn't matter what. His heart swelled at the idea that Lyle might take to a regular job with a regular paycheck and even have a role model and mentor in Earl. Maybe he would want to enroll in the Greenville Tech program. He and Earl agreed to meet for lunch at noon on Wednesday at the Poinsett Club in Greenville. "There's no fool like an old fool," Lee said to himself when he ended the call. His fantasy of Lyle's new life deflated like a punctured tire. It dissipated in a cloud of cannabis smoke.

H E took Smoky for their morning walk. He turned left toward the ravine, and when he got to the McBee house, he could hardly stand to look at it, empty, deserted, and deteriorating. He saw the ghosts of the little McBee boys daring to pet Smoky that first time, looking up at him in wonder at their bravery. He wanted them to be okay, to have their father home, reformed, and for their lives to be settled and happy. The image of the Dodge being towed away last night still burned in his mind. It was a good car, good enough, and Del needed it. How that travesty would be resolved, he didn't know.

Well, he counseled himself, none of this was his business.

Marcus and Del would have to work things out themselves. Marcus would have to deal with the Dunlaps. The twins were young and resilient, and this was just a bump in their childhood. An adventure, really, sleeping at Sarabeth's. So many families suffered so much worse (including his). He would stop by Sarabeth's after lunch and see how things were going there. Maybe Del would have decided that it was time to go home. She and Marcus would fade from memory (as so much did these days), and he'd be back to a quiet life.

ON his way to town for his lunch date with Earl on Wednesday, he had to drive by the Dunlaps' to get to the county road. He made a concerted effort not to look toward their place with all the damn wrecks in the yard. The last thing he wanted to see was the McBees' Dodge sitting there on flat tires. He breathed a sigh of relief when he got to the county road leading out of Blue Ridge. There was no actual town of Blue Ridge—just a Dollar Store. The joke went that Blue Ridge was not a place but a state of mind.

Over the last five years, the area had changed, was changing every day, with new houses and even a couple of subdivisions springing up. There were still some derelict houses, seemingly unfit for human habitation, though humans did inhabit them; there was an assortment of trailers in various states, including abandoned, some nicely-tended red-brick homes with white trim on large lots, and a few incongruous McMansions, as if Blue Ridge was a gated community. There were still a couple of horse pastures and some remaining open fields and forests, the way most of it had been when Lee bought his double-wide back in 1996. Twenty years ago. Time flies. It also drags.

He passed Sandy Flat Cafe, "2 hotdogs, 89 cents," turned onto Fews Bridge Road and then onto Pine Log Road to get to the Tigerville road and Highway 25. Travelers Rest had sprouted fast food restaurants along a single mile of the highway, as abundant as mushrooms after a rainy spell: Chick-fil-A, KFC, Wendy's, Hardee's, McDonald's, Burger King, Waffle House, Bojangles, Taco Bell; it was amazing! He breezed past Furman University and the Cherrydale shopping center. Closer to town, the Poinsett Highway was lined with Mexican groceries and taco joints, discount stores, beauty salons in concrete block buildings, anonymous strip malls, an empty Pizza Hut, millions of used car lots. City Arsenal sold guns, and Duke Sandwiches, which had once been great—he had practically lived on their pimento cheese on white bread at one time in his life—were now expensive inferior imitations. This low-rent economy was the alternative to the booming, prosperous downtown of Greenville.

In town, he drove slowly down the tree-shaded Main Street. He came to Court Square, the heart of Greenville since the 1800s. Here was the (now) elegant, refurbished red-brick Poinsett Hotel, built in 1924, the grand dame which had been through numerous incarnations of her own, including being a run-down retirement home for the elderly. Around 2000, it was renovated to become the Westin Poinsett Hotel as part of Greenville's revitalization. It flanked the cream-colored Greenville County Courthouse, where, Lee knew, his father's lynching trial had been held in 1947.

When he was in therapy with Beverly Proctor, she had encouraged him to read about the murder and trial, which, because of the sensationalism of a lynching with twenty-eight defendants, had been covered extensively in local and national newspapers and magazines, including *Life*. He'd tried looking through the large file the library had accrued on the case and had even made copies of some of the stories, but he found he had no appetite for such research.

Let the past stay the past.

EARL was already at a table at the Poinsett Club, a private club housed in a red-brick Colonial house built in 1904 by a textile executive. He had on his same summer uniform he'd worn since high school: a polo shirt with an alligator logo—this one baby blue—khaki pants and loafers without socks. He sported a Coppertone tan from all the golf he played. Lee knew people who had outgrown their childhood faces, unrecognizable in the present. But despite all the decades that had passed, Lee still saw his little brother's face in his features—still the irrepressible child he had been, only with jowls that sagged. The rest of him was now inflated; he'd gained upward of fifty pounds over the years. "Long time, no see, Junior," he said, rising to slap Lee lightly on his back, despite the fact that they had just seen each other at the Golden Corral on Saturday—a lifetime ago to Lee. Lee was named for their father, Lee Trammell; Junior was not a moniker he cherished.

"I'm having the deluxe burger with cheese," Earl declared, not even looking at the menu. "Beth is nagging me to lose weight. She wants me to eat more vegetables. I tell her potato chips with onion dip *is* a vegetable."

Lee ordered the same. He had already asked about Earl's sons and Beth at the Golden Corral—"all doing great" blah blah—so he cut to the chase.

"Do you think you could find a job for Lyle at the dealership?" His heart beat harder than felt safe.

"How is Lyle? I can't remember the last time I saw him. I know he's been a challenge."

Lee wondered how much he could say. But his need for help with Lyle made him spill the beans. "He's a pothead."

"A what?"

"You know. Someone who smokes marijuana. Weed."

"A pothead, huh!" Earl chuckled a little. He stirred sugar into his already sweet ice tea. "Well," he said after a thoughtful pause, "that's not as bad as those opioids we're hearing about. And from what I understand, marijuana is not necessarily addictive."

"I don't know about that," Lee said. "But I want him to straighten out, get away from bad influences. I was thinking if he had a regular job, he'd have to get to work on time, have a regular paycheck. Have to answer to some authority. You maybe could keep an eye on him. Be a role model of sorts."

"I've already raised my boys," Earl said, chuckling a little but pointedly. "What kind of job do you have in mind? What kind of skills does he have?"

"I was thinking maybe in the shop. He's always fooling around garages, working on cars," Lee said lamely. He didn't actually know if Lyle knew a thing about cars, aside from being able to open the McBees' hood. He was sweating under his arms. "I've talked to him about going to Greenville Tech. Getting a degree in automotive technology."

"And what did he say?"

Lee was silent. He felt the wind leaving his sails. It was hopeless. Even if Earl managed to scrounge up some kind of little job for Lyle, he'd be in over his head with the guys in the shop. He wouldn't last a week.

He just shook his head. They sat in silence for a few

moments as the waitress set down their plates. "I'll see what I can do," Earl said. "I'm not promising anything. But I'll talk to Buck in the shop."

"I'd appreciate that," Lee said. "Thank you, Earl."

They settled down to eating for a few minutes. "I really like the burgers here," Earl said as he squirted ketchup on his fries. "But the ones at Grill Marks are great too."

"There's something I've been wanting to ask you," Lee said. "What do you remember about our father?"

"Daddy? Well, I was only three when he died," Earl said. "Let's see. I remember that he was a lot of fun. Chasing us around to scare us. Like he was a tiger. Or maybe it was a bear." He squinched his face, pondering. "I just have vague memories, if they even are memories. Maybe Mother told me things that I think I remember. Like how he'd always come in and kiss us goodnight, no matter what time he got home. He drove a cab, you know." He paused to take a big bite and chewed thoughtfully.

"Don't you think it was odd that Mother didn't have any pictures of him around and never talked about him? Like he never existed."

"I don't remember that," Earl said. "She talked about him, Junior. Of course she was working all the time after the accident. And she wasn't a big talker." He stopped chewing and looked at Lee quizzically.

"Accident?"

"You know, he was killed in a car crash—driving the cab." He commenced chewing.

"Do you ever think about what he did? Does it ever bother you?"

"He drove a cab. Nothing wrong with that."

"The lynching."

"Daddy wasn't involved in any lynching, Junior!" He looked at Lee in astonishment. "What the hell are you saying? You're off your nut!"

"Don't you remember me telling you? About Daddy? How he was part of a lynch mob. They abducted a Black man out of the Pickens jail. There was a trial. In the courthouse on Main Street here in Greenville. You and I were there with Mother. All twenty-eight of the cabbies got off."

"When did you tell me about this?" Earl asked indignantly. He removed the half-chewed piece of burger into his napkin. "I don't remember you telling me a thing about any lynching!"

"You don't remember something like that?"

Earl sat in silence. He pushed his plate with the rest of his lunch away. "Are you sure you told me? Maybe you just meant to. Or thought you did. I'm sure I'd remember."

"It was after Mother died. She told me on her deathbed. She felt we had a right to know. I didn't tell you right away. But then I decided you had a right to know."

"I'm sure I'd remember something like that. Where were we when you told me?"

"You'd gotten a new boat. A Mastercraft. You took me for a ride on Lake Hartwell. We anchored at a small island. I told you the whole story that Mother told me. Don't you remember that?"

Earl was shaking his head. "What did I say?"

"You just listened. You didn't ask any questions. Like you couldn't absorb what you were hearing."

"Well, if you say you told me, you did." He paused, looking past Lee out the window to Williams Street. "But there's nothing we can do about it now, Junior. It's too far in the past.

The past is over. I live in the present . . . and the future. You should do the same."

They sat in silence for several minutes.

"Dessert?" Earl finally asked. "I hear pecan pie is a vegetable." When he smiled impishly, Lee saw in his wrinkled bloated face the little brother he had watched grow up happy and carefree, chasing butterflies, riding his three-wheel trike, marching forward through high school, popular, athletic, normal, shedding any troubles that might have changed his trajectory. He was bulletproof. Untouched. His little brother Earl. While Lee carried the burdens of the world on his shoulders.

"I have a situation going on," Lee said. He hadn't intended to mention the "situation" with the Dunlaps, Marcus, and the goddamn tires. But now, he felt like unburdening himself. He told as succinctly as he could how he had come upon the Dodge, finding Del McBee and the twins at the empty house, about the Dunlap lads. How someone punctured the four tires and how Marcus McBee had shown up at the same time as the Dunlaps last night. "And Marcus actually let them tow his car to their place." The story sounded crazy even to him.

"So you think the Dunlaps punctured the tires? Why would they?"

"Racism. Meanness. Marcus and Del are Black. The Dunlaps fly a huge Confederate flag in their sorry yard, like a big middle finger. They don't want the McBees in the neighborhood. Or anyone like them."

Earl nodded his head. "I see. But why is all this your problem?"

Lee was silent for a long moment.

"Atonement," he said at last.

CHAPTER TWELVE

DRIVING OVER TO Sarabeth's, he wondered if he should tell Del about the car. He certainly didn't want to tell her that Marcus had been at the Hidden Valley house with a gun or that he'd let the Dunlaps tow the car away. He had no idea why, and he had no idea what the Dunlap lads had in mind. Might they rise to the occasion and make things right? He thought he detected something a little better in Matthew than his initial impression of him as a redneck racist cracker. But he was going on mighty slim evidence and speculation. Hope and a prayer, like they say.

He couldn't even feel hopeful about Earl arranging a job for Lyle. For starters, Lyle didn't want a job. At twenty-four, he'd never really had one. What he did for weed money, or food, Lee had no idea. He was just crashing at the Dunlaps' (the way he'd crashed at Sarabeth's), and apparently that was okay with the lads. Just another stray dog. He wondered if the Dunlaps were selling marijuana. Where would they get it, and—suddenly *he* got it: they were growing it. Of course! Out behind the house— where their supposedly esteemed great-grandfather had farmed the land "with plow and mule." Maybe Lyle was the mule!

And then there was Marcus. He needed to talk to Sammy about how to get him to AA. If he didn't get help with his drinking problem, and if Del returned home, it would probably be *deja vu* all over again. He felt a certain paternal feeling toward Del. Whatever. He just liked her. You could tell when someone was good. Solid.

SARABETH'S red Fiat was not in the driveway. She'd be at her paralegal job at Campbell, Smythe and Morrow. He rang the bell. There was a delay, and he heard excited shuffling behind the front door and some muffled giggles: the twins. When Del opened the door, she gave him a broad smile. "Mr. Trammell!" she said. "Come on in. We been expecting you."

"Lee," he said. "None of this mister stuff."

"Okay, mastah." A broad smile.

Something smelled wonderful: chocolate chip cookies.

"We made cookies!" Jackson said. James ran into the kitchen and brought back a napkin with a perfect golden cookie. He held it up to Lee, who bent over and almost touched his nose to it, taking in a big whiff. "Ahhh," he said to the excited boys. He took a bite: "Perfection."

"Did you bring Smoky?" Jackson asked, his face hopeful. "Is he in the car?"

"I miss Maybell," James said sadly. "And I bet she misses me."

Del and Lee exchanged a sympathetic look. "I'm sure she does," Lee said.

"And Dad misses us too," Jackson said. "We're going home tonight!"

"Well, that's great," Lee said, raising his eyebrows at Del.

"Come sit down," Del said. "Coke or ice tea?"

Lee had eaten maybe a fourth of his burger, his conversation with Earl being too intense. He'd had the leftover meat put in a box. Smoky might forgive him for being gone so long if he got that hamburger meat.

"Are you our uncle?" James asked.

Lee laughed. He wanted to say, "Do I look like your uncle?"

"I'm your friend," he said, "who likes you very much."

"It's time for you boys to go out back and practice your badminton. Then you can show Uncle Lee how well you can hit the birdie." She winked at Lee.

"We don't have a net," Jackson complained, sticking out his lower lip, whether in real frustration or for show, Lee couldn't tell. "It's no fun."

"We pretend there's a net," James explained.

"Out the door, you two," Del said. "And play nice. Don't make me come out there."

They slammed the kitchen door, and in a few minutes, Lee saw them through the kitchen window, in the backyard, batting the bedraggled birdie, which looked like it had been caught in a crazy whirlwind.

"They're great boys," Lee said. "I really enjoy being around them."

"Thank you. They have their moments."

"So you're going home this evening?"

"Just for a visit," Del said. "We're coming back here to spend the night. Sarabeth couldn't be nicer or easier. I swear she's an angel."

"I suspect she would dispute that."

"I just want the boys to see their father. He's cooking Sloppy Joes. He'll come get us about six, and after supper, I want him to run us out to get the Dodge. It's just sitting out there at that empty house, and I need it. I'm worried about it. There'll be time for Marcus and me to talk later. Tonight is for the boys."

Lee held his tongue. It wasn't his place to try to explain about the car. "How are you feeling about things?"

Del tilted her head, taking her time answering. "I can't impose on Sarabeth forever. I miss Marcus. How he hit me is fading into the past." She grimaced slightly. "The boys really miss their daddy, and he misses them. It doesn't seem fair to keep them from him."

"Do you think you can get him to go to AA?"

Del's face filled with consternation.

"I don't know."

"Does he have any friends—maybe from childhood or school—who might talk to him? Maybe someone at church? Maybe get him to go to a meeting?"

"We just gradually stopped going when the boys were little. But I want to start back. Especially for the kids. There's a little church in Nicholtown. It's been there forever. Maybe thirty people in the congregation. It might be easier than going to a big church like Long Branch. And as for his 'friends,' I'd say they're part of the problem."

"Okay," Lee said. He stood up. "And good luck tonight. I hope it goes well. It's a good start." He paused. "I think I mentioned to you that I have this childhood friend. He's been sober for years. I could ask him if he'd talk to Marcus."

Del nodded. "I don't know. I'll see what Marcus says."

ON his way home, he thought about his conversation with Del. He felt encouraged. Sort of. People were surprising.

Maybe Marcus would stop drinking. It was a good possibility, considering all he was giving up if he didn't. Maybe he was the kind who could have a beer or two and stop at that. He didn't really know. Maybe he would actually go to AA. He would feel Sammy out, and maybe Marcus would accept Sammy's help.

Still, as he neared Hidden Valley Road, he felt melancholy. He knew the feeling well. Why, when a few minutes ago, he was thinking things were going pretty well, everything considered? But now, after the conversation with Earl, thoughts of his father began to creep into his mind like a fog spreading in the bottomlands. He knew he needed to shake the feeling before it developed into a black hole that could suck him under. Over the years, he'd learned the signs, enough to take action. He would get his dog. He would take him for a treat—a small ice cream cone for both of them at the ice cream shop in Travelers Rest. And then a walk around town, Smoky enjoying a change of scenery, the chance to sniff and piss on every post and pillar. And these small pleasures might shift his mood.

At Pink Mama's, he got two one-scoop cones of vanilla. Smoky was excited out of his mind, his eyes lasered on Lee's every move. Lee sat on a pink wrought-iron bench outside and licked his own dripping cone, while Smoky, commanded to sit, kept his gaze plastered on his cone. He was not allowed to stand and demand. "No snatching," Lee warned him as he held the cone down to him, but the ice cream scoop was gone in a big gulp. There were a few customers there, who smiled at Lee and Smoky, and he smiled back, feeling better. Dogs were the great equalizers. The great peacemakers and friend-collectors. Unless, of course, they got into fights. He thought back to that scene in the yard where Smoky, Maybell, and the black-and-white Dunlap bitch had worked things out. "Good boy," he commended Smoky and offered the empty cone to him. Smoky took it delicately, dropping it on the pavement before eating it there.

He hoped the ice cream wouldn't give Smoky diarrhea. He could hear Smoky's response in his mind: *It won't, and if it does, it will be worth it!* "Easy for you to say," he spoke aloud to the dog, who was swirling his pink tongue around his black muzzle in search of any remaining ice cream. "You won't have to clean it up." He laughed to himself. He felt better. Looking around, he saw that it was a rare summer afternoon: Hot, yes, but not so hot that they couldn't take a little walk around town. Not so hot the pavement would burn Smoky's paws. If only an ice cream cone could solve all the problems people in his world had as easily.

They walked down the main drag through town. When the Swamp Rabbit Trail, a one-hundred-year-old railroad track, was converted to a bike path, it had been extended from Greenville to Travelers Rest. TR, as it was known, had come alive. Formerly a somnambulant little village, the main store of which was a Feed and Seed back when, now it was bustling in comparison, with several nice restaurants, a gourmet pizza place, a couple of brew pubs, and various shops for tourists and locals to browse.

Suddenly his heart began galloping. He realized he was approaching the café where he and Margo Williamson first had lunch ten years ago. The town had changed so much, he hadn't recognized the site. The café was gone, and now the place was a yarn shop with brightly colored balls of yarn and knitted sweaters and scarves in the windows. Back then, it was the short-lived Moondog Café; it had seemed to want to cater to hippies, forty years too late. Tofu and kombucha had been featured in chalk on the black signboard outside, but the menu was standard café food. Now he stood staring at the balls of yarn and sweaters, as if he might take up knitting.

Was it merely an accident that he had wanted ice cream today and found himself walking to this spot? He was suddenly flooded with Margo Williamson, a woman he hadn't seen in eight years! How he wished he could talk to her now, tell her about his day! It was like a physical pain, so strong was the longing.

One day—not long after she joined the library staff and surprised him by telling him they were going to become very good friends—she asked if he'd like to drive up to Travelers Rest over the lunch hour. She wanted his opinion of the "big ol' monstrosity" she and her husband Joe had bought. She explained that Joe was pulling off layer upon layer of wallpaper and cleaning decades of grime from every surface on the second floor. This future bed-and-breakfast was Joe's idea, she explained on the twenty-minute drive. She indicated, vaguely, that some of his business dealings had not worked out back home in Minneapolis. The bed-and-breakfast was a dream of his. "He romanticizes the South," she said, rolling her eyes.

She parked on the street in front of an undistinguished Victorian, circa 1890, a few blocks off Main Street. He saw immediately that renovation of the place would be impossible. Too large; too expensive; too run-down. They stood there under a giant live oak with roots that had uprooted the sidewalk; they looked at the house for a few endless moments. Lee hadn't known what to say, so he said nothing, nor did she.

They went up on the front porch, which had sunk on one end, and she said, "I'd invite you in . . ." but he quickly demurred, saying he'd just wait. She disappeared into the house, and he heard her call up the front stairs, "Honey, want to go to lunch? A friend from the library and I are going to Moondog." Lee couldn't hear the answer. When she reappeared, she explained that Joe was in the middle of—she wasn't sure what, something to do with a bucket and scraper—so he wouldn't be able to join them. They didn't mention the house or Joe again.

At the Moondog Café, they had the special of the day, beef stew, and it was really good. There was a homemade yeast roll and ice tea. Even though he was nervous, he found conversation surprisingly easy; no long awkward silences. She was fifty-nine to his sixty-five, and she looked directly at him with her gray-green eyes as she told happily about her first library experiences as a child, borrowing books from a one-room library heated by a wood-burning stove in her small hometown in Northern Minnesota. "So becoming a children's librarian was the bee's knee." Her face was lovely, beguiling.

She asked how he got started in the library biz. He explained about working as a page in high school and all through college and how after college, he was grandfathered in at the library. "It was on North Main Street then, housed in an old school building, long gone now. I loved that library— the wooden card cabinets with their little drawers filled with cards, all the titles alphabetized. I was sorry to see them replaced by computerized catalogues."

"Not everyone would agree with that!"

Called out, he had to laugh. He told how he'd gotten his master's in library science at the state university in Columbia, living in government housing for $75.00 a month.

"A scholarship paid my tuition," he explained. "About three thousand for the whole degree."

"What drew you to be a librarian?" she asked. "Aside from it being a job. You've spent your whole working life in a library."

No one had ever asked him such a thing. He had taken it so for granted he drew a blank, and had to think about it for a few minutes.

Finally something came to him. "It's the order in libraries that I'm drawn to—the lack of chaos." He hadn't realized this was true until he spoke it. "The companionable silence, people absorbed in their solitary pursuits, the subtle turning of pages. And I like how every book has its place, and that place is known. And there are so many books. All free."

"Free to borrow!" she corrected, grinning.

"Touché."

"Was there chaos in your life when you were growing up? That made order a value?"

Her invitation drew him out. "In a manner of speaking," he said. "My father disappeared when I was six. That's when the chaos began. I didn't know what had happened, and no one explained. But everything changed." He paused. "I was forty before I learned the truth."

"Which was?"

He looked away from her. He found himself telling her how his father had been involved in a lynching back in 1947. "He was acquitted along with twenty-eight other defendants. It was huge local and even national news. He committed suicide within a year of the acquittal."

She was silent for several moments. "That's a terrible story. So sad. I'm sorry."

"For most of my life, up until I was forty, I suffered from depression," he said, unable to stop himself. "My therapist said it was grief. Stuck grief."

"What happened when you were forty?"

"Oh. My mother told me the truth. When she was dying. About my father. It explained the chaos and the loss. And it began to free me."

"So the truth set you free."

He had never thought of it that way.

H E and Smoky turned off Main Street and walked the few blocks to where Margo and Joe's bed-and-breakfast was going to be. In the two years the Williamsons had owned the place, it had never come close to opening. Now the old mansion, with its steep gabled roof, turrets, and chipping, faded pastel paint, was even more decrepit than it had been when they tried to renovate it. A panel of eight mailbox slots on the front porch indicated the house had been turned into rental rooms.

Gone, gone, gone!

I T had been eight years since he'd seen her. He'd told himself he had moved on. But if life had taught him one thing, it was that the things that really mattered to you were always there, still waiting for you.

CHAPTER THIRTEEN

HE LAY DOWN on his bed, and Smoky crashed on the floor next to him. Their sugar highs had worn off, and now they were zonked. Staring up at the popcorn ceiling, Lee reviewed the status quo: First Earl, and his startling admission that he didn't remember or know about their father's past. Had he been living in a cave? No, he'd been living in pleasant suburban neighborhoods, moving up from a modest one-bedroom duplex to a two-bedroom ranch house to a bigger brick split-level house with four bedrooms and two-and-a-half baths. For all those years, he'd been climbing the ladder at Davis Ford, working long hours, raising his good sons, taking nice vacations to the beach and the mountains, playing golf, being a solid citizen. Maybe he had repressed the knowledge about their father, or maybe he didn't want to remember. Maybe he had it right, that the past is past. Dead. Gone. But was it ever, really?

Then there were Del and the twins. He wondered how it had gone with Marcus. Had Del even brought up AA? Probably not. This was a "pretend-everything-is-okay" evening for the kids. There would be time for such a discussion later. At least he hoped there would be. He wondered if Del was capable of following through. The suck of the familiar and easy might prove stronger than what was hard. Well, he would follow through on his part. He'd call Sammy and talk to him about AA and Marcus. AA was the only thing he could think of that might help, but what did he know?

Then there was the trip down memory lane in TR. He thought about getting out his safe deposit box of important papers and taking a look at Margo's letters, all of which he'd saved. The box in his bedroom closet was radiating radioactive commands to be opened. But he knew what that would lead to: commotion. In his mind, in his heart. He'd had enough commotion for the day.

It would be good to spend more time with Sammy, not just at the monthly Lunch Bunch buffet. They didn't get together as often as they should since Sammy lived out at Lake Harwell. And the mole the dermatologist had removed from his scalp was cancer. Sammy said they were going to do a sentinel lymph node biopsy to see if it had spread. Lee was worried, and he told Sammy to let him know as soon as he knew something.

He had known him forever—since that first day in third grade after his mother had moved them back to Greenville. Sammy came up to the new kid and asked if he wanted to fight. Fearing the worst, that this big kid might destroy him, Lee held his breath and shook his head. "Okay," Sammy said and patted Lee on the back. "You have made a wise decision."

After that, they sat together every day at lunch, not just that year but all through grammar school, junior high, and high school. They saw each other through broken marriages, divorces, deaths, Sammy's alcoholism, and Lee's depression as best they could, each damaged but in different ways.

THE following Saturday they met for lunch at the S&S Cafeteria. They pushed their trays down the steam table line, which had, in Lee's opinion, the most desirable food in town. You could select from among fried catfish, fried chicken, turkey and dressing, chopped steak, beef stew, flounder almondine, and liver and onions. But what Lee always went for were the vegetable choices: yellow squash casserole, fried okra, collard or mustard greens, green beans cooked with fatback, pinto beans, mac and cheese, and of course, corn bread at the end of the line, and always, always ice tea. The same cashier had been there twenty years. They took their silverware rolled in a thin napkin and sat down in a booth with cracks in the Naugahyde in a quiet corner.

Sammy had shrunk with age—as had Lee. But Sam was still a big guy for an old guy, and he pronounced himself healthy except for some pesky little diabetes and a little scalp cancer. He took his tea unsweetened, and both passed on the spread of desserts, Sammy shielding his eyes from them.

"What's going on with that thing on your head?" Lee asked after Sammy said a perfunctory blessing on fast forward. There was a new, larger white bandage now, and a lot of Sammy's white hair had been shaved around that area.

"Melanoma," Sammy said, picking up his fried chicken with his fingers. "The big C. Or I guess that's the big M. I had this mole that kept bleeding. I didn't pay it much mind. They dug it out, but now it's spread to the nearest lymph nodes. The good news, if you can call it that, is that it hasn't spread any further. The place itches like crazy, but I try to keep my dirty paws off it."

"My God, Sammy," Lee said. His stomach had taken a fast elevator ride down. "I'm really sorry to hear this." He eyed his vegetable plate ruefully. "Will you keep me posted?

"Sure will," Sammy said. "I don't feel sick or anything." But he looked a little sick—not physically exactly but maybe emotionally—as he said this. "So let's move on. What's up with you? You said you wanted to talk to me about something."

"Well, for starters, Lyle is a pothead."

Sammy's eyes, the upper lids drooping to the point where he could barely see out, popped opened wide. "Say what?" His white eyebrows were a bushy mess in desperate need of a trim.

"I didn't even know I knew the term 'pothead' a week ago," Lee groaned. "And now I toss it around like a hippie."

"Hippies went out in the seventies, Lee. Are you sure you know what a pothead even is?"

Lee rolled his own eyes, his saddlebags underneath instead of on top. "He smokes marijuana. Pot. You know."

"Oh well," Sammy shrugged. "I smoke a little weed myself. But I'm not what you'd call a pothead, Lee. Marijuana relaxes me. It's way better for me than alcohol."

"Is the world going crazy?" Lee asked dramatically. "I come here to get counsel from you, and you turn out to be a doper!"

Sammy laughed. "Tell me what's going on. Is Lyle seriously addicted? Is it messing up his life?"

Lee sighed deeply and found himself starting in on the saga of Del, the car, and the damned punctured tires again. "And then there's Marcus," he said. "And the Dunlap lads and their humongous Confederate flag. They live down the road from me—you know, that big white two-story farmhouse with the dead dogs in the road."

Sammy grinned and shook his head. "All this is getting to you, pal. But what does it have to do with Lyle?"

"He's living there. With the lads. Fine fellows, those, as

you can imagine. They punctured those tires, I'm pretty damn sure. Because the McBees—Marcus and Del—are Black. And then Marcus let them tow his car to their junkyard!"

"Are you sure these so-called Dunlap lads punctured those tires?"

"Who else!" Lee practically shouted. "And there's more. Marcus hit Del, and now she's living at Sarabeth's with the twins. Cute nine-year-old boys. Marcus drinks, and I want him to go to AA. I want you to . . . I can't think of the word."

"Sponsor."

"Yes. I want you to sponsor him."

Sammy shook his head. "What does Marcus want?"

Lee looked down. He stirred his yellow squash casserole and ate a green bean shiny with grease, but he'd lost his appetite.

"I assume he wants to live with his wife and children. I imagine he doesn't want to hit anyone. Just the normal things."

"Who appointed you their white savior?" Sammy asked.

"I don't know. God. Jesus. Mary. When someone is going under, aren't you supposed to throw them a lifeline? You're the only lifeline I've got."

"It would be better, in terms of AA, if he went with someone he knows and trusts. Another Black dude. Maybe someone he knows in their church."

"Am I gonna have to strangle you?" Lee asked. "Will you at least consider it? And I want you to talk to Lyle. You're someone who could talk to him. Okay, so two lifelines."

Sammy regarded Lee with a bemused expression. "I just love you, man," he said.

HE stopped at Winn Dixie that night and bought a rotisserie chicken, which would last him several days. He opened the last can of Campbell's pork and beans. He turned on the TV in the living room, put out his placemat with its view of Mt. Rushmore, and settled down to pretend to watch the news while he ate, though it was just background noise.

After he'd washed his plate and tidied up the kitchen, he felt the pull of the safe deposit box in the bedroom closet. He'd known that was coming. He got the key from his red sock and brought the box out and set it on the dining table, eyeing it like it might bite. Margo's letters were at the very bottom, as if to hide them from someone—Lyle—opening the box after he was dead. He'd have to destroy them before that! Not that they were romantic but just that they existed.

His hands rested on the top of the box. He hadn't looked at her letters in two years, a feat he prided himself on. He knew if he succumbed now, he was in trouble. The box was Pandora's box; he wouldn't be likely to stuff back in all the memories and desires housed there. But he unlocked it and opened the lid.

On the top was his father's pistol and the heavy box of bullets. He lifted the gun and laid it on the table gingerly, along with the bullets. It disturbed him to even see the pistol. Maybe it was time to get rid of it. But how? You couldn't just throw a gun in the Reedy River, could you?

Under the gun in manila envelopes were the deed to the trailer and his two acres, a property insurance policy, a deed to the burial plots he had bought for himself and Elaine, back when, children though they were, they had first married at twenty-five; the plots would never be used, at least not by them. He had a list of instructions for his death. Lyle had power of attorney, and Lee had signed a healthcare directive; he didn't want to be resuscitated; none of that intubation and "clear!"

shouted over his dead heart. He wanted to be cremated, his ashes strewn in the woods behind the trailer. He intended to die in the trailer, no nursing home for him. "But they all say that," he said to Smoky, who was lying with his head on his front paws, watching him. He set those papers aside.

And here was a photograph of his beloved dog Mutt, lying in yellow fall leaves, his pixie face alert. He paused a moment as the latent love and grief swelled for a long moment before subsiding.

Next was a black-and-white picture of his mother, the only one he had. She was sitting in a straight-back chair with baby Earl on her lap and Lee pressed against her leg, staring straight into the camera, unsmiling. He couldn't recognize where the photo was taken or remember who took it. She was so young! She had a round, childlike face and blonde hair cut short. Bangs. She might have been the third child in the picture. She had given birth to Lee when she was seventeen. He hadn't realized how young she was when he was growing up. Age, years, meant nothing to him then: she was Mama.

Next in Pandora's box were the Xerox copies he'd made at the library of news stories about the lynching and trial. He hadn't read them but figured he might want to one day; that day had yet to come. One sheet contained the mug shots of all twenty-eight cabbies arrested and acquitted. He studied them: They were a motley-looking crew. How to describe them? He had seen their like all his life. Growing up, he could have become one of them. No handsome, privileged looks, no Harvard or Princeton grads (or college grads at all, nor even high school in most cases); none of them had had many advantages in life. Somehow he'd managed to pull himself up, get a college degree and a master's, have a profession: librarian. It wasn't doctor or lawyer, granted, but it was respectable, white collar, and secure as long as he'd performed.

He studied the headshot of his father: Lee Trammell. Did he look any different—any better—than the rest? He looked heartbreakingly young himself! He'd thrown away his life at twenty-four—the same age Lyle was now. Had set his wife and sons adrift. What might life have been like if . . .

There was a knock on the door. Lee was startled. No one ever knocked on his trailer door, especially at night. Never. Smoky went into defense mode, barking aggressively, rushing to the door to confront the robbers or murderers. Lee had meant to put a peephole in the front door, but since no one ever visited, he'd never gotten around to it. He was afraid. His mind was running around like a trapped mouse. Maybe it was just Lyle. But he knew Lyle wouldn't knock.

He laid the papers back in the box, put the gun on top, and closed it with shaking hands. The knock came again, more insistent. He cussed whoever it was: He wasn't deaf! Could it be the police? Was there bad news? Lyle! He shoved the box into the closet and went to the door: "Who's there?" At least his voice didn't quaver.

"Yo. It's me. Marcus."

Lee drew back a little and opened the door. "Smoky, settle down," he said sharply, and the dog quieted. The hair on his back settled down, and when Marcus, standing under the front porch light, held out his hand, Smoky licked it apologetically.

"You got better manners than Maybell, Smoky," Marcus grinned. Lee noted he had good teeth, straight and white. "Good dog," and he rubbed Smoky's pointy head. "I'm sorry to disturb you like this, Mr. Lee. Can I come in for a few minutes?"

"It's just Lee. Lee Trammell. Junior. Is something wrong?"

When Marcus stepped into the trailer, suddenly the living room became smaller. He must have played basketball—and football—before he had to drop out of school. Lee was struck again with what a handsome face Marcus had, high cheekbones, deep-set eyes, a high forehead, his hair closely, neatly cropped. He moved like a dancer, easy and graceful, as if he was always hearing music in his head.

"Nothing's wrong, sir. Lee sir. I mean beside all that's wrong. I apologize for busting in on you like this." He kept petting Smoky while he tried to explain.

"Come and sit down, Marcus. It's fine. I'm glad to see you. Would you like something to drink? I mean a Coke or glass of water?" They sat down opposite each other, Marcus sprawling in the La-Z-Boy rocker, Lee's chair, and Lee upright and uptight on the couch.

"Nice place," Marcus said, looking around. He sighed, ran his hand over his head as if he could pull an idea out of his scalp.

Lee gave it a few beats, unable to think of what to say. "So…"

"Uh," Marcus said, as if he'd found the thread. "I just wanted to talk to you."

"Of course," Lee said, his head spinning. "About the Dodge."

"No, no, not that. I saw Del the other night."

"How did that go?"

"Just great!"

Lee was silent, waiting.

After a few long moments, Marcus said, "The only thing … she wouldn't let me touch her."

Lee waited again.

"I guess she isn't over it. She said you know someone who could maybe . . . for these meetings. I know about 'em. I just never thought I needed that kind of thing. But Del. She's tough. She said AA or . . ." He let her ultimatum hang in the air.

"I did tell her that. And I did speak to Sammy about you. He's an old friend of mine. He had a really awful drinking problem. It ruined his life for many years. Until he finally joined AA. He's been sober for maybe ten or fifteen years. But he still goes to meetings."

"I don't have that kind of problem," Marcus said quickly. "I didn't mean to hit Del, man. It was just . . . for a moment I just . . . I don't know. Slapped her. To shut her up. She said she told you. But I love her! That's the thing. She's the best thing that's ever happened to me." He lowered his head and shook it. Lee was afraid he was going to cry. He looked back at Lee, an earnest expression on his face. "I was loaded I guess, and when she started in, something in me just snapped."

"Like it's snapped before."

Marcus nodded slowly.

"Don't you think it could happen again?"

Marcus tilted his head back, his Adam's apple popping out from his throat. He took a long time to respond. "I don't really think so, sir. I don't intend to ever let it again."

"That might not have been the real you, Marcus—the you who has a job, loves his wife and children, whom I believe is a good guy. But don't you see? The alcohol took over. It was stronger than you."

Marcus took this in as they sat in silence. He leaned forward, resting his elbows on his knees, holding his head in his big hands. He stayed that way for several minutes. Lee waited.

"Did you tell that Sammy dude about me?"

"Yes, what little I know."

"And what did he say?"

Lee laughed. "He said he loved me."

Marcus stared at him. "Say what?"

"You'd have to have been there. But yes, I think he'd be happy to at least meet you, talk this over. I can introduce you. Giving up drinking isn't easy. You have to really be ready. From what I've heard."

Marcus nodded. To Lee's relief, he didn't say he was ready. Time would tell.

CHAPTER FOURTEEN

A FEW DAYS later, he woke to the phone ringing before eight o'clock. What the heck! He used to have a quiet life, and now there were people knocking on his door in the middle of the night and the phone ringing at ungodly hours in the morning. He swiped his cell phone on, and Earl's cheery voice came booming through. "Up and at 'em!" he practically yodeled.

Lee swung his legs over the side of the bed, trying to get oriented. Morning. Phone call. Brother Earl.

"It's . . ." he tried to focus through bleary eyes at the small clock on his bedside table. "It's eight o'clock in the morning, Earl!"

"I know. I've been up for hours. I have news for you."

At this Lee woke up. "What?"

"I might have a job for Lyle." He paused, waiting for Lee's reaction.

"Wow."

"There are maintenance things he could do around here, washing cars, taking out the trash, sweeping. And I talked to this one guy in the shop, Buck Anderson, great guy, been with us for years. Nothing goes on in the shop that Buck doesn't know about. He has twins about Lyle's age, they haven't been easy sledding either, in and out of trouble, just juvey stuff, though I think one of them did a little time. Never mind, he knows what raising boys is like. Anyway, he said he could teach Lyle a few things in the shop when he has time. How to change spark plugs, stuff like that."

Fear flowed through Lee. "Earl, that's great," he said weakly. "I mean, thanks a million. I really appreciate this. I hope Lyle will take advantage of such a great opportunity." He paused, grimacing. "I don't actually know if he wants a job."

"Everybody wants a job," Earl said. "And if he doesn't, I'll kick his ass!"

Lee rolled his eyes. "Well, it's worth a try. Let me talk to him first, Earl. Feel him out."

"Okay. But I want to see this pothead, Lee. It's been years since I laid eyes on li'l Lyle. I raised two boys myself. Ever' time they got out of line, I jerked a knot in their tails. And look at them now: productive members of society! Good citizens with good jobs, is what I'm saying, Lee. Married to beautiful wives, gave me two beautiful grandchildren each. They go to Christ Church School, expensive, I'm paying, but golly, I can't tell you the good job that school does, gives them every advantage. I'm a lucky man, Lee."

Lee was silent, feeling a headache coming on.

"Okay, you talk to him first, and then I want to talk to the li'l pothead. I'll have him come in and meet Buck. I'm Lyle's great-uncle, and pun intended, I haven't exactly been a great one. That's on me, Lee. I owe him one."

THAT afternoon he walked over to the Dunlap place. All he could do was talk to Lyle, present the situation. He'd ask that he at least meet with Earl, visit the shop, meet with—what was his name? Buster? Butch? Maybe that was too much. Just meet with Earl once, and then see.

The pack of black-and-white spotted dogs came storming out to the road, howling like banshees, surrounding him. He recognized the fat one who'd come to the McBees' that time. "Hi there, doggie!" he faked affection in an exaggerated syrupy voice but didn't sacrifice his hand. "Good girl!" She came waddling and wagging up for a pat on the head. "You guys are better than a doorbell."

He'd had the perspicacity to bring Milk Bones. But bringing them in his pants pockets had been a mistake. Now the pack surrounded him, sniffing treats and threatening to get at them any way they could. Lee grabbed them out of his pockets and tossed them as far away as he could. The pack scattered in pursuit, gobbled them up, and came back for more. Matthew Dunlap came out the front door and down the three steps. "Git! Git, you mangy critters!"

"They're okay," Lee said. "I only lost one finger."

"Well, I'm glad about that." He was wearing a long-sleeved light blue Oxford cloth shirt with the sleeves rolled to the elbows and frayed khaki pants. He shook Lee's hand, surprising him.

"What's that one's name?" Lee asked about the fat one that seemed to be the leader of the pack.

"That old bitch? Spot. And that one there is Spot II. Then there's Spot Junior and Spotty. Spot the third is asleep somewhere. A few other Spots. What brings you here today?"

"Is Lyle here? I'd like to talk to him." Lee noticed the pickup truck was gone.

"They went into town to rob a bank."

"Okay. When will they be back?"

"It depends on how many years they get."

Lee looked around the yard. There was the McBees' Dodge, still sitting on its flat tires under a pecan tree. "I see you haven't made much progress there." He walked over to the car, and Matthew joined him. "The McBees need this car, Matthew."

They stood looking at the car in silence. "Just tell me this," Lee finally said. "Why did y'all do it, Matthew?"

"Matt."

"Just pure meanness? Bored out of your minds, so you thought a little vandalism might make the night go faster? Or because the McBees are Black and you wanted to give them a message?" He could feel the heat rising to his face.

"You think I punctured these tires, don't you?"

Lee threw back his head. "Let's not play this game—Matt."

"I didn't do it, professor. But I know who did."

"I was a librarian."

"Even worse!"

"Okay, I'll bite. Who did it? Why don't you just tell me if you know so much?"

"Follow me."

MATTHEW kicked open the front door, which stuck at the bottom. The interior was gloomy and looked exactly like a stage set where four debauched young men would live. Lee had been too distracted to look around much when he'd tried to talk to Lyle about enrolling in Greenville Tech, but now he surveyed the scene. Boxes of Saltines, packages of Fig Newtons, cigarette packs, and empty beer cans covered the coffee table;

once-white T-shirts, sneakers, and gray socks caked with red mud littered the floor; girly magazines were splayed open on the old couch; there were dust mice and piles of crumbs everywhere, as if someone had stomped on graham crackers. There was an open fireplace with a wrought iron frame that apparently hadn't been used in decades and a tall wooden gun cabinet with a glass front displaying six or eight rifles. Lee glanced toward the open door to the kitchen where piles of dirty dishes tilted precariously in the sink. The counter space was cluttered with a stack of cheap paper plates, a gallon of milk, half-full, bags of potato chips, an open carton of onion dip, and two packages of Oreos; six-packs of Cokes and two Bud Light cartons littered the floor beside the old Frigidaire.

They passed Lyle's room where the door was closed and climbed the staircase, which had worn oak steps slightly sunken in their middles and a solid oak banister. It used to be a nice house, Lee could tell, not a fancy place but solid in its construction. The banister was loose. There was a landing halfway up the stairs, and at the top were four closed doors. "My room," Matt pointed out the closest one on the right, then Mark's, then the bathroom, and then the one on the far left: Luke's. It was this door he opened. He moved back so Lee could step inside. "Welcome to Luke's world," he said.

Lee's breath caught. Over the bed was a poster-size black magic-marker drawing of a crude swastika. A large Confederate flag and a poster of Robert E. Lee in his Confederate uniform, looking slightly off-camera, bearded and balding, were hanging on the side walls. Taped to the closet door was a crudely printed poster in all caps: WE MUST SECURE THE EXISTANCE OF OUR PEOLE AND A FUTURE FOR WHITE CHILDREN. "Existence" and "people" were misspelled. A shiver went up Lee's spine. A tattered gray Confederate uniform jacket hung from one of the posts of the high, unmade mahogany bed. Several tear-outs of Playboy bunnies were taped on the ceiling above the bed, and magazines were strewn across the floor. Lee picked one up: *American Renaissance.* He'd never heard of it, but fanning through the pages, he got the message.

"My God," Lee said. "Y'all are white supremacists!"

Matthew snorted. "That's a four-syllable word, above my pay grade, but hell no, Jesus! Just Luke. Mark and I live in the present, not the past. We're just poor white trash. Of course we're racists, but so are you. You were raised in the South. We consider ourselves 'recovering.'"

Lee looked Matthew in the eye. "So Luke punctured those tires."

Matt nodded his head. "Just like you thought. Because those folks are Black. You got that right. But it was just Luke. Mark and I didn't know anything about the tires 'til you came by that day."

Lee felt a little weak. He considered sitting down on the bed, but the gray, filthy-looking tangled sheets repelled him. "What do you intend to do about it?"

Just then they heard the pickup truck grinding into the yard.

"I intend to make it right."

"Do you have a timeline on that?"

"I'm working on it," Matt said.

OUT in the yard, they found Mark, Luke, and Lyle unloading boxes of groceries from the back of the pickup. They'd been to Costco in Greenville.

"What you doing here?" Lyle said to Lee. The dogs were swirling around, wanting in on the action. "I thought you'd had enough of neighborly visits."

"I'd like to talk to you for a few minutes, Lyle."

"We'll get the rest of the provisions," Matt said. "You go on and talk to your dad."

"Granddad," Lyle corrected.

"Whatever," Matt said. "Just give Pops a little time of day, Lyle. We'll finish up here."

Lee couldn't help staring at Luke. He had that same sullen look he'd had the first time Lee saw him. His hair was cut in a bowl cut, which made him look like a simpleton, and maybe he was. His neck was thin, as if you could encircle it with one hand and squeeze, which Lee felt like doing, and his frame was frail, undernourished looking. He kicked at one of the dogs when it came too close. To Lee's amazement, there was a swastika decal on one of his cheap tennis shoes. Licking his lips, he stared at Lee with what struck him as a "Don't tread on me" expression.

Lyle led Lee into the house, and they sat down on the ratty sectional couch. He got out a plastic baggie from a bookcase crammed with old paperbacks, stuffed a pipe with weed, and lit up. After a few long seconds, he exhaled the smoke toward the ceiling.

Lee looked on in dismay, but he had bigger fish to fry than lecturing Lyle about pot.

"Your great-uncle Earl called," he waded in. "He wants to talk to you about a possible job opportunity at the Ford dealership. Minimum wage stuff but a foot in the door." Lyle looked blank, as if he didn't know who Earl was. "You know, my brother Earl."

Lyle was dragging on his pipe, filling the air with that skunk smell.

"I don't think I'd fit in there," he finally said. "I know how to change a tire. That's about it."

"Well, you wouldn't be changing tires there, you'd be washing cars and sweeping. Scrubbing toilets. But there's a mechanic in the shop willing to teach you some things."

Luke and Mark came barging into the living room and plunked down on the couch.

Mark lit up a pipe while Lee, silent, watched. "Don't mind me," Mark said. "Want a toke?"

"I might get a job at the Ford place," Lyle informed the others. "Could I smoke on the job?" He let out a stream of smoke. This question brought on a burst of laughter from Mark and Luke.

"Come on, Lyle," Lee said with surprising authority. "You and I are going to take a little walk."

"But it's hot out."

Lee took him by his arm, impressively muscular, and jerked him to his feet. "See you lads later."

He marched Lyle out the door, still holding onto his arm. "Ouch!"

When they reached the road in front of the house, and the dogs retreated back to the yard, he said, "I need to talk to you, Lyle. I can't do that with you smoking pot and the lads looking on. Okay?" He let go of Lyle's arm, and they started walking in silence in the direction of Lee's trailer.

"I have things I need to tell you. Important things that you need to know. Let's get Smoky. He'd appreciate a walk."

When Lee unlocked the trailer door, Smoky came rushing out to sniff the stranger, who froze with his hands stuck to his sides. "He probably smells pot and Spot and Spot and Spot *ad infinitum*," Lee explained. "Smoky, this is my grandson, Lyle. You know him. Be nice, he's family." When Lyle reached out to stroke him, Smoky shirked back, too many strange smells, until Lee coaxed him to make nice.

He leashed Smoky, and they started down the road to the left, toward the ravine. After a long silence, Lyle said, "What does that in . . . fin . . . something mean?"

"*Ad Infinitum*. Forever and forever."

"*Infinitum. Ad Infinitum*. What's so important that you want to tell me?"

Lee gave a huge sigh. "When your father was killed, you were two years old, Lyle. Do you remember him?"

"Of course not. I've seen pictures. I look like him."

"Yes you do. Well, how can I explain this? When he died, I was in bad shape myself. And losing your dad just—it was just horrible. And it meant I lost the chance to make up for what a terrible dad I'd been to him."

"Wow, dude, you been terrible to everyone!" Lyle said. "A real wrecking ball."

"I certainly could have been better to you. And I'm sorry, Lyle. I want you to know that. When you came to live with me, I didn't know how to relate to you. A fourteen-year-old teenager. I hadn't a clue. I was a mostly solitary introvert with a tendency toward depression."

"You weren't exactly a barrel of laughs. But don't worry about it, man," Lyle said. "I lived. And you got me out from under Olive and Sam's hand-wringing." He paused to light a cigarette. "They were actually pretty good to me. Better than I was to them. They put up with a lot. It was time for them to cut me loose."

"You were running away all the time. They were basket cases."

Lyle was silent.

"Anyway, Lyle, here's what I want to tell you. Up until I was about forty, I was a mess myself. Depression with a capital 'D.' But I never really felt that word fit. My therapist back then said it wasn't depression. It was grief. Whatever, it was like a big black cloud hung over me, and my feet were stuck in deep mud."

"Very poetic," Lyle said.

Lee laughed a little. "Okay. I agree. But I want to tell you this. I think you need to know. When my mother was dying, she told me about my own father. I was six when he disappeared. He left a hollow crater inside me where he'd been. Mother never talked about him, as if he'd never existed. But when she was dying, she told me he'd been part of a lynch mob that took a Black man from jail. They beat and stabbed a confession out of him off Bramlett Road. Then they shot him to death with a shotgun. Twenty-eight cabbies, including Dad. They were all arrested, tried, and acquitted. But within a year of the verdict, Dad hung himself.

"Who was this dude?"

"Your great-grandfather. Lee Trammell. My father."

"Why are you telling me all this?" Lyle kicked a stone off the road. They had come to the vacant McBee house and stood looking at it while Smoky ran around back, investigating.

"Because it happened. Because it's part of your history. Because you have a right to know. And maybe it might help explain the way I was. Am."

"Why were they acquitted if they did it?"

"They killed a Black man. He'd been arrested on

suspicion of killing another cabbie. White. They were all white. That's the way it was back then."

"Did the Black dude do it?"

"We'll never know. There was some evidence. But never a trial." Lee took a deep breath. "Regardless, he would have been convicted and executed summarily. That's also the way it was back then."

They walked in silence until they came to the ravine. They stood on the road looking down into it without speaking.

"Matt showed me Luke's room," Lee said. "Are you part of that?"

Lyle snorted forcefully. "All that stupid Nazi nigger-hating shit? Hell no! That's just Luke. Matthew and Mark neither. But they look after him. I don't know if you noticed, but he's not all there. We all try to keep an eye on him."

"Is he dangerous?"

Lyle took his time responding. "Well . . . Luke's too out-to-lunch to be dangerous. But for a while there, he was hanging with some bad dudes. Losers. Full of that same crazy shit he's got in his room. Did you see that Confederate uniform? He used to do enactments, only to him I think they were real. Matt cut him off from all that. He spends a lot of time in his room looking at porn sites, poor fucker."

"So he punctured the McBees' tires."

Lyle nodded. "Correct. Usually Matt keeps him on a tight leash. He locks the doors at night. But he must have forgotten one night because Luke snuck out. He hated having a colored family down the road."

"But y'all are flying a huge Confederate flag!"

"Fuck that," Lyle said. "That's just for Luke. He really wanted it. Matt didn't see having a humongous fight over it."

Lee whistled for Smoky, who came running, panting, and went to Lyle for some vigorous rubs.

"I wish you weren't mixed up with that crowd," Lee said. "You could come live with me, Lyle. You still have your bedroom at the trailer."

"I'm not 'mixed up' with any crowd. I like it there. And I can smoke there. I don't think you'd exactly go for that, Lee."

"Probably not." They walked in silence back to the trailer. "So can I tell Earl we'll meet with him? He wants to see you. He wants to do you a favor."

"Okay."

"Well, then," Lee said, feeling both encouraged and unnerved. "I'll let him know."

"Whatever. Hey, man, look!" Lyle said. "Some fool torpedoed your mailbox."

Lee frowned. "Damn! Hit and run, the bastard."

When he and Lyle lifted the mailbox, the post was broken. "Damn." They lowered it back to the ground where it rested on the shoulder. Lee stooped over and pried open the door. Just the usual grocery store flyers and junk mail. But there was also a cream-colored envelope with his name and address handwritten in blue-black ink.

CHAPTER FIFTEEN

LEE HAD ARRANGED for Marcus and Sammy to get together to talk about AA. The latest cancer update from Sammy was that his sentinel lymph node biopsy—"those of us in the know call that puppy SLNB," Sammy reported—revealed some cancer cells; he could have a lymph node dissection now to remove all the lymph nodes near the cancer on his head, or the oncologist could watch the lymph nodes closely by getting an ultrasound of them every month. "I'm not too keen on having my pate, what's left of it, scalped, so I'm opting for plan B."

"Is there anything I can do for you? How you holding up?"

"I'm fine, considering I'm mostly bald and have a dome full of cancer. And I thought bed bugs were bad. But anyway, I think it went pretty well with Marcus. He's a good guy. I'd say we hit it off. Great personality, and he has good intentions. I'm not sure how he'd take to meetings, though—all that higher power stuff. He doesn't think he has a problem. I told him I've been sober for fifteen years and I'm still an alcoholic. Having a beer or two on the weekends with his homeboys, it's an important part of his life. But it's the beers after that . . ."

"Did you tell him he can call you anytime he's getting in trouble?"

"I wrote my number on a paper napkin at Starbucks. The damn pen leaked all over my hand, so Marcus got some wet paper towels with soap from the bathroom. He said, 'This'll take the black off—course I've never had much luck with that myself.'"

They both laughed. There was something appealing about Marcus. Lee wanted things to go well for him, for him and Del and the twins to be okay. About his ability to control his drinking, he hoped Marcus wasn't just whistling Dixie.

"Keep me posted on what's happening on top of your head. And inside it, too."

MARCUS called to report on the meeting with Sammy. "Man, he told me 'bout the cancer. That's rough. But he seems to be handling it. I appreciate that he didn't put the full-court press on me. I'm a social drinker, man," he told Lee on the phone, "not a hard-core drunk."

"So, will you go to a meeting with Sammy?"

"Maybe. But for now I'm just gonna try it on my own. Three beers, that's my absolute limit. Most times I'll stop at two. That's my plan."

"Well, good luck," Lee said. "And you can call Sammy if you need a little support, you know. Or me. Will you do that, Marcus?"

"Will do. But I'm gonna take care of my own shit. You wait and see."

Lee was silent for a moment. Then he broached a subject he'd been thinking about for a few days.

"Marcus, my brother is a salesman at the Ford dealership. I'm getting together with him soon, and I'm going to ask him how much a set of new tires is or if he has any good used ones from a trade-in. We got to get that Dodge on the road again. You've got your Pontiac, but Del needs her car. Can you put some money on it?"

"I thought that Dunlap fool said he'd take care of it—the one with the scruff on his face. They ruined my tires, bro. They got to make it right!"

"You might be waiting a long time for that. And by the way, it wasn't Matt who did the tires. It was the youngest Dunlap, Luke. As a message, let's say. Matt didn't even know about it at the time."

"I don't give a damn if their dog done it! Who's gonna pay for them tires?"

"Maybe your insurance would cover them. Can you look into that?"

There was dead silence on the other end.

"I'm sure Earl would give us a good price. I'm planning to chip in. We just need to resolve this issue."

"Those racist motherfuckers—sorry, Mr. Lee—those racist assholes need to make it right! I'm gonna go have a little come-to-Jesus talk with them!"

"Maybe it's time to involve the police," Lee said. "Maybe we should have done that in the first place."

"What they gonna do? Arrest those honky motherfuckers—sorry, Mr. Lee—on my word? Out in Greenville County? I most definitely don't think so!"

"Okay, calm down. I agree. But don't go out there, Marcus."

"Motherfuckers!"

"Let me talk to my brother. I'm seeing him on Monday.

Just wait a couple of days. We gotta get this behind us without starting a race war."

"Del wants her car back. I had to tell her what happened to it. She's mad as a wet hen, and she just might go out there herself. I told her I'd take care of it so I gotta—and soon."

"Tell her not to go out there," Lee said.

"Those honky motherfuckers!"

"I'm going to take care of it, Marcus. Just let me handle it."

"Why you, Lee? You got a dog in this fight?"

Lee paused. "I guess I do. A very old dog."

H E hadn't opened the letter with the familiar blue-black writing on the front. It had been three days since he'd gotten it out of the mailbox, put it on the kitchen counter, and eyed it as if it were a bomb, which in a way it was. Whatever it said, it would upset the equilibrium, such as it was, of his quiet life. In a way he resented her reappearance in his life. He hoped it wasn't bad news—she was sick, maybe dying. That was the most likely reason she'd write; she'd feel compelled to let him know. They had been close, after all, despite the years of silence that had passed since. He still cared about her. Always would. He was angry at her for stopping writing the way she had; but maybe she had her reasons. She was married, for one.

It was a Sunday night. He couldn't eat his dried-out re-microwaved rotisserie chicken and congealed Stouffer's mac and cheese. His stomach refused. The time had come. He turned off his phone, though someone calling was unlikely. He sat down in his La-Z-Boy in the living room and looked at her handwriting. It hadn't changed, the way his had. He used to have a serviceable script, but it was chicken-scratching now. He'd been a good typist—had to be at the library.

He even evolved into a master of research on the computers. But he didn't have a computer now—didn't want one. He had his cell phone, and that was as much technology—and typing—as he cared for.

He had a gold-plated letter opener; of course it wasn't real gold-plate. He slit the back of the envelope open and lifted out her folded letter. "Well, here we go, Smoky," he said. He felt as nervous as a teenage boy on a first date, not that he'd ever had that experience.

Dear Lee,

I know this letter comes as a surprise, and perhaps not a welcome one. I owe you an apology. Do you know the term young people use for what I did: "ghosting"? It means you simply drop someone with no explanation by not returning their letters, calls, or emails. It's a terrible thing to do to someone, a cowardly thing, and I did it to you, Lee. I stopped writing, with no explanation, and I didn't answer your letters. I'm sorry. I'm really sorry, Lee! It was cruel, and I know it hurt. I don't know if I can explain. I don't know if you can forgive me.

It had to do with Joe, of course. I didn't love him, not the way I wanted to or should. I knew you were the one. I was in love with you, and I loved you, which is different. I felt guilty writing you, guilty for how much your letters meant to me, how much you occupied my thoughts. I knew I had to stop. Cold turkey. What an expression.

Joe and I married young, had children, grandchildren— the usual story. We were always kind to each other. We raised wonderful kids and have wonderful grandkids. But he wasn't my soulmate. What a ridiculous term, like something out of a romance novel! I don't even read romance novels! But all the world's great literature (well, not all but a lot!) deals with couples who are soulmates—usually star-crossed ones. Romeo and Juliet. Heathcliff and Catherine. Vronsky and Anna. Gatsby and Daisy. Like us. Oh I sound ridiculous!

I didn't even consider divorce. I knew that would hurt everyone: Joe, my daughters, even me. I thought maybe that's just how marriage is; how life is. Maybe I was a coward.

I'm embarrassing myself here. But it's just so good to talk to you! To try to explain. A year ago, Joe became ill. Lung cancer. He died this past winter. And now I feel free to write you, without the guilt. I don't know how you'll feel about hearing from me, Lee. A lot of time has passed. Maybe you're mad at me. But I hope you're well. I hope you're happy. Well, I know happy isn't exactly your "thing." But I hope you're content. I hope you'll write back. I won't blame you if you don't. But I hope you will.

Margo

H E sat there for a long time, just holding the letter in his lap. Margo! How could he be mad at her?

He loved her.

H E was picking Lyle up at ten o'clock the next morning to go to the Ford dealership to meet with Earl. Lyle had agreed to go, maybe out of curiosity as much as anything. But Lee would take any interest Lyle had in anything besides smoking pot as a good sign. It was unlikely that a job would come of this meeting. But Earl said he wanted to see Lyle again, and Lee could ask him about a deal on tires.

The dogs at the Dunlaps' recognized him and came wagging up, sniffing his pockets and crotch for Milk Bones. Knowing what he was in for, he had brought them in a plastic bag, and now he tossed the treats as far from him as he could:

"Go get 'em, Spot, Spot Jr., Spot the third, Spotty, Spotless, and Shout-out." It pissed him off to see the Dodge still sitting in the yard with flat tires. He kind of liked Matt, wanted to, at least, and he wanted to believe he was a good guy, that he had good intentions. Naive! he scolded himself. He looked up at the Confederate flag, which was flapping in the light breeze, making an annoying clanking sound, and allowed himself a cuss word under his breath.

No one was in the yard, so he had to knock on the door. No one answered, of course, so he opened the door, kicking the bottom with his foot where it stuck. Couldn't one of the lads fix that door?

"Lyle?" he called into the apparently empty house. Maybe they had all gone to rob a bank again. He knocked on Lyle's door. No answer. He hesitated before opening it. He half-expected to find him dead on his bed. Could you O.D. on marijuana? But aside from the overwhelming smell of weed that rushed out the door, the room was empty. Lyle's things were in disarray, the way they always were when he was a teenager living with Lee. Picking up his room was one battle Lee had surrendered to Lyle. There were bigger battles, like his coming home at night.

He went up the stairs to try to find someone, and when he stepped onto the landing halfway up, there was Luke, pointing a long-barrel rifle at him from the second floor. Lee's legs evaporated under him, and he gripped the railing. Luke looked more idiotic than usual, his baby-face blank under his stupid bowl-cut. He could be anybody or nobody. He didn't utter a word, letting the rifle speak for him.

Lee, his trapped heart trying to flee, had one terrifying thought: He would never get to see Margo again. He'd die on this filthy landing, his chest blasted by what he realized now was a Civil War musket. He'd seen them in the Confederate Museum in Greenville.

"That looks like a Civil War replica."

"It's not a replica," Luke said. "It's the real thing. A Springfield."

"Wow," Lee said. "It must have cost a lot of money."

"I know who you are," Luke said, ignoring the small talk. "You're that nigger-lover that lives on our road."

Lee was silent. Finally he said, "We use the word 'Black' now, Luke."

"Why you creeping around up here?"

"I'm looking for my grandson. I'm taking him for an interview. At the Ford dealership. Is he around?"

Luke seemed to have lost interest. "He's out back. With the others."

"Well, then," Lee said, "I better go get him before we're late. Nice to see you, Luke."

WHAT the hell was that! he wondered as he scrambled down the stairs on trembly legs. He looked back, and Luke was watching him, still pointing the gun in his direction. Lee forced himself not to run down the final steps. He went through the kitchen and out the screened back porch (where the screens were coming loose from their wood frames, he noted) and stepped outside onto the crumbling back step, almost twisting his ankle. What he saw there stunned him: Lee knew every vegetable grown in the South—corn, okra, tomatoes, soybeans, half-runner and Blue Lake beans, cucumbers, eggplant, peppers, zukes, and squash—all of them. But this was no vegetable he'd ever seen.

"Yo, Lee," his grandson called to him from the middle of the field. "Be right with you." Lyle was wearing a red baseball cap backward, and his white T-shirt stood out brightly against the bright spiky green leaves. He was carrying a big straw basket with leafy stalks.

Matt came out of a shed to the side. He was in overalls, a plaid shirt, and a straw hat, looking for all the world like a gentleman farmer from the 1850s. All he lacked was a corncob pipe and a few slaves working the field. Maybe that was Lyle's and Mark's job.

"So this is the farm," Matt said when he came up to Lee. "Not exactly what my great- grandfather grew, but I guess times have to change."

"Luke just pointed a gun at me," Lee said.

"Dear God," Matt said. "I'm sorry about that. That old musket isn't loaded and never will be. There's no ammunition for it."

Lee didn't know what to say. He was still a little breathless from the encounter.

"Is that crop what I think it is?"

"Depends on what you think it is. If you're thinking cannabis, bingo! Mainly hemp but a few Mary Janes hanging out here and there with the boys. For private use, shall we say."

"Hemp. Like rope."

"Hemp like CBDs."

"I don't understand."

Matt smiled. "Why would you? Hemp and marijuana are derived from the same plant, *cannabis sativa.* But marijuana contains more than .3 percent THC—which is what produces that wonderful high your grandson craves—while hemp contains less than .3 percent THC—tetrahydrocannabinol."

Lee turned to stare at the hemp field, trying to process what he was hearing.

"We're licensed by the state. When the plants mature, we'll take them to a hemp processing facility in Travelers Rest—also licensed. They'll be processed there to extract the cannabinoids used to manufacture CBD products."

"And what the hell are CBD products?"

"All kinds of things. Things you consume, things you rub on your body. Things that help people with pain, inflammation, anxiety, insomnia, seizures. There's a lot of medical research behind it, Lee. It does a lot of good for so many people. Our guy in TR oversees the production of medicinal gummies containing CBD."

Just then Lyle came up to where they were standing. "Go put on something besides filthy jeans," Lee barked at him.

Lyle didn't answer, but Lee thought he detected something like "shut the fuck up" as he went in the screen porch door.

"High school is never over," Matt mused. "For the parents as well as the children."

"This has nothing to do with high school! I just want him to make a good impression."

"And how long can he keep that up?" Matt asked.

Lee ignored that comment. "I see you haven't made any progress with the tires!"

"I'm sorry about that," Matt said. "I know it's frustrating."

"You're sorry about a lot of things. Tell Lyle I'll be in the car."

He waded out through the dog pack again and leaned against his Camry on the shoulder of the road. He couldn't tell which was more mind-blowing, the rifle pointed at him or the hemp plot out back. He couldn't believe Matt had a license to grow something akin to marijuana. Hemp! That was for rope, not gummies! And what exactly were gummies?

He had to get Lyle out of there. If only he would show an interest at the Ford place, see what an opportunity a job there would be! When Lyle appeared, Lee was surprised to see he had dressed appropriately. He had on khaki pants that Lee thought he recognized as a pair he had given him for his twenty-first birthday, three years ago. Not a lot of wear on those, he thought. And he actually had on a nice white Oxford shirt with the sleeves buttoned at the wrists.

"You look nice," Lee said. "But you could use a haircut." *Oh why can't I stop?* he screamed at himself inside.

Lyle didn't answer, just stared out the passenger window as they started toward the county road. They rode in silence. Lee debated telling Lyle about the musket incident but decided to pass. He had different rows to hoe—hemp rows.

"That's quite a crop out back," he finally said.

"It's a pretty good business," Lyle said, still staring out the side window.

"Is there actually money in it?"

"It's a living. But for Matt, it's a calling."

"From what Matt said, it's not just hemp."

"Oh that. Just for us and a few friends."

"So you don't sell it."

"No." Lyle paused. "Not much."

"You could go to jail!"

Out of the corner of his eye, he saw Lyle shrug.

"Listen to me, Lyle!" Lee practically shouted. "Pot is messing up your life!"

"It is? How is that, Lee? I'm happy enough."

"But . . . you're not a productive member of society."

Lyle laughed long and hard. "Society is getting along just fine without me."

"But don't you want a wife and children?"

Lyle didn't miss a beat. "You didn't."

CHAPTER SIXTEEN

OUT ON THE strip, the Davis Ford Dealership was a wonderland of huge glass windows and a spit-polished showroom filled with shiny new automobiles, which, Lee mused, if they were women, would have been high-fashion models. Lyle seemed stunned by the sight; he'd probably never been in a new-car dealership, Lee realized—not that he had either. Once Lyle got his bearings, he wandered around the floor, peering in the new cars, checking out features posted on yellow printouts on the passenger side windows. In an alcove Lee found him staring at a royal blue sports car like no vehicle he'd ever seen. "I'll take this one," Lyle said, patting the long low hood.

"Don't touch it!" Lee exclaimed.

A young salesman about Lyle's age in a light blue seersucker sport coat came out of one of the open cubicles that lined the back wall, looking to Lee like a cougar that had spotted its prey. "I see what you have your eye on," he said to Lyle, coming to stand beside him. "This little beauty will make your heart sing! Orders open at $400,000."

"What do you think, Lyle?" Lee said. "Should we take it?"

"I wouldn't complain."

The salesman was in on the joke, such as it was. "All I need is a little down payment."

"That lets us out," Lee said.

"Wow," Lyle said. "What's it doing here?"

"Just a loaner. A way to get people into the showroom. Word gets around, people come in just to see it."

"And maybe buy a Ford Escape," Lee said. "What's one of those go for?"

"We can work with you," the salesman said. "Let's say $25,000 to get the conversation rolling."

"I'm afraid we're not in the market," Lee said. "Would you let Earl know we're here, please?"

Lyle was circling the car.

"Certainly. He's probably on the phone. He's always on the phone. You must be his brother and nephew. Can I offer you some coffee or water while you're waiting?"

"What an amazing design!" Lyle exclaimed to the salesman across the car. "The aerodynamics are mind-bending."

"Ford's rebooted the GT. 600-horsepower, twin-turbo, carbon-fiber monster. Zero to sixty in 3.4 seconds. 6-speed manual. Fun little car to drive! Not that I have, or ever will."

"We're fine," Lee said, and he sat down on a backless love seat. Lyle was still talking about the car to the salesman. Lee observed him: he had a good strong build, a pleasing face without being too movie-star, his long brown hair streaked blonde by the sun—he did need a haircut. Dressed nicely, he was attractive and appealing—a far different look than he had around the Dunlaps' dog pound.

Earl appeared, coatless with his own white Oxford cloth shirt with the sleeves rolled to the elbows, khaki pants, and his signature Weejun loafers and no socks. He and Lyle actually bore a family resemblance, or maybe it was the clothes. He went over to where Lyle was still ogling the GT, and they admired the car together. "Bet you'd like to go for a spin in this little beauty!" Earl said.

Lyle smiled and shook his head. "I wouldn't want to get hooked on it," he said. An unfortunate choice of words, Lee thought. Lyle was already hooked on enough in his opinion.

"Well, not a chance anyway," Earl said. "No one drives this car. We don't even get the keys. It's just for show for a few weeks. But believe me, I'd give my left nut to take a spin."

THEY went out a side door and into the large brightly lit repair shop where eight cars were raised on lifts. Men wearing dark blue coveralls were working under them, with tools and equipment scattered around the cement floor. Earl moved Lee and Lyle from bay to bay, speaking to the men, introducing his guests. The teasing flew fast and furious. "Whoa! We can sure see who got the looks in the family," one older grizzled-looking fellow poked Earl, and Earl retorted that he was sorry the cataract surgery hadn't worked. Another mechanic with a grease-smeared face came out from under a car and offered his oil-covered hand to Lyle, who hesitated for just long enough for Earl to exclaim, "Don't touch that hand! We know where that hand's been."

"Ever'body knows where it's been," another chimed in, and several guys laughed. A middle-aged fellow who looked like he was a weightlifter stopped what he was doing under one of the cars and came over to where they were standing. He had a neatly-trimmed graying beard and a sunburned face. "This is Buck," Earl introduced him. "He gets that toasted look from riding his hawg." They shook hands all around, and Buck said to Lyle, "Earl told me you might want to learn the trade. I'll show you around."

While Buck took Lyle around the bay, stopping to introduce him to some of the guys working on cars, Lee observed Lyle. He seemed to feel comfortable around the mechanics, who were friendly and willing to explain what they were working on. "A lot of what we do has to do with the new computer systems in cars these days. Technical stuff," he heard Buck tell him.

"How'd you learn all this?" Lyle asked.

"My dad had a garage, so I learned it from the time I could walk, seems like," Buck said. "I just always loved cars. And then when things began to get complicated, technical, all this computer stuff, I took courses at Greenville Tech in the automotive tech program."

"Cool. I've considered that myself."

Lee pulled Earl to the side. "That Dodge with the four flat tires is still sitting out there at the Dunlaps' under a pecan tree where it'll probably be forever. Could you give me a good price on four new tires or maybe used ones in decent shape?"

"You still driving that old Camry? How many miles on that thing?"

Lee shook his head. "The odometer doesn't work, but last time I looked, about 105,000."

Earl threw back his head and laughed. "Does Lyle have a car?"

"That's a problem."

"Tell you what. Here's what I'm thinking. I hire him at the minimum wage level. Can't bump him up at first just 'cause he's family. He's unskilled, but there are things around here he could do. Wash cars, sweep out the garage, clean toilets, stuff like that. Do a little work in the garage if one of the guys has something he could help with. I like the kid's looks—handsome like me," and for an instant, his teenage face grinned at Lee through the sagging jowls.

"He's twenty-four," Lee said.

"How can that be?" Earl mused. "Time flies. Anyway, I could loan him one of the used cars we have on the lot. Where's he living?"

Lee grimaced. "Well, he's 'crashing' at the Dunlaps' place just down the road from me. Where the Dodge is."

"Sounds lovely. Well, he's gotta have some way to get in from that outback. Nothing fancy but if he wants the job, a loaner could be part of it."

Lee was moved. But following on the heels of his gratitude was fear that Lyle would blow this chance. He had no idea how he'd react to the job offer, such as it was.

"I'll talk to him about it," he said. "This is very generous of you, Earl."

"No, I'll talk to him. In my office," Earl said. "Mano to mano. Alone."

"Without me?"

"You'd just get in the way," Earl said, slapping Lee softly on the back. "Let Uncle Earl handle this."

HALF an hour later, during which time Lee sat outside the repair shop on bench in the shade, Earl and Lyle came out of the showroom. Lee thought he detected a change in Lyle: he didn't look so lost, if that was the right word. There seemed to be an ease or camaraderie between Earl and him. He hadn't realized that Lyle was capable of losing his habitual slouch and his face, relaxed, had what was possibly a smile.

"Let's go out here to the lot and pick out a loaner," Earl said as Lee joined them. He didn't dare ask what had transpired, but Lyle must have accepted the job.

There were dozens of rows of used cars.

"This one's in pretty good shape," Earl said of a black Jeep. "Only seventy thousand miles on it. Runs good except it'll need a quart of oil a month."

"That should do fine," Lyle said. "I'll take good care of it, Earl."

"Okay, then," Earl said. "We'll get the keys, and you can drive 'er home. Be here at 8:00 sharp Monday morning. And Lee, I'll be looking into those tires."

AFTER Lyle got the car keys, Lee walked back with him to the Jeep. "So you're taking the job," he said. "That's really great, Lyle."

"Earl's a good guy." Lee was afraid he was about to say, "I wish he had been my grandfather," but he didn't. "I'll see how it goes," he said, and then he fell into his habitual closed-mouth silence.

Lee thought about saying something supportive, encouraging, how proud he was, but it was a little early for that. He had to bite his tongue to stop from saying Lyle couldn't smoke pot on this job, or be late, or . . . And he couldn't help thinking about the Dodge sitting on flat tires in the yard at the Dunlaps'. He sighed.

There would undoubtedly be some joyriding in that Jeep.

CHAPTER SEVENTEEN

SINCE HE DIDN'T have to take Lyle back to the country, Lee decided to go by Sarabeth's and see how Del and the twins were doing. He knew from Marcus that Del's patience had run out about getting her car back and no wonder. He just hoped and prayed she wouldn't get Marcus to take her out to the Dunlaps' so she could confront them herself. He needed to tell her that he was about to resolve the situation and that she'd soon have her car back good as new.

As he drove out to Chick Springs, he thought about the response he would write to Margo. She'd been so honest in her letter, and he wanted to be honest in his. He was a little intimidated by her candor. He knew he'd had feelings for her, but it surprised him to have her state so bald-facedly she had feelings for him. It was a little frightening. He would of course express his sympathy over Joe's death. She was probably rebounding from the loss. Maybe she was at loose ends, shaken at being alone, a widow. What did she mean by "soulmates"? She was right, that was the stuff of romance novels. And she lived in Minnesota, a state he would have trouble finding on a map. She had children, grandchildren: a life.

He lived in a twenty-year-old trailer by himself on a country road in upper Greenville County, South Carolina. He had a pothead for a grandson who didn't much like him, a brother he wasn't particularly close to, and a good dog. In the light of day, it didn't seem he had much to offer.

DEL came to the door barefoot, wearing shorts and a berry-colored T-shirt down to her hips. She was a thin, handsome woman who exuded an air of accommodation tempered by a steely strength. He waited for the boys to come running, but no boys. Only the empty sound of a TV on in the den.

"Where are they?"

"Come on in, Lee. They're at day camp at Paris Mountain State Park. Sarabeth dropped them off on her way to work, and another parent is bringing them home. Ice tea? Water?"

They sat down in the den with colored plastic glasses of tea. "How are they taking to camp?"

Del explained that at first they were intimidated, especially shy James. They weren't the only Black kids, but they were still in the minority. But it didn't take long—"like about three minutes"—for them to get into it. "Now apparently Jackson is the leader of the pack. They're learning how to sit in a canoe without tipping it over. Of course it's more fun to tip it over. They got to ride a pony. They've never been close to a pony, and now James is begging to get one. And they've learned three swimming strokes in the lake, in spite of weeds and bream that nip. But I tell you, Lee, it's quiet as a tomb around here." She shook her head. "Quiet! The very thing I've been wishing for since they were born, and now it's driving me crazy. Without my car, I'm homebound in this white suburban 'hood. It's a good thing I'm not a dude, or a police car would to be following me on my walks."

"You're about to be liberated," Lee said.

"'Free at last, free at last, thank God almighty I'm free at last!'"

"Isn't that kind of sacrilegious?"

"I'm sure Dr. King wouldn't object."

Lee smiled and nodded. He took a sip of his ice tea. "I guess Marcus told you about Sammy."

"From what I hear they hit it off."

"That's what I hear too. How did it go the other night? Are you and Marcus getting along?"

"We're . . ." she searched for the word ". . . good. He's on his best behavior. I'm waiting to see if it holds. I'm not giving him much leash yet, though. He hasn't been drinking as far as I know. He really liked that AA guy—Sammy—but he hasn't been to an AA meeting yet. We're moving back to Nicholtown tomorrow. Sarabeth is getting it on with a guy, and she needs her space. And I'm homesick for my own things . . . and my own man." She gave Lee a telling wink.

"I get it." He laughed. He just loved Del. *Please let it go well at home for her.*

"So Marcus told you what happened to the tires."

"Yes he did! And he had certain choice language for that creep. Which I won't repeat in polite company. I told him I'd set him straight when he takes me out there."

"Don't go out there, Del. I'm about to take care of it. I have a lead on some tires. My brother Earl at the Ford place. I talked to him today. He's going to get the tires. It'll only be a couple of days, and then you can forget those idiots."

"'Idiots' is too mild a word," she said. "I haven't forgotten that disgusting rag on their flagpole. What century do they think they're living in? They can just crawl back under whatever rock they crawled out from."

When he got home, Lee was surprised to see Matt and Lyle with a posthole digger, a bag of instant concrete, and a 4x4 wood post at the edge of his driveway. His old mailbox was still lying like a fallen soldier on the shoulder. Matt finished digging out a deep hole, and Lyle centered the new post in it. They grinned when they saw the look on Lee's face.

"Fellows," he said. "You don't have to do this."

"Like you were going to do it," Lyle said.

"Good point," Lee acknowledged.

"I have set many a mailbox," Matt said, wiping sweat off his forehead with a huge white hankie. "You don't live on this road without your mailbox being a casualty ever so often. Sue Ellen delivers mail with one hand on the wheel and the other on her phone, reading Facebook and slinging our mail in the direction of our boxes. She's been known to take out a box or two."

Lee smiled at the picture, but he had his own thoughts about who might have run into his mailbox. "Do you need a level?" he asked. "I used to have one around here somewhere."

"Like last century," Lyle said. "We got one."

"Lyle came driving into the yard this afternoon in that hot black Jeep looking like the cat who swallowed the canary."

"The canary who swallowed the cat," Lyle corrected and burped long and loud.

"How can you do that?" Lee asked. "Spontaneously like that."

"Full of gas," Matt offered.

"Listen, Matt, that Jeep's a company car," Lee couldn't help warning.

"Old man thinks we're gonna drive to New Orleans on a lark."

"You'll be lucky if it makes it to Greenville tomorrow," Matt said.

"So did Lyle tell you about his new job?"

"Pur-ty cool," Matt said. "Hand me that tape measure," he pointed to one on the ground. He and Lyle measured. "Forty-two inches high," Matt said. "That's what we're after."

"I sure appreciate this," Lee said.

Lyle set the post into the hole, and Matt tore open a heavy red bag of Quikrete fast-setting concrete and poured it around the post. Lyle poured water from a bucket into the hole, where it immediately made friends with the concrete.

Matt retrieved the mailbox from the shoulder. "Doesn't have much of a dent in it. The door still opens and closes. She'll do. Let the post set up good, and I'll come back tomorrow and drill the box back on. Lyle'll be at his big job."

"Yeah," Lyle said and shook his head. "Cleaning shit off toilets." But he didn't look displeased.

AFTER Lyle and Matt left, Lee got his bag of groceries out of the car and opened the door to a welcoming Smoky, who raced to bring a stuffed monkey from his toybox to tug with Lee. Lee had gotten him a big raw bone from the butcher, and he let him out to gnaw on it in the grass out back. It was late afternoon, the June sun still high and hot, but the picnic table was in the shade, and there was a breeze. After he put away the cold stuff, he got a can of ginger ale from the six pack he'd just bought and went out and sat down at the picnic table, helping his creaky knees squeeze into the tight space between the table and attached bench. He popped the top on the can and took a long swill. Warm, but all in all, he'd had a pretty good day.

A better-than-most day, in fact: Lyle had a job, at least for a few days; he trusted Earl would get those tires for the Dodge; he felt Marcus would not relapse, and if he did, he'd have Sammy to answer to; Del and the boys were moving home; the twins would have their parents back together, and hopefully the family would be resuming a normal life; Sarabeth had a new flame; and Matt had proved to be a thoughtful and handy neighbor.

The only dark spot was Sammy's cancer. It didn't sound good; how could it? But at least Sammy had sounded like his usual unperturbed self. Maybe his equanimity was related to his having overcome alcoholism. He'd seen the bottom of the well, and now everything up top looked if not like sky, at least manageable.

He took Margo's letter out of his pants pocket and laid the envelope on the weathered gray wood of the picnic table. He used to have some stationary he'd bought at Walgreens. But after a year had passed and Margo hadn't responded to his last three letters, he'd thrown it away with confused and bitter feelings. Neither of them had ever mentioned The Kiss in their letters. What was there to say? A lot, but they left whatever it was unsaid. For years he had replayed that good-bye kiss in his mind, analyzing it, trying to determine which of them had instigated it, deciding it was spontaneous combustion, but most of all trying to keep the feeling it gave him alive. But now when he thought of it, he couldn't arouse the passion it once held. Too much time had passed.

He tore a page out of an old spiral notebook he kept around and spread Margo's letter on the table, reread it, and then folded it back into the envelope. He intended to write from the heart.

But what? First, he would express his surprise at hearing from her after all this time. He'd express his condolences over the death of her husband but say that he was glad to hear she was okay. He paused. A yellow jacket was sitting on the opening of the ginger ale can. He brushed it away gingerly, but it buzzed angrily, refusing to retreat, and as soon as he resumed thinking about his letter, it alighted again on the can's top, claiming the drink. How awful it would be to find a yellow jacket in your mouth!

He got up, stiffly—*because you're seventy-five, you old fucker*—and poured the rest of the ginger ale out at the edge of the yard. So there! If I can't have it, neither can you! He threw the can in the recycling bin beside the gas grill, which he never used, and put the metal lid on tight, feeling a smug satisfaction that he had thwarted the bee. But when he sat back down, again having to help his ancient legs squeeze into the tight gap, there it was, even madder than before. A grim expression came over Lee's face. *I'm not playing this game.*

He called Smoky in, and with index finger and thumb he lifted the slobbery dog bone off the kitchen floor, where Smoky had dropped it. He wondered what part of the cow this big bone came from. It was enough to make one a vegetarian. He wrapped it in foil and put it in the freezer. He glanced at the clock on the stove. Almost six o'clock, time for the evening news. But who cared about the news? He had a job to do. He was going to write Margo or die trying. Not a particularly far-fetched idea at his age.

He sat at the dining table. His chair was wobbly, something he hadn't noticed before. Maintenance was nonstop.

He tore another sheet from the spiral notebook. He didn't have to make this into a PhD thesis:

Dear Margo,

Thank you for writing . . .

He got up to get a glass of water, which required cracking open a tray of ice. Several cubes leaped onto the floor, and he had to bend over to pick them up, which activated a pain in his left hip. He sat back gingerly in the chair, which emitted a groan.

It was good of you to write. I . . .

He should offer his condolences about her husband. But he didn't give a damn about Joe, didn't know him from Adam. Since she'd explained so openly about her own marriage, it seemed important to tell her about his, and why it hadn't worked out.

"I was just a kid," he began. But he'd been twenty-five when he married Elaine. It seemed important to tell her about Sammy, his best friend, how they'd married a week apart, and how both marriages were on the rocks within five years. But hadn't he already told her all this on one of their walks? Anyway, he wanted to tell her how Sammy had been sober now for years, was still going to meetings, and how he was helping a friend, Marcus, who had a drinking problem, but he, Sammy, had cancer on his scalp. He wanted her to know about Marcus and Del and the twins. But that wouldn't make sense if he didn't tell about the damn Dodge and the four flat tires . . .

He had lost the thread of what he wanted to say. Writing her was different from talking as they'd walked around the historic neighborhood behind the library or through downtown Greenville on their lunch breaks. Maybe he should email her or call her. But that would be so awkward. He wouldn't be able to say what he needed to say. Which was what? He stared out the dirty window over the sink. It needed washing inside and out.

Why had she even tried to open things up between them again? He had come to terms with her going dark without a word. He was angry at her for that, and now he was angry at her for writing a cockamamie letter trying to open things up again! Telling him she had feelings for him! It *was* cruel and it *did* hurt! And what did she mean by "I know happy isn't exactly your 'thing.'" How presumptuous of her. Really! He was plenty happy. Happy enough. What did she want, to be pen pals again? She thought they were soulmates? She was obviously having a late midlife crisis. And he was old! He had just turned seventy-five! The horrible thought of sex reared up in his mind like a furry penis with big paws and crooked teeth. Did she think they would be like young lovers rolling around in the hay? Straw gave him hay fever! He was working himself up into a frenzy.

He looked down at his sheet of notebook paper. All he had written was *Dear Margo*. The page was so white, so empty.

He scribbled across it in his big looping scroll: *PLEASE COME FOR A VISIT!*

THE next morning around ten o'clock, Matt came over to see if the cement had set properly and the post was straight. Lee saw him out the front window and went out with Smoky to speak to him. He'd walked over from the Dunlap place, and of course Spot, her overused tits hanging down, had accompanied him. Smoky was overjoyed at the company, and they took off around back so he could show her his graveyard of fossil bones.

Matt, satisfied that the post was solid, the right height and vertically straight, had brought a piece of wood cut a little larger than the base of the mailbox. With his battery-powered drill, he drilled holes in the wood, screwed it into the top of the post, drilled more holes in the bottom side panels of the mailbox, and screwed the thing on. All this he did without measuring. The guy's a genius, Lee surmised. He got his letter to Margo from the house, deposited it in the dented mailbox, and put the red flag up for Sue Ellen.

He invited Matt in for a cup of coffee or whatever was his pleasure. A glass of water, thanks very much. After the perfunctory conversation about the weather—hot and humid, probably a thunderstorm in the afternoon—feeling hospitable, Lee indicated for Matt to sit in his recliner. Lee himself sat on the couch, which he noticed had a dip in the cushion and in need of... oh, never mind.

"I'm glad you came by, Matt. Thanks for the mailbox fix."

"I figured I owed you."

This remark was a little enigmatic, but Lee had something more important on his mind: "It's time we had a little talk."

"I figured this was coming sooner or later. Okay, shoot."

Lee studied Matt. That brown, mountain-man beard almost obscured his features. He had the long thin nose of mountain people, the kind who had settled Appalachia generations ago. He was looking at Lee, his eyes direct and blue. Serious. Kind. It occurred to Lee that Matt had a lot on his plate, running that zoo down the road.

"Listen, Matt. Do you realize there are serious penalties for growing and selling marijuana?"

"I'm aware of that. Just so you know, I rarely indulge myself," Matt said. "I can't afford to. I have the farm and two brothers to look after. They've been my responsibility since Dad walked out. Ma was never a factor. Your grandson and Mark are more at risk. I lecture them all the time—never have more than an ounce on you, no driving while or after smoking, no selling. If they got nabbed, they'd be looking at simple possession, a first offense—$650 fine and up to thirty days in jail."

"What about Luke?"

"Luckily he won't go near grass. Not his thing. I used to be quite a stoner myself though."

"Really."

"Yes, really. In Iraq. We smoked a lot of ganja. I mean *a lot*. It was the only thing that got us through. Bravo company. Fourteen fun-filled months in a bomb-infested neighborhood in east Baghdad. I was a sniper."

Again that serious direct look.

They were both silent.

Matt tossed his head back and snorted bitterly. "No weapons of mass destruction. No stockpiles of WMDs. Just millions of dead Iraqis and too many guys like me who enlisted for the noblest of reasons—to get away from home—coming back in body bags or maimed or traumatized." He was silent again. "Well, you know all this."

"I'm so sorry."

"I used to wake up screaming from nightmares of dead Iraqis in bed with me. I couldn't go out in a crowd. I thought about suicide all the time. They gave me pills—as many as thirty a day. Turned me into a zombie. Weed was the only thing that helped with the PTSD. So I started growing my own. But then I saw the risk I was taking. Mark and Luke— well, they need me to manage things. When the state issued twenty licenses to grow hemp, I was first in line. We only grow a few marijuana plants in the field."

"But Lyle. Isn't he addicted? He's got to get away from . . . the farm."

"Lyle wouldn't do well in jail. He knows the risks. The limits. He's a recreational user, Lee. There's a distinction between that and an addict. And he's smart. It's unlikely he'll get busted."

"Do you think he'll keep this Ford job?"

"I'll kick his ass if he doesn't."

"I want him to move out of your place. He could come here, but I don't think he will."

"Do you know he and Sarabeth are shacking up again?"

Lee was shocked. "No I didn't!"

"Maybe that'll work out."

"Not if he's a pothead."

"I'll talk to him," Matt said. "You stay out of it."

"Why is everyone always saying that to me? Okay. But soon. Like tonight when he comes back from town."

"Will do."

"And here's another thing I've been wanting to talk to you about."

"Luke."

"Right."

"I suspect he did my mailbox."

"It's a possibility."

"Do you think he's dangerous?"

"You mean like Dylann Roof?"

"He seems cut from the same cloth, Matt. All that white supremacy stuff, the neo-Nazi decal on his shoe, pointing a gun at me, calling me a 'nigger-lover.'"

"He's not dangerous," Matt said, shaking his head. "He's play-acting. A fantasy role. Like you and I used to play cowboys and Indians. Luke couldn't organize a lemonade stand. All our guns are locked up. If I thought he was dangerous, I'd be the first one to blow the whistle on him."

"I'm not convinced."

"You can take my word for it. I know him. I know what he's capable of—and not."

"So what about the tires, Matt?"

"Those tires are something between me and Luke. He's going to be accountable. I'm working on it."

"You're always working on it," Lee said. "My brother at the Ford place is going to get Marcus some replacement tires. I hope you'll be willing to pay for them."

"How is Marcus? Give him my regards."

"Something tells me he won't appreciate any 'regards' from you. He'd appreciate some replacement tires for the ones Luke punctured. And his wife is about to go ballistic. So this has to get resolved and soon."

"It will. But you have to give me more time. To deal with Luke."

Lee studied Matt, who was looking down. "What is it with Luke?"

"Well, that's what I'm working on."

CHAPTER EIGHTEEN

A WEEK LATER Lee was still feeling disturbed and agitated.

What Matt told him about Luke had hardly been reassuring. Words didn't mean much; he wondered if Matt might be in denial about Luke. How do you know if someone is dangerous, or just play-acting? Did anyone close to Dylann Roof know he was capable of walking into Mother Emanuel Church, only to pull out a Glock handgun and kill nine African Americans in a Bible study class? Could anyone who knew him have stopped him? Did his father know? His mother? Anyone? And what could they have done? Notified the police beforehand? Luke was over eighteen. He could buy a gun legally in South Carolina. There were no age requirements, permits, or licenses required to buy a rifle, and the Dunlaps had a whole supposedly locked cabinet full of them.

It distressed him to know what had happened to Matt in Iraq. Matt was a good guy, in Lee's opinion. He'd had to claw his way back to some kind of normalcy, to nights that didn't include dead Iraqis in his bed. He gave him credit for trying to care for his younger brothers, and he showed some entrepreneurship in trying to make a living from farming hemp.

But whether he had a reliable take on Luke, Lee couldn't tell. It definitely concerned him.

Then there was Lyle. Lee had forced himself not to call him. It was torture, but he had to give him some time and space. Nor had Earl called to report on how Lyle was doing or if he was even showing up. And nothing about replacement tires. A week wasn't that long, Lee reasoned, though it was a lifetime. And to top it all off, he hadn't gotten any response from Margo. She would have gotten his letter. She'd had plenty of time to respond. Well, maybe not by letter, given the postal service these days, but she could have called. Life was waiting. Someone famous said that. Well, it was. And waiting was hell.

The only thing that really helped calm his nerves was taking his evening walk with Smoky down the road to the ravine. A couple of mimosas, also known as Persian silk trees, were in bloom, fanciful Asian ornamentals, incongruously at the edge of a Southern forest. When he was a boy, their blossoms were the most beautiful thing he'd ever seen: starburst puffs of pink filaments touched with yellow at the base on graceful horizontal limbs, the foliage lime green and fern-like. Later he learned mimosas were introduced to the United States in the 1700s and were considered undesirable because they were invasive; their seedpods were toxic to dogs and livestock. Things were not always the way they appeared. He leashed Smoky until they were well past them.

This particular evening, though it was still in the eighties, watching a small breeze rustle the tops of the loblolly pines helped him get a grip. Maybe Lyle would take to his job. Maybe he would realize he had to move out of the Dunlaps'. Maybe he and Sarabeth would make it. Maybe . . . He stood in the middle of the deserted road, watching leaves in the forest moving from an invisible force. You couldn't save some people. They had to save themselves.

Maybe Margo's silence *was* her answer. She had surmised that he was senile: *Come for a visit!* Indeed. No wonder she hadn't bothered to respond. As for the damn tires, he no longer gave a damn. Damn! His heart in his chest ached, and he put his right hand against it, talking soothingly to it, the way he used to do as a child when he missed his father: "It's okay. Everything is all right. God loves you." Even though by seven he no longer believed in God or Santa Claus.

He had come to the McBees' empty house. What the hell! Marcus's Pontiac was in the drive. What the hell was he doing here? A bad feeling came over him. As far as he knew, Marcus didn't have a key. But perhaps Del had given him the one she'd used when Lee first found her here. Something made him doubt that. And hadn't Marcus understood he had no business out here, given the punctured tires?

Smoky was investigating the car, sniffing around it. Lee knew before he looked what he would find: a drunk Marcus in the backseat, sleeping it off. And that was what he did find.

He banged sharply on the back passenger side door. Was Marcus dead? Dead drunk, more likely. Lee could see his chest rising and falling, his head lolled to one side. He was going to have a terrible crick in his neck. When Lee opened the door, Marcus almost rolled out, but that jolted him awake. Lee shoved him into a more upright position on the backseat. He smelled strongly of hops and had drool down his chin. There were seven or eight beer cans on the floor. He blinked and blinked, trying to wake from the nightmare that was his life at this moment.

"Why here?" Lee asked.

Marcus looked up at him blearily, but when he recognized Lee, he popped more awake. He ran his hand all over his buzz cut and managed to swing his feet onto the ground, but he didn't try to stand up.

"I'm really soused," he murmured in a ridiculous imitation of what a drunk would sound like. But it was no imitation.

Lee was so disappointed—distraught, really—that he felt like sitting down on the grass and crying. The ghosts of those little boys, Jackson and James, came running through his mind, throwing the stick for Smoky. How they had laughed and competed with one another, but kindly. How they gobbled hot dogs at his house and slept like babies in Lyle's bed. And Del. That lovely, strong, dignified woman. Her love and her hope. He caught Marcus by the front of his T-shirt before he could lie back on the seat and pulled him to his feet, even though Marcus outweighed him by maybe fifty pounds. His left hip cried out, protesting. Once Marcus was on his feet, holding his upper arm in a death grip, Lee made him walk a few steps, though unsteadily.

"Keys," he demanded, and Marcus pointed to the ignition.

"Get in the car," Lee ordered. "Not back there!" as Marcus slumped toward the backseat. "Front." He helped steer a shuffling Marcus into the passenger seat and closed the door carefully, though he felt like slamming it on him. He let Smoky in the backseat and started the Pontiac. It was big and heavy compared to his Camry. He backed carefully out of the red dirt driveway. Tears felt trapped in his chest. Why did people ruin their lives? Why did they mess up and hurt other people? Why did *that* have to be human nature? If there was a God, why did He let man invent alcohol? And marijuana? Why wasn't the world as it was good enough for people?

He pulled Marcus's Pontiac into the driveway at the trailer. What else could he do? He didn't want to have it at his place, but there was no place else to take it. Hopefully Luke wouldn't drive by. Marcus was beginning to come to. He looked around, not recognizing where they were. "My place," Lee said. "You're about to drink a shitload of coffee."

Marcus nodded. "Jesus, man . . ."

"Shut up," Lee barked. "There will be plenty of time for contrition later."

Smoky jumped from the backseat into the front to get out of the car. He licked Marcus's cheek and neck, the beer-flavored sweat. "You've been on a bender," Lee observed. "How long?"

Marcus shook his head.

Lee helped him walk unsteadily into the kitchen. He steered him to the couch—no La-Z-Boy for him! He loaded up the Mr. Coffee machine with coffee, making it extra strong, while Marcus looked around.

"You live here?"

Lee didn't bother to answer.

"How much rent you pay?"

"I own it," Lee snapped. "Does Del know?"

Marcus shook his head.

"Well, if you haven't called her, I'm going to. She'll be worried sick."

Marcus looked stricken. "Tell her I'm sorry."

"I don't think she's going to exactly appreciate that sentiment."

While the coffee was brewing, Lee dialed Sammy. Why hadn't Marcus called him? Well, back to human nature.

"I got Marcus here," Lee said when Sammy answered his phone. "Drunk as a skunk."

There was a pause on the other end. "Shit! Where you at?"

"Trailer."

"On my way."

Lee poured Marcus a mug of black coffee. "What happened?"

Marcus shook his head.

"When did you eat last?"

Marcus shook his head again. Shame emanated from him like an odor. "I got fired."

A spark of compassion flared in Lee's chest. He preferred anger. Judgment. Again his thoughts flew to Del. "Have you been with Del? Did you hurt her?"

Marcus looked at him in shock. "Hurt her? I love her, man," he said. "I don't deserve her."

"True. But where were you last night?"

"I didn't go home." A long silence. "I was . . . elsewhere."

Whoring, Lee thought, but he didn't say it. He squelched the sarcasm of asking if he'd had a good time.

"I'm going to have to call Del," he said finally. "She needs to know where you are. That you're safe."

Tears came to Marcus's eyes. He nodded.

"Do you want to call her?"

Marcus shook his head.

Lee dialed the number. She answered immediately, her "hello?" rippling with anxiety.

"It's Lee. I have Marcus. He's with me at the trailer. He's okay."

There was a long silence. When she didn't speak, Lee told her about how he'd found him at the Hidden Valley house, how he'd been on a bender but was coming around.

Lee waited. Del didn't speak. He realized you could hear

a broken heart over the phone. He told her Sammy was on his way.

"Don't y'all bring him home!" Del said. "He's not welcome here."

"We'll work things out," Lee said, idiotically. He didn't know what else to say. "I'll bring the Pontiac..."

She hung up the phone.

He and Marcus sat in silence until Lee heard Sammy's Corvette squeal to a stop on the road out front. Sammy strode through the kitchen door. "Bro!" he said to Marcus. "What the fuck! You should have called me!"

Marcus, shame-faced, shrugged.

"Who wants scrambled eggs and toast?" Lee asked. He had gotten a dozen fresh eggs yesterday, and now he was about to use them up. He had made an hour trip to Lizzie MacKensie's chicken farm, just to help play the waiting game.

He and Sammy sat at the table, and Marcus sat on the couch with his plate in his lap. Lee had made instant Sanka for himself and Sammy, and he poured more hi-test for Marcus. The eggs were a goldfinch yellow; Lee had poured a little half-and-half in them. The three men ate in silence. The toast was stale, store-bought.

Lee deposited the plates in the sink. "What next?" he asked.

"We'll talk about this later," Sammy said. "We'll process it."

Marcus, who seemed totally abashed, just nodded. "Cat got your tongue," Sammy chided. "All you drunks want to do is get shit-faced and hunt wo-man."

"Geez," Lee said. "Hunt 'wo-man,' Sammy?"

"What guys in the service used to say," he said. "Okay," he said to Marcus. "Get up. You're coming home with me.

We'll deal with the rest tomorrow."

Marcus stood up shakily. He towered over Lee by what felt like a foot; Lee took his arm to steady him. "Thank you, man." He looked defeated, and Lee guessed he was. It would be a long, hard road back, if there was a "back."

"You're in no condition to drive, Marcus," Lee said. "And we can't leave your car here." He glanced at his watch. It was 9:30, almost his bedtime. He sighed. "I haven't told you this, but one of those guys down the road—the youngest one, Luke—let's just say he has a 'thing' about Blacks. And it's not a good 'thing.' He's the one who punctured your tires. Not Matt or Mark. They didn't know. If we leave your car here, I might be dealing with four more flat tires tomorrow."

"Jesus," Sammy said. "Let's go! I'm missing my show."

"But . . ."

"Leave the car to me," Lee said.

AS soon as he heard Sammy rev his motor and lay rubber as he took off toward the county road, Lee dialed Lyle's cell phone. It rang and rang, and then when he was about to give up, Lyle answered.

"I need your help."

"Are you okay?" Lyle said with some alarm in his voice—gratifying to Lee, who never got any indication Lyle cared about him one way or the other.

"Yes, fine. But I have a problem." Feeling weary, he told the story of finding Marcus and of needing to deliver his car to Del in town. "Can you follow me in and bring me back here?"

Lyle was silent for so long that Lee wondered if he was stoned.

"You okay? I mean to drive, Lyle."

"Of course," he said. "Just tired. Let me put on some pants. I'm at Sarabeth's. I'll be there in twenty."

Lee dialed Del and told her he and his grandson were bringing her the Pontiac. She didn't ask any questions; maybe she knew. She told him not to ring the doorbell; she didn't want to wake the boys up. Lee wanted to say more, he didn't know what, but Del just mumbled thanks and was gone. It was just as well. There would be time to talk—he hoped—sometime in the light of day.

After he hung up, Lee paced a little, nervous about the unexpected chance to get to talk to Lyle. And not just alone but locked together in the small cab of the Jeep on the drive back. He was afraid of what he might learn. As far as he knew, Lyle was still going to work, but he didn't really know. The times he'd passed the Dunlaps' place, the Jeep wasn't there—a good sign. He wanted to ask him how the job was going and about the hemp business Matt was running. And what about the marijuana mixed in with the crop? Could he get Lyle to move out? And he had plenty of questions about Luke. He still felt shaken by how Luke had pointed that rifle at him, the fact that it was an unloaded replica be damned. He'd encountered the crazy brother living in the attic, like something out of a gothic novel. Did Matt have to chain him up at night? To keep him from running loose and puncturing Black people's tires? Or worse? Not that there were many Black folks who lived in Blue Ridge. Marcus and family had been an anomaly: one that Luke took it upon himself to eliminate in his own creative way.

He heard Lyle pull into his drive behind Marcus's Pontiac. Smoky, already excited by the visitors that night, set to barking. Lee let him out to check out Lyle, who was standing beside the Jeep, smoking a cigarette. Smoky charged at Lyle, then recognized him and took to sniffing the million or so scents on him. After Smoky had a long pee, Lee called him inside, told him to guard the castle, which meant sleeping on the couch, grabbed Marcus's car keys, and went out to the Jeep.

"Whadup?"

"Marcus was here." He paused. "He couldn't drive home. Too drunk."

"Y'all got drunk? I didn't know you had it in you, Lee!"

"No, no, for Pete's sake! Let's just get going. I can explain more on the way back if I have to. We're taking the Pontiac he drove out here back to his wife in town. He didn't want to leave it here—if you get my drift."

"Check."

Lee paused before opening Marcus's car door. "Thanks, Lyle," he called to him. "I really appreciate this."

"Of course," Lyle said, surprising Lee with his equanimity. He had expected some sarcastic lip.

Lyle followed Lee as they drove past the Dunlaps' and turned onto the empty county highway. So Lyle had been at Sarabeth's. This was a good thing. He hoped it was, at least. Sarabeth was a good influence—unless Lyle was a bad influence. He tried to think what to say to Del. He'd have to explain about finding Marcus. But how to offer . . . what? Encouragement? Hope? Consolation? A solution? If this was the end of their marriage, what a shame. He'd read what the experts say, that alcoholism was a disease. It wasn't a character flaw, was maybe even genetic. He didn't know, and he didn't care; he wasn't a psychologist. What difference did any "reasons" make when you were in pain, as he was sure

Marcus was—and now Del? "The devil made me do it" was as good an explanation as any.

The lights from Lyle's Jeep were steady in his rearview mirror. Buddy, Lee's son and Lyle's father, must have been drunk when he drove into that truck on the Asheville highway. What devils chased him? Might Lee have slain those demons if he had been a real father to Buddy?

They were entering Nicholtown, winding through its crooked streets. It was a beautiful balmy night, with Black folk out on their front porches, visiting and drinking together in small groups. Someone had set up a card table, and men were playing cards, laughing and teasing. Lee pulled in front of Marcus's house. No lights were on, the house appearing asleep itself. Lee, stumbling in the dark up the cement steps, knocked very softly on the door, and it opened immediately, as if Del had been standing behind it. It was hard to see her face, and that was just as well. Lee had had enough looks at pain that night. He handed over the Pontiac keys, and they were both silent, staring at each other in the faint light from the living room. "Okay," she finally said, without asking a single question. Then, her manners not deserting her, "Thanks." She closed the door, and he heard her turn both locks.

His old knees barely cooperating, Lee began carefully and fearfully working his way down the dark stairs with no railing. If he fell, he'd break a seventy-five-year-old hip, probably the one that was always biting him. But a strong hand reached up to him, which he grasped with both of his, and Lyle helped him maneuver the last steps. When he reached the *terra firma* of the yard, Lyle released him.

"Thank you, son," Lee murmured. "You saved my life!"

"Or at least your neck," Lyle said lightly. "Let's not get too melodramatic, Lee."

They got in Lyle's Jeep, which required Lee to practically vault up to get in his side. He'd never been in a Jeep.

"You'll have to direct me out of this maze."

Lee did his best, though Nicholtown *was* a maze, especially in the dark.

"So what's going on? The guy was drunk at your house? If you were having a party, the least you could have done was invite me."

Lee snorted. "Rain check. I was walking by the house earlier where Marcus and Del used to live. Before that Confederate flag drove them out."

"I doubt a flag could do that."

"Well, regardless. Marcus was there, drunk in the backseat of the Pontiac. He has a drinking problem."

"Noted," Lyle said. "So you brought him to your trailer."

"I was afraid to leave him there. Especially with that white supremacist maniac in your attic."

They drove in silence until they had cleared the city limits and were on the road lined with every conceivable business, none of them big or prosperous. "I guess his wife knows. What I'm not sure, but she didn't ask a single question about why I was bringing Marcus's car home, not him."

"Probably seen it before. Mind if we stop?" Lyle said. He pulled into a Clock Drive-In that looked open, though there were no cars in the parking lot.

"Good idea," Lee said, though he couldn't imagine eating. He'd had some of the rich scrambled eggs himself, on top of his early supper of a turkey TV dinner, and now all he wanted was to get home and crawl into bed. But if Lyle was hungry, so be it.

They ordered at the counter where a sleepy-looking clerk with a massive eruption of acne on his face repeated two double cheeseburgers all the way, fried onion rings, and two drinks before he disappeared into the kitchen supposedly to cook. When Lee tried to get an Orangeade from the drink machine, it spurted ice cubes all over the dirty floor. "I'll take over," Lyle said. "I have a PhD in drink machines."

They sat in a booth to wait on their burgers. "So how bad a drinking problem does the dude have?" Lyle asked.

"Bad enough that I don't know that his marriage can survive it. They have two young sons who need both of them. Anyway, Marcus is a serious binge-drinker. He's with Sammy now. Do you remember Sammy? I called him for help. He's an AA professional."

When the clerk brought their burgers, they ate in silence at first. "This is really good," Lee said. "I hadn't realized how great a greasy, calorie-laden, cholesterol-busting drive-in burger with cheese could taste at eleven o'clock at night."

"You gotta get out more, Lee."

"I suppose I'll pay for this later."

"Tums."

As they ate, Lyle said, "I'm surprised you haven't called me. To see how the job is going."

"Don't think I haven't wanted to," Lee said. "But I wanted to give you a little space." He paused, looking out the dark picture window at the car lights going past. They were the only ones at the Clock. The counter guy was reading his phone. "So . . . how's the job going?"

Lyle snorted. "Like they say in your pal's AA—one day at a time. Ask me again this time next week."

"Well . . ." Lee said, not sure what to ask, there was so

much he wanted to know. But he was wary of pressing Lyle. Before he could come up with something, Lyle said, "That Buck. Hellava nice dude. I think he likes me." Lee heard something in Lyle's words, or maybe his voice, that almost moved him to tears. Someone—Buck—was being nice to him, maybe seeing something in him to nurture. Lee started to say, I'm sure he does, but stopped himself. Too smarmy. Better to just listen.

"And Earl. He's certainly taking his role as unc seriously. It's sort of hilarious. He pretends to be checking on things in the shop, just to make sure things are going okay for me. I actually like having somewhere to go in the morning, having something to do. Not that I like getting up so fucking early. But then when I'm there, there's stuff to learn. Maybe that will wear off, but for now—it's okay."

"I'm glad to hear it," Lee said. "This is good." His heart sang.

"Well, you know now that I'm seeing Sarabeth again."

"Oh my God!" Lee said. "That poor girl! Listen, if you're planning to use that young woman—for a crash pad, or . . ."

"Sex." Lyle was grinning across the table at him. Lee grimaced anyway.

"She's like a daughter to me, Lyle. I'm warning you."

"Does that make her my grand-sister?"

Lee had to think a minute. "Your great aunt. I think."

"Then it's not incest."

"Stop it, Lyle!" Lee barked, but he laughed. "I'm trying to have a serious conversation here!"

"Sorry, old man. I can assure you my intentions are honorable."

"She's not interested in a relationship with a pothead, I can tell you that. I have it on good authority."

"I heard it from the horse's mouth too. She should have been a cop, the way she can lay down the law. I told her I'm not addicted. I can give it up. In fact, I already have. Earl told me I had to my first day at work. Pot-free for a week. Almost a week."

"What about withdrawal?"

"Don't be so dramatic. I'm not a drug addict, Lee. I just like the way it makes me feel. Which is good good good. I could use a hit right now, given the way this conversation is going."

They ate in silence for a few minutes.

"Listen, Lyle, there's something else I want to talk to you about. Matt told me about the hemp business. He said marijuana plants are mixed in with the hemp plants."

"Ah yes. The Mary Janes."

Lee sighed. "I'm afraid for you. I'm afraid you might get busted."

"Busted, huh. You've certainly learned the lingo. Just so you know, most of the plants are hemp. Just a few marijuana plants scattered around. No one will notice. They look just like hemp. They're the same plant, actually. Did Matt tell you he has a commercial hemp license?"

"He told me."

"Do you know what CBD is?"

Lee sighed. "Enlighten me."

"It's legal in South Carolina, and it makes people feel good. It's kinda like weed but weaker, and it doesn't make you high. He sells it to a company that makes gummies out of it. Matt really believes in the benefits of CBDs. He has a Jesus complex about it. He wants to help people who are hurting or anxious or whatever. Maybe because he's been there, big-time."

"I don't care if he *is* Jesus," Lee said. "I just don't want you to get in any trouble."

"Registered. Let's get moving. I have to be at work at 8:00 tomorrow. That ought to make you happy."

"It does. And would those gummy things help my aching hip?"

THEY rode in the dark down the county highway for a while.

"I might get a Jeep," Lee said. "I like this vehicle."

"It would take ten years off you."

Lee laughed. "That'll be the day." He felt good, despite the indigestion. A greasy hamburger at midnight was wonderful, but then it hardened in the stomach like the instant cement surrounding his mailbox.

"Do you ever hear from my mother?"

Lee was taken by surprise. He had to search his aging memory for her name: grind, grind, the slow computer of his brain searched. Lights from an occasional car going the opposite direction toward town flashed by them.

"Rebecca. Becca. And no. I never do."

"Me neither," Lyle said. Lee sensed his shrug next to him in the dark Jeep.

"Do you know why she didn't want me?"

Lyle had never asked him about his mother. Lee had never met her. As soon as Lyle was born, she left the baby with her parents and moved out West. Colorado, maybe, he wasn't sure. Olive and Sam were good people, overwhelmed by a situation they were unprepared for. Becca herself had been an unwanted surprise, Olive told him, and by the time Lyle was fourteen, they felt too old for a teenager like Lyle. Of course, Lee was too old too, at sixty-five.

"Do you keep up with Sam and Olive? Ever see them?" Lee asked.

"Not really. I think I bring back bad memories."

Lee was silent for a while. They were turning onto Hidden Valley Road. "It's true Becca didn't want you when you were born. But she was almost a child herself, unmarried and pregnant with evangelical parents who were deeply ashamed of her and the pregnancy. At least that's how I read it at the time. And then Buddy was killed, and Becca was in no position to raise a child. That's how I read it now. It really had nothing to do with you, Lyle. You were an innocent baby."

"And then I became hell on wheels for Olive and Sam."

"I just hope you know I love you, Lyle," Lee said, and embarrassingly, his voice broke and those old-man tears filled his eyes. "And I'm proud of you."

"Or at least you plan to be," Lyle said. "If I can keep this job."

They were almost at the Dunlaps' place. "Just let me off at the driveway," Lee said.

"You sure?"

"Yes, I want to walk. It's not that far. And the night will help clear my mind. Which has been blown plenty tonight."

"Okay," Lyle said, pulling into the Dunlaps' dirt driveway.

"Thanks for the help tonight, Lyle," Lee said. He vaulted down from the Jeep and stepped back so Lyle could pull into the yard. He parked in front of the porch and with a backward wave disappeared into the house.

Lee stood on the soft shoulder of the road in the dark. For once there were no Spots around. Lightning bugs were flashing in the woods, and katydids were filling the night with their insistent vibrating sound. Somewhere far away a barred owl hooted "Who cooks for you? Who cooks for you all?"

And now as he tilted his head back, he saw how amazing the night sky was: clear and crystalline, with a billion stars, timeless. He identified the Milky Way, easily, but he wasn't certain about Sagittarius, the archer drawing his heavenly bow. A feeling of peace came over him. All in all, everything considered, it had been a good night.

When he stepped onto the asphalt to start home, he couldn't stop himself from glancing over at the McBees' Dodge under the pecan tree. He wasn't sure—but in the moonlight, it appeared to be sitting on four fully-inflated tires.

CHAPTER NINETEEN

FIRST THING THE next morning—for Lee that meant 9:00 a.m.—he walked back over to the Dunlaps'. He hoped he wouldn't find Lyle there; by now he should have been at work for at least an hour. As he came up the drive, he noted that the Confederate flag was missing. Peculiar. But what he thought he'd imagined in the moonlight the night before was perfectly real in the light of day: the Dodge was riding high on four new tires.

The lads were sitting around the spool top table, drinking coffee out of tin mugs. When Lee looked at Matt, he was grinning, his lips bright pink inside his brown beard, his blue eyes crinkled in amusement. Mark, shirtless as usual, was chuckling, probably at Lee's expression.

But Luke scowled. He turned his head aside as if the sight of Lee revolted him, and before Lee reached the spool, he got up and went into the house.

Matt shrugged. "Coffee?" He poured Lee a mug from a blue-speckled enamel pot sitting on the ground.

"So," Lee said. "New tires."

"Fairies came in the night," Mark said. "You know, like

the shoemakers' helpers. Well, not really in the night; more like about 5:30 yesterday afternoon. We were afraid you'd drive by and see them. Spoil the surprise."

"Well I am surprised," Lee said. "I thought I was seeing an apparition last night. I've wanted to see that car on four inflated tires so bad, I thought I was dreaming." He raised his eyebrows and opened his hands in a gesture of "Tell me."

Matt and Mark high-fived one another. "You tell," Matt said to Mark.

"Those helpers who came were your brother Earl, his man Buck, and a young mechanic from the shop. Lyle talked Earl into giving us a good price on some new tires. And he did. Ate some of the cost himself, no doubt."

"That would be Earl," Lee said. "He'd want you to pay for them, but he'd also chip in."

"They brought the tires out after work," Matt said. "And a couple of car jacks, and a big piece of heavy plywood. We know how to change tires, but Buck knew what to do a hell of a lot better than us. Course it being four tires, it took some time. Luckily you didn't drive by and see them."

"I never thought I'd see the day," Lee said. He paused. "I got the feeling just now that Luke wasn't exactly happy about it though. Or to see me." He raised his eyebrows in question.

"Oh don't give li'l Luke a thought. He's jess licking his wounds," Mark said.

"He holds you responsible for those Black folks moving in down the road, 'replacing' us," Matt said, shaking his head.

"Jesus," Lee said. "I didn't even know them when they moved in." He too shook his head and muttered the "f" word under his breath. "How did you deal with him—about the new tires?"

"I sold his Confederate musket," Matt said matter-of-factly. "It took me a few weeks to find a buyer. That was the best punishment I could think of, instead of wringing his neck for puncturing the tires in the first place. It paid for the tires. I figure justice was done. Maybe you noticed the ol' Stars and Bars is gone."

"I certainly did."

"Matt told him he was sick of all his white supremacy shit," Mark smirked. "'Bout time."

"Jesus again," Lee said. "How did Luke take his medicine?"

"Sulked. Told me he hated me." Matt shrugged. "I been dealing with Luke his whole life."

"He has these loser friends," Mark said. "They have this whole fantasy thing about how Blacks are raping white women, shit like that. Not that they call them 'Blacks.' They're all full of shit, hate, and big talk 'bout how they're gonna stop 'em from taking over the country. That gang couldn't stop a guy from opening a bag of peanuts."

Lee glanced toward the house. He saw a figure peeping out the attic window, but quickly the face was gone.

"Is he dangerous?"

Matt and Mark were silent. "We keep an eye on him," Matt finally said. "He's a little strange. But dangerous? I wouldn't say so."

MATT agreed to follow Lee into town to return the Dodge to Del. Lee was afraid to leave it at the Dunlaps' another hour. He'd had enough flat tires to last a lifetime. Lee drove his Camry, and Matt followed him in the McBees' car. The thing Lee most wanted in the world was to get that car back to its rightful owners, in addition to hearing from Margo.

Matt parked the car in front of the McBees' house while Lee went up the steps, cursing again the lack of a rail to hold on to. When he knocked, per usual Maybell put up a furious barking spree behind the door. Marcus cracked the door just enough to keep the dog from rushing out, grasping her by her choker collar. Lee was surprised to see him. He had assumed he'd spend the night at Sammy's, drying out. The whites of his eyes were bloodshot. He hadn't had a shower and was still wearing the soiled white T-shirt and jeans he'd been in last night when Lee found him.

"Who is it?" he heard Del call from the back.

Marcus didn't meet Lee's eyes. He went through the "let Maybell smell the back of your hand" bit. After she'd licked Lee's hand, he patted her on her broad flat head, her little slanted eyes looking up at him beseechingly: "Wuv me!"

"I didn't expect to see you here," was all Lee could think to say, but his eyebrows shot up.

Marcus ignored the implied question, turning away to call to Del, "Put May in the bedroom and come see who's here." Lee heard her calling the dog in a high-pitched voice: "Come to Mama, Baby, that's my good girl!" and the dog went racing down the hall, its feet sliding on the bare wood. When Del came out in a few minutes, wearing an apron, she nodded politely at Lee but didn't say a word, which surprised him. But of course, given the circumstances . . .

"I've got a surprise for you," Lee said to her, trying to pump things up a bit, but his elation at returning the car was losing air fast. He would have liked to ask when Marcus had come home last night and in what condition. But that would have to wait.

At that moment the twins, rubbing their eyes and look-ing sleepy, came out of their bedroom in their pajamas. They stared at Lee like they didn't recognize him. Was that because a white man had never come knocking on their door? Did a white man signal trouble in some way? Or was it that they were aware of their parents' trouble?

"Hi boys," Lee said.

"Did you bring Smoky?" Jackson asked, yawning broadly.

Marcus went out the door, and Lee watched him join Matt at the Dodge on the street in front. They did some kind of fancy fist bump Lee wasn't familiar with.

"It's back!" Jackson yelled when he saw the car. James parroted, "It's back!" They went running out the door, and Lee followed.

Marcus was walking around the car, inspecting each tire. "Brand new!" he exclaimed. "Way better than the ones we had."

Del stood in the open doorway, looking at the Dodge. "Brand new tires," Lee said to her. "You'll be riding in style." What a thing to say, he chastised himself. He felt thrown off.

Del was studying Matt.

"Oh, that's Matt Dunlap," Lee said quickly, and Matt came in the yard and up the steps. He offered his hand to Del. "He's a neighbor of mine," Lee said, and he felt a blush bloom on his face, as if he'd done something wrong.

"I know who you are," Del said, ignoring Matt's hand.

Matt backed down to the bottom step. "I can imagine what you think of me, ma'am," he said. "And I don't blame you. I just want to apologize for all your trouble. I won't even try to explain. It's a complicated story. Sometimes family is complicated," he trailed off. "But I'm sorry."

Lee looked at Del's face. He knew disgust when he saw it. She was thinking of that Confederate flag and the racism behind her punctured tires.

He turned to find Marcus. He'd gotten in the driver's seat of the Dodge. "Want to go for a ride, Honey?" he called to Del. "Try out our new tires."

"I wanna go," Jackson yelled, and James echoed, "I wanna go."

But Del had disappeared back into the house.

Matt and Lee exchanged a glance.

"Y'all come too!" Marcus exclaimed through the open car window. "Come on, Lee! Matt, get your butt in the car! We're gonna go for a joyride!" He raced the engine, and the boys climbed in the back seat. Things felt off kilter. "You go on," Lee told Matt. "I'll visit with Del." He watched as the car pulled slowly away from the house, and then he heard the squeal of new tires as the car disappeared too fast around a sharp curve at the end of the block.

"Del," he called from the open front door. "Can I come in?"

"If you want to," she called from the kitchen. Maybell, released from the bedroom, came racing out again, all wiggles and licks now.

He walked slowly down the hall to the kitchen. Del had her back to him; she was stirring something on the stove, and she didn't turn around.

"That smells good," he said.

"Just chicken and rice," she said.

"My mother used to make that. With celery and onion. The celery was what made it good."

She turned to look at him. "Have a seat," she said, indicating a chair at the kitchen table.

Lee sat down. The table was covered with open envelopes and loose papers, bills and various notices.

"What going on, Del? I thought Marcus was with Sammy last night, sleeping it off."

"He lost his job," she said flatly. "They caught him smoking pot out back at work. That's why he went on a bender. They're replacing him with that white guy who's been wanting his job." She gave Lee a long, accusing look.

A horrible sinking feeling came over him. "Where did he get it? The pot."

"I think you know."

He remembered how Matt had passed around a joint that night at the empty house when they towed the Dodge. Marcus must have sought him out, and of course, ol' Matt was a willing dealer.

"He's lucky they didn't turn him in to the law. I've given him two weeks to find a place."

Lee was speechless. Silent moments passed as Del stirred the chicken and rice more vigorously than she needed to, Lee noted.

"Do the kids know? About you asking him to move out?"

"Not 'til he gets a place. I'm sure they know something's up. He came in stinking of beer last night around two. He barely made it to the couch. This morning he's acting all sweet like nothing is wrong, but everything is wrong. And some things can't be fixed."

"Don't say that, Del," Lee pleaded. He didn't know what to say. He prayed Marcus and Matt weren't out smoking dope with the boys in the car right now. Surely even they had more sense than that.

"I didn't know about Matt," he said. But that wasn't

exactly true, was it? He just didn't know that Matt was selling to Marcus.

"I know you don't feel this right now," he said. "But Marcus is a good man. He's definitely lost, but people can learn. They can change, they can grow. I know it sounds hollow right now, Del. But don't give up. Don't give up on Marcus. It's not over."

"You've got some nerve," Del said. "You don't know Marcus. You don't know me or our marriage!"

Lee, chastised, was silent.

"I was raised in the church," Del said. "I fell away when I married Marcus. But now I'm starting back. There's a little church right here in Nicholtown where everyone will know my face. It's the one thing I've got to hold onto right now."

"WHAT was that?" Matt asked when they were in Lee's Camry on the way back to the country. "Looks like there's trouble in paradise."

"There is," Lee said grimly. "And I think you know why."

They rode in silence as they cleared town and were on the Poinsett Highway. Neither spoke until they turned onto the county road.

"It was just once," Matt said.

"Oh sure," Lee said bitterly. "Like I can believe anything you say. Do you think once doesn't count? You told me you don't smoke yourself. You don't sell. Can I believe anything you say?"

"Marcus just showed up out of the blue. Looking to score. I figured I owed him. I gave him a couple of joints."

"Well, that was enough to get him fired from his job, and now he'll probably lose his wife and children."

Matt was silent.

Lee felt like slapping him and he might have, except he was a gentle guy—plus he was driving. He felt like crying. It was Marcus, it was Del, it was the boys, and it was Matt. He had grown to like him. Trusted him!

"Who are you?" he said, turning to glance at Matt. "Who are you really behind that big beard? Is anything you've ever told me true? How can I believe anything you've ever said?"

They were turning onto Hidden Valley Road.

"I fucked up," Matt said. "I'm really sorry. I just hope I can regain your trust someday."

Lee pulled onto the shoulder in front of the Dunlap house. "Unlikely," he said.

<h1 style="text-align:center">CHAPTER TWENTY</h1>

HE WAS STILL waiting for a response from Margo. At times he wondered if she was pulling a disappearing act again, but then he reasoned that as opposed to him, she had a whole life to keep her busy. His letter had probably stunned her into silence. The Fourth of July came and went, thank goodness. Down at the Dunlaps', there'd been rockets and Roman candles exploding in the sky, and a warlike barrage of firecrackers. He could only imagine how the Spots enjoyed that, and as for a trembling Smoky, he shoved his face behind the toilet, believing he was hiding his whole body. There was nothing Lee could do to reassure him that it wasn't the end of the world.

When he drove by their place, he couldn't help glancing over to see if the lads were out and about. He missed Matt, in spite of himself. What a jackass he'd been to give those joints to Marcus! So what if he thought he owed him something for the flat tires fiasco. Matt was an evangelist for the saving powers of pot. He didn't foresee that Marcus would be an idiot and smoke on the job. According to Sammy, Marcus was now renting a room over a storefront in San

Souci. He'd finally agreed to go to one of Sammy's AA meetings; he told Sammy he had "dug" the others' stories and struggles. Sammy thought there was a good chance he'd go back to meetings, and he would keep after him. He'd found work, another auto parts wholesaler out on I-85, but a lesser position with less pay. Del was going back to teaching in the fall. All this Lee learned from Sammy; he hadn't heard from Marcus or Del.

ONE evening when he was watching *Dancing with the Stars,* his phone rang. He stared at it, knowing it was her. He let it ring three or four times, figuring that when he answered, his life would change—he just didn't know in what way.

"Hi," she said.

"Hi."

The years fell away.

"I always seem to be owing you an apology," Margo said, and he could hear the smile in her voice.

"You certainly do." Smiling too.

"I went to the North Shore for the Fourth with the family. Ten of us, four grandchildren under twelve." She paused. "And I needed time to think about your invitation."

"It was a bit stark, wasn't it?"

"It got right to the point." She laughed, and everything about her came back to him. The essence, one might say. The Margo-ness of her, which he had loved then and loved now, hearing her voice.

"I do want to come for a visit," she said. "If you'll still have me."

"I will," he said. He almost said, "I do."

He told her about the trailer, how she might not be

comfortable staying there, and there were no motels within thirty miles. Nonsense! She'd love to have a "trailer experience." She laughed just the way she used to. He'd never invited her to the trailer during the two years when she was in town; he hadn't thought it proper somehow.

"You can meet my dog. Smoky. You'll like him. And he'll love you."

"I'd love to meet Smoky. And I'd love to see you, Lee. It's been too long."

They made their plans. She would come for ten days.

HE was invited to Sarabeth and Lyle's—they were a couple again—for dinner the next night. Shaken and excited, he told them over shrimp and grits that a friend was coming for a visit for ten days. She was flying to Greenville from Minneapolis. They'd stared at him. "Wow," was all Sarabeth could produce.

"That woman from the library," Lyle guessed. "Did you two have 'a thing'?" He grinned, and Lee blushed.

"I don't know what 'a thing' even is," Lee retorted, "and no, no 'thing.' She's a friend, Lyle. Men and women can be friends, you know."

"I see," Lyle had said, rolling his eyes. "Friends. Well, is this friend going to be staying at the trailer?"

"What's wrong with that? She'll be staying in your room, in case you're wondering."

"I'm sorry to be the bearer of bad news, Lee, but the trailer is a dump."

"Stop it, Lyle! You'll hurt Lee's feelings!"

"I still have a little time to tidy up," Lee said.

"Tidy up."

"You know, pick up and put up and . . . She said she wants

to stay at the trailer. She insisted! I warned her!"

"Let's move on," Sarabeth said. "We have something to tell you, Lee. A big announcement! I'm pregnant. We're pregnant," she grinned over at Lyle, whose face flushed.

Lee looked from one of them to the other. They were watching for his reaction. He was shocked. Lyle was just twenty-four. And they'd been back together for only a couple of months. But Sarabeth was definitely a stabilizing influence; she was thirty, and she wanted a child.

"Congratulations, you two! This is wonderful news! Wow! I didn't expect—"

"Well," Sarabeth said, "It *was* kinda an accident. But I'm not getting any younger. And

now that Lyle has this job and has stopped doping..."

"You really are off pot?"

"I told you I wasn't addicted," Lyle said. "And Sarabeth . . . well, she wants a baby, and she doesn't want to give birth to a li'l pothead." He snorted and reached over and took her hand. "*We* want a baby, I better say, or I'll be in the doghouse."

"I'm so happy for you guys. Will this make me a great-grandfather? I feel old before my time!"

"You are old," Lyle said, though not unkindly.

THE next Sunday Sarabeth and Lyle showed up at the trailer. Lyle's Jeep was loaded with a vacuum cleaner, a wet mop and a dry mop, a new broom and dust pan, two buckets, rags, Ajax, Windex, Bleach, Clorox, Pledge, Murphy's oil, white vinegar, and twelve rolls of paper towels. They ordered Lee to take Smoky for a drive and not to come home for at least four hours. He had no idea where to go. He went up to Asheville and drove fifty miles along the Blue

Ridge Parkway, stuck in slow-moving tourist traffic, fuming. The idea! The nerve!

But when he came home, he couldn't believe the transformation. Sarabeth had brought a new oilcloth tablecloth with bright red poppies on a green background, Lyle had cleaned all the windows inside and out (amazing the difference that made), the countertops had been scrubbed clean of their sticky residue, the round rag rug, vacuumed, was cleaner than it had looked in years, the wood cabinets were cleaned and oiled to a dull glow, the sinks, showers, and tub were scoured of soap build-up and the faux-wood floors of general grime. The place stunk of cleaning products but Sarabeth said that would dissipate in a few hours. Lee felt like those people on *Extreme Makeover: Home Edition* when they return to find their crappy house miraculously transformed. He was moved and grateful, shaking his head, exclaiming over and over at what they had done, thanking them profusely.

Sarabeth had bought new bedding and towels. She had taken Lee's sheets ("Did these really used to be white? Well, say goodbye, you'll never see them again!") and made the bed with new cream-colored 400-thread percale sheets and a cotton quilt in the old timey wedding-ring pattern, in shades of cream, navy, and patterned blue patches. The towels were light blue. Lee didn't know what to say, but he stammered out, "It's all so beautiful!"

"Pottery Barn," Sarabeth declared.

"Lee's more a Target man," Lyle said.

"Sears," Lee corrected. Not that he'd bought any new linens or towels since he moved to the trailer twenty years ago. Was there still a Sears in Greenville?

"Thank you, kids," he said, laughing. "I don't know what to say."

"Just invite us over to meet the gal," Lyle said. "She must be pretty special."

TIME crept and sped, crept and sped, and then he was at the airport. He used to come out here when he was young. That was in 1962, when he was twenty-one years old. He'd finished junior college and was working as a page at the Greenville County library to make enough money for classes at Clemson that fall. On balmy summer evenings, he'd drive his mother's ancient Chevy from downtown to watch the construction of the new Greenville-Spartanburg Airport. Make that "Jetport," though no one called it that. The airport was being constructed on a large parcel of open rural land called Flatwood between Spartanburg and Greenville. He'd walk out the concourse of the modern new terminal to see how the runway was coming along. At 7,600 feet, according to newspaper reports he followed, it would be long enough to accommodate jets when they did arrive.

The runway had centerline lighting, the first civilian airport in the nation to have it. Before then, airports had lighting only on each side of their runways. At night those lights illuminated the misty darkness as far as his eye could see, stretching into the future. Out there in the middle of nowhere, the new airport was futuristic. Did he imagine that he might fly away someday, that he might escape? He could no longer remember. If he had such ambitions back then, they were lost to time. What he'd longed to escape was inside. Back then, there would be no lifting off from the mud that bound him to the earth, from the weight that pressed down from the sky above. In the fifty-five years since those youthful visits, he'd never taken a flight. But now, at this very moment, he realized he had escaped the mud and the weight, and he felt, if not weightless, then free—and happy—in a way he couldn't have imagined.

There was something about a new baby on the way that filled him with wonder and hope.

He felt closer to Lyle than he ever had, and he adored Sarabeth, sure that she was good for Lyle. And in a short while, he would see Margo again, something he'd never dreamed could happen. When he put that ridiculous note—"Please come for a visit!"—in the mail, it had been like wishing on a star. He hadn't believed such a wish could come true.

He was here too early. Margo's plane from Atlanta wouldn't land for another hour, that is if there were no delays. She'd be spending ten days with him. It was hard to imagine. It was also a lifetime if things didn't go well. If he'd been more nervous, he would have dropped dead.

Now, for something to do while he waited, he went out the glass doors to the "airside garden" with its spirited fountains and concrete benches, which provided an attractive area to view the distant mountains and planes landing and taking off. Very thoughtful and attractive. Not that he gave a damn. He was too anxious for aesthetics. He watched a couple of planes take off and a couple land. The airport was busy. In this empty time between before and after, he found himself pondering where the years had gone. When you're twenty-one, you never stop to think "I'm young." When you're seventy-five, all you can think is "I'm old!"

Make that seventy-six, he corrected himself. He had passed yet another birthday in May, with only a small—a very small—celebration: he and Sammy had gone to O.J.'s meat-and-three for lunch, where Sammy had treated him to a slice of coconut cake.

But he didn't feel old. Or at least not now, not at this moment. He felt like himself, ageless, timeless, the self he was outside of time, age, and encroaching infirmities. He wondered how he would find Margo. She was sixty-nine now, practically a baby. Was there still time for   . . . what? She was coming for a visit, damn it, he scolded himself, that was all, not to marry him! She had a whole life, a family, a hoard of nine or ten of them, back in Minnesota. He could never move there. And she would never move to Blue Ridge. But they had ten days, and he determined to make the most of them. Unfortunately, her visit came in the summer's hottest month. But they could walk with Smoky to the ravine in the early mornings when it was still cool, and he would show her how the bright green kudzu sculpted the whole landscape there. They would eat late dinners at the picnic table out back in the evenings when the heat relented, and the katydids struck up their frantic din in the trees—*katy did! katy didn't!*— to Lee the very heart of summer and one he'd never tire of. They'd . . .

Lost in reverie, he was jolted to realize a Delta plane was landing. It came in fast on the long runway, braked to slow down in front of the airside garden, then made a neat turn and taxied to a gate. There was a time when debarking passengers came down a plane's stairs and walked from the plane to the concourse, rather than through an elevated jetway. Now TSA wouldn't let anyone without a ticket out to the gates. They'd agreed to meet at the baggage claim. He hurried inside to the carousels, wondering if he would even recognize her.

A JUMBLE of passengers was vying for their suitcases, which were spit out roughly onto a circulating belt. He scanned the crowd, but there was no one he recognized. Then he spotted an attractive-looking older woman with short curly white hair standing over by the exit door, looking calm and poised, confident she would be found. When she caught sight of him, she smiled and waved, and started toward him, walking at her usual fast clip. She had always reminded him somehow of a pony. Not that there was anything remotely horse-like about her. But there was something jaunty. Her face—intelligent, kind, serious but ready for a laugh—would please just about anyone. She was standing beside a carry-on suitcase, wearing a blue-and-white seersucker skirt and jacket and tennis shoes, and she had a big red bag over her shoulder. He went toward her as she came toward him, and they paused a long moment, just looking into one another's smiling eyes. They embraced. They held on long past a casual hug.

THE landscaping on the median from the airport back to I-385 was particularly lush and beautiful now in summer. There were all sorts of conifers and evergreens, deodar cedars, arborvitae, hinoki cypress, junipers, some trees blue with airy needles, some a dense dark green, some bright, with every blue-green shade in between. It had always been important to the early planners to have such a beautiful entrance to the airport. Over the years, the landscaping had matured, but Lee could remember its infancy. Margo exclaimed over the amazing lushness. "I remember why it's called Greenville," she exclaimed. He didn't disabuse her of that thought, despite the fact that Greenville was actually named for the Revolutionary general Nathanael Greene.

They made small talk as they drove through Greenville—her flight, her white hair, which she'd let go "age appropriately natural," the people they'd both known at the library, the changes in town since she'd left, with Margo marveling at all the crepe myrtle trees along the way with their extravagant displays of pink, rose, white, or lavender blossoms. "I've missed those!"

But as they neared Blue Ridge, he began to get cold feet. What would she think of the trailer—he was suddenly embarrassed about it—and what would they have to talk about for ten days? It felt awkward, two strangers about to run out of conversation. They'd covered the obvious topics, her two daughters and four grandchildren, how she was doing since Joe's death, their health and aches and pains. He could think of little to say about his life that didn't seem, well, either boring or too complicated. He'd put a beef stew in the Crock-Pot for dinner in honor of that first lunch they'd had back in Travelers Rest at the Moondog, which she probably wouldn't even remember, and she probably didn't eat beef, and it was too hot for beef stew. Maybe she was allergic to dogs, though she hadn't said so. She'd probably insist on sleeping in the "guest room," Lyle's old room, instead of in his room, as he intended, with its queen-size bed and brand new bedding.

"I'm so glad to be here," Margo said as they turned onto Hidden Valley Road. "I know you're worried about the visit," she added. "Don't be."

"Does it show that much?"

"Well, I know you, Lee. It's been a long time. But I felt I knew the true you then, and I feel that now. I just feel happy in your presence. I intend to lap that up while I'm here."

He wanted to blurt out "I love you," like he had a Tourette's tic but luckily stopped himself. They drove by the Dunlaps' where Matt was standing at the edge of the drive, as if he'd been watching for them. He and Lee met eyes briefly, and when Lee gave a wave, he felt a pang. "That's my neighbor Matt," he said to Margo. "One of the Dunlap lads, as I call them: Matthew, Mark, and Luke."

"Duh," Margo said.

"I'll tell you all about them sometime."

He was pulling into the trailer's driveway. "Be it ever so humble . . ."

Margo was silent as she took it in. "Wow." There was a pause. Then, "It doesn't get much more . . . vintage than that." Another pause. "It's so . . . you."

For some reason this made them both laugh.

CHAPTER TWENTY-ONE

LEE WORRIED ABOUT whether there would be any drama in the neighborhood with Luke on the loose. Whenever he drove by the Dunlaps', he tried to see if he could spot him, but no sightings of the crazy in the attic. He wondered if maybe Luke had moved away—where, he couldn't imagine. He hadn't spoken with Matt since the "joint episode," which at first seemed an unforgivable lack of judgment on Matt's part but gradually had dulled in importance. It was hard to hold onto as the crime of the century. Matt may have even thought he was doing Marcus a favor, substituting pot for booze.

He hadn't heard from Marcus or Del, and he missed them—but he wondered if he wouldn't be welcome back in their lives. He knew from Sarabeth, who kept up with Del, about Marcus's new job at another car parts warehouse. Del would be teaching tenth grade in the fall, and the boys would be starting fourth grade. And from Sammy, he knew that Marcus was going to weekly meetings. He and Del weren't living together, but Sarabeth thought it was just a matter of time.

And Lee was busy with other things, to say the least: Margo's visit: the event of a lifetime, as he saw it.

Ten days were clearly not enough. By the fifth day of her visit, this had become abundantly clear to Lee. He wasn't sure about Margo. She hadn't brought it up. As far as he was concerned, the visit had gone wonderfully. No awkward moments, no running out of things to say; it felt both amazingly new and exciting and also as if they'd always been together, not in an old hat way, but in the best way—as if they were meant to be. But she had another home, in Minneapolis, full of family and friends, and he really couldn't imagine she'd want to spend much more time in rural South Carolina. It was not an even match-up.

Lee had won the battle that she must sleep in his room with its fancy new Pottery Barn bedding, not Lyle's room. Thinking he needed to entertain her, for the first several days after their early morning walks to the ravine down Hidden Valley Road, Lee had planned daily outings—the art museum, Asheville, Falls Park—despite temperatures rising into the nineties by noon. At last Lee announced, "That about exhausts the local entertainment I have to offer," to which Margo responded, "Good. I'm exhausted! Let's stay home."

They quickly discovered they had in common a love of afternoon naps. Was there anything more desirable on a summer afternoon when the air conditioning was on high, making a steady white noise, than retreating to lie with a sheet lightly over you while you drifted off to Nirvana? On the seventh day of the visit, Margo appeared in the door of the guest room, where Lee was snoring lightly, having dropped off to sleep almost as soon as he hit the bed. She came over to him and lightly stroked his forearm. He woke, startled, and looked into her gray-green eyes. "Why don't you join me," she said, not a question. "It would be so nice, don't you think?"

Not a question. Smoky, nothing if not adaptable but confident of his place as a dog-human, followed them into Lee's room and asked to be let "up" on the queen-size bed. "Oh for Pete's sake!" Margo said. "Okay, uppy Puppy, you rascal." She patted the pile of blue patchwork quilt pushed to the foot of the bed. Smoky leapt up, circled, "dug" a time or two, and settled down happily with the pack for his nap too.

Lee, unnerved, didn't know what to do: lie there straight-armed like a board? Should he touch her? Was she wanting sex? If so, she was looking in the wrong place! But Margo was making her nest in the crook of his arm, snuggling next to him, resting her head on his shoulder, her open palm riding the rise and fall of his chest. He inhaled the clean smell of her hair. Prell? He adjusted himself to get more comfortable and listened to her calm, slow breathing. She had fallen asleep! It occurred to him that they fit together like correct pieces of the McBee boys' Mt. Everest jigsaw puzzle.

Naps led to nights together, and nights led to what Lee had never dreamed possible, even though he'd made a visit to his doc when he knew she was coming to Blue Ridge. He'd known Doc Cobb for three decades, and yet he felt like a teenager asking for rubbers at the local drugstore. He'd blushed painfully as he explained that he had a friend, a *woman* friend, coming for a visit and . . . Doc wrote the prescription without a word but with a big grin on his grizzled face. He handed it over with just a few words of advice: take it a half-hour to an hour before you expect to need it, and take only one (as if Lee would OD on Viagra!). Lee had it filled at a Walgreens where he was unknown in Greenville, feeling deeply ridiculous and obvious (and old).

One night, lying next to Margo in his shorty pajamas,

his arm under her shoulder in her sleeveless nightgown, her head in the crook of his arm, he felt her hand sliding down his chest over his pot belly, and then his eyes popped wide open at the next sensation. Unfortunately, it was just a worm, but what a worm! A worm that felt good, real good, a worm that was waking up from a long slumber, a worm that was rising to the occasion, raising its little hooded head: More! More!

"You smell so good," he said into her ear when she raised up to kiss him. "Jergens," she said. He caressed her loose breasts, and kissing her came naturally. He nuzzled her hair. "I've dreamed about this," he said, amazed. "I just thought it would be too hard . . ."

"Well, it's not *that* hard!" she said, laughing, putting her hand down below to feel. "I think I can fix that," and she disappeared under the covers.

When she was back in his arms, she pulled out a little bottle she had tucked under her pillow. "Silky," she said. "I came prepared, just in case. The travel size, so it wouldn't be confiscated by TSA." She took his hand and squirted some on his fingers. "Your turn. Think you can find it?"

Sex obviously turned her into a comedian.

NOW with only two days left of her visit, he had to broach the subject of her extending her time, his heart aching at the thought of her leaving. He was cupped against Margo's back, their hands entwined together against her belly.

"Would you consider staying a few more days?" he whispered. He stopped himself from saying "please." He didn't think that was fair. "I know it's asking a lot."

She was silent. He wondered if she could feel his racing heart against her back.

"I didn't book a round-trip ticket." A long pause. "I thought this might happen. I thought ten days might be too short. But I didn't know how it would go, for either of us."

"And?"

"I'm thinking two more weeks. Maybe three."

THEY spent peaceful evenings, sometimes playing Scrabble or working on a jigsaw puzzle. They were both readers, favoring novels and memoirs. They'd discuss the ones they'd read in common, sorting out any plot points they'd missed or forgotten and assessing the prose or choices the authors' made. On this particular night, Lee was reading *The Lords of Discipline,* set at a fictional military college based on The Citadel, full of over-the-top (at least he hoped it was over-the-top) plebe torture. Margo was reading Joan Didion's memoir about the year after her husband's death. Lee looked up to see her sitting with the book turned down on her lap, staring into space. Outside the katydids were filling the night with their hysterical urgency.

"Are you okay?" he asked.

She startled, brought back to the present. "Yes, I'm fine. I'm not sure I like this book though." She shook her head. "But reading it makes me think about Joe's death."

"Do you want to talk about it?"

"Not really. It was hard but not terrible. He was in hospice, and they took good care of him. But the funny thing is, we were closer than we'd been in a long time." She looked over at Lee in his La-Z-Boy. She patted the couch, and he came over and sat next to her.

"I do want to tell you about it. Not so much his dying, or even our marriage. But what came afterward."

"I want to hear."

She nodded. "For many years, we lived together not really as man and wife. More like pals. Friends. But his dying brought us closer. There was a sweetness in it. We'd been together forty years, after all."

Lee was silent. He put his arm around her shoulder, and she smiled at him but removed it. "Thanks. But I'll get a crick in my neck." He'd imagined that Margo had had a happy, close marriage, and he'd tried not to be jealous, though he'd wished he was the one married to her. She'd never talked about Joe or her marriage back when they took their lunch-break walks. He'd assumed it was none of his business, private, and he was just happy to be in her presence.

"There's more to the story of Joe's death." He glanced at her. The floor lamp by the couch cast a golden light on her face.

"Okay," Lee said, feeling a ripple of fear. "Tell me."

She nodded. "A few weeks after he died, a woman we knew, Julie Wanamaker, called and asked if we could have coffee sometime. It seemed odd, since she and I had never gotten together like that. Our kids had gone to the same schools, but in different classes, and we knew each other casually but not well. I'd always liked her. I figured she wanted to express her sympathy or was reaching out because I was alone. But it wasn't that. She wanted to tell me something." She paused, shaking her head a little. "She and Joe had had an affair." She gave this a beat or two. "I've always hated that term. I've always felt it was demeaning. To the people in love."

She paused, as if considering this. He waited, wondering what might be coming next.

"Anyway, of course I was shocked. I hadn't imagined that Joe would fall in love with another woman. But why not? I saw that she was attractive. But just average—like me. A good person. It had gone on for five years, including after he got sick. He never told me. Julie cried as she told me all this in her living room. I was surprised, yes, even shocked, but I don't know if I can explain this, Lee. It made me glad. Glad that Joe had had that happiness. That love in his life. I mean it probably made him guilty and all that, but I knew instinctively that he had loved her. In a way he couldn't love me. That was just the way it was. And I felt happy. I don't know if you can understand this. I hardly do myself. But I felt happy that Joe had found this happiness in his life that we hadn't had together.

"But here's the thing I want to tell you. It freed me. It made me angry that I'd wasted so many precious years loving you—yes, loving you!— and keeping that to myself. Not acting on it. Denying myself. While Joe found love and acted on it. But once he died, once I knew about Julie, I had to rethink everything. I took some time to make sure. We're both old, Lee! A lot of time has passed. I wasn't even sure if you were alive or well. But I decided to take a chance. I sent you that letter. And when you wrote back, 'Please come for a visit!' my heart nearly burst. With joy."

A S the weeks of Margo's extended visit clicked by, Lee again braced himself for her departure. But with a couple of days to go, Margo announced that if he would have her, maybe she would stay a little longer. Maybe another month or two. She didn't have anything pressing to get back to at home. She really wanted to see the fabled color as the leaves turned in the North Carolina mountains. So if he didn't mind, she'd stay on a while. *Mind!* Lee shouted inside, but he played it cool and said, simply, he'd like that. Big smile.

LYLE and Sarabeth invited Lee and Margo for an end-of-summer cookout, so they could meet Lee's "girlfriend," as Lyle put it. Sarabeth also invited Del, Marcus, and the boys. Del and Sarabeth got together every so often: a visit to a nail salon to have manicures and pedicures; an occasional "girly" movie as Marcus called them while he took the boys fishing; or clothes shopping at the mall. Del was counseling Sarabeth on morning sickness. According to Sarabeth, Del and Marcus were living together again, apparently happily aside from the usual couple grouses, which she and Sarabeth enjoyed sharing. Marcus was singing in the choir at church, and to her knowledge, he wasn't drinking. In Sarabeth's opinion, their ship had righted itself.

Lee was so happy to see the McBees again. When Marcus tried to thank him, Lee cut him off, mumbling about bygones, and Del actually gave him a hug, unexpected from someone normally so reserved. While the guys cooked on the Weber in the driveway, the boys played badminton in the backyard with an excited Smoky and a new birdie and actual net. Their peals of laughter were music to Lee's ears.

As they sat around the dining room table eating burgers, Lee noted that maybe Sarabeth had what she'd wanted ever since she'd gotten involved with Lyle: a normal life. It didn't seem that much to ask, but then, everything considered, it was. Before dessert, a whipping cream pound cake Del had brought, Marcus produced a little wrapped present out of his pocket and handed it to Lyle. Lyle, surprised, unwrapped it: a wooden clothes pin. He gave Marcus a questioning look.

"For changing all those diapers!"

Del reached over and took Sarabeth's hand: "My wish for

you is—(suspenseful pause)— twins!" A big wink and every-one laughed as Del and Sarabeth hugged.

Lyle told stories about the guys in the shop—like the time they wired an old car horn to the brake lights in Lyle's Jeep, so whenever he hit the brake, the car honked. "Another time they asked me to diagnose a car that was in the shop. I took it for a test drive and when I got back, I told them some-thing serious was wrong—it was clunking like it might throw a rod. I didn't actually know what a rod is or if cars throw them." They all laughed. "Anyway, the guys stood around looking serious and worried, shaking their heads, muttering about thousands of dollars in repairs. Until Butch pulled off the hubcap and rocks tumbled out!"

"I suppose that's what's known as male bonding," Lee speculated. He couldn't recall seeing Lyle so at ease and comfortable with himself. Lyle finished by announc-ing—given how much he had to learn and with this new bun in the oven—a nod to Sarabeth—that he'd enrolled in Greenville Tech's Automotive Technology program. He'd be starting in the fall.

"Gosh, why didn't I think of that?" Lee said, giving him a nudge.

CHAPTER TWENTY-TWO

ONE MORNING THERE was a soft knock on the door. Smoky began barking, his hackles raised, ready to defend the castle. Margo and Lee looked at one another, four eyebrows raised, two thinning ones, two plucked ones. No one ever came knocking. Margo, lying on a yoga mat on the floor, paused her stretching, and Lee laid his crossword puzzle on the side table of the couch. He turned down the volume on the record player. He had a big collection of classical, jazz, and swing records he had collected over the decades. Lyle teased him about still playing records—even CDs are extinct! he exclaimed—but Lee loved the look and feel of vinyl records. And his 1980 Yamaha turntable still worked like the day he bought it. He held Smoky by the collar to restrain him.

When he opened the door, a stranger was standing there with a huge bunch of blue hydrangea blossoms. Smoky was wagging and straining to greet the guest. Lee met eyes with the man: Matt Dunlap. Sans beard. His face looked exposed, naked without the squirrel's nest. His cheeks were gaunt, his eyes as blue as the flowers he held; he looked younger and more vulnerable than he had when half his face was hidden.

His expression was shy, abashed, and touchingly beseeching.

"Lyle told me you have a guest." He actually stammered. "A lady friend. These are for her." He thrust the flowers at Lee. Then he fell silent.

"Matt!" Lee exclaimed. "Glad to see you." And he was. "Come in and meet Margo."

Matt looked uncertain. "I'm still sorry for what happened with Marcus," he mumbled. "I was so stupid."

"We all make mistakes, Matt. I've made plenty. I've missed you!" Saying it, Lee realized it was true.

Margo had come to the door.

"This is Matt Dunlap," Lee said. "Our neighbor down the way. He brought you these."

Margo took them in hand. "They're absolutely beautiful! The size of these blossoms! And blue! Thank you! Did you grow these?"

"Well, they did that on their own," Matt said with a shy grin. "Once the bushes are established, as these have been for years, they do fine on their own. I just give 'em a drink of water when I think of it."

"Blue flowers are my favorites. Won't you come in? A cup of coffee? Maybe ice tea?"

"They're the only flowers on the farm. They're blue 'cause of the acid soil."

"Come in," Lee said, holding the door open wide. "We got some catching up to do."

After he'd closed the door, they heard a plaintive whining. Lee let a bloated-looking Spot in. She and Smoky began sniffing each other's privates. "Knock it off, guys," Lee said. "No manners," he sighed to Matt, who was looking more relaxed now. "Sit down, sit down."

"Am I interrupting?" Matt asked perfunctorily, perching on the edge of the couch. "I should have called."

He glanced at Margo anxiously, but Lee filled in the silence with a bit of their past, how they'd met at the library, how she was visiting from Minnesota. "I'd always wanted to have a trailer experience," Margo said. Lee chuckled, but Matt looked mystified.

"Don't mind her," Lee said. "You know how these Northerners are. What you been up to, Matt?"

Matt gave a big, involuntary yawn. "Well, right now the hemp crop is taking all my time."

Margo took the bait and asked him about hemp. Matt was a willing teacher: he explained how he was growing an acre of hemp behind his house. "You wouldn't believe how complicated it all is. We have to make sure the harvest produces a legally compliant crop that tests below .3 percent THC and is safe to ingest."

"How do you harvest it?" Lee couldn't resist asking.

"Well, because I have a small farm, we harvest by hand. We use tobacco knives."

"And then what?"

"We load the plants onto a trailer and take them to Travelers Rest to the facility there for drying and curing. The thing is, it's mainly just Luke and me and a gal who's helping with the harvesting. We have to cut the stalks before they get too mature, otherwise we'll produce plants with THC higher than the .3 percent."

"And the hemp is used for . . ." Margo asked.

"Now there's a soft pitch," Lee said.

Again, on cue, Matt spoke passionately about CBD products and how they help people keep inflammation down and block pain receptors. "It's a non-intoxicating way to help with a variety of physical and mental issues."

"I've heard something about it," Margo said. "Do you think it would help the arthritis in my thumb joints?"

"Absolutely. There's research. I'll drop some cream by," Matt said. "After our crop is processed by the plant in Travelers Rest, the CBD will be infused into things like body butter, honey, gummies, even pet tinctures. In case you're wondering, growing hemp isn't illegal; we have a state license."

"That's all very interesting, Matt."

"Don't encourage him," Lee said, "or we'll be here all day."

"Not possible," Matt said, missing the jab. "Right now, I'm working morning, noon, and night." He yawned deeply again, as if to prove his point, and now Lee saw that he really did look exhausted.

"Isn't Mark helping with the harvesting?"

"That's what I came by to tell you. Mark joined the Marines. He's in basic training at Parris Island. Learning how to rappel down a wall and shit like that. So Luke and I are managing the farm. Or trying to."

"Mark enlisted?"

Matt nodded. "I know. It seems unlikely. But he wanted to get away from here. I can't blame him. It'll actually be good for him. He won't have any trouble with basic training, or deployment, for that matter. It's his only shot for college. So it makes sense." But he didn't look happy about it. Lee felt shaken by this news. Afghanistan came to mind.

"Obama promised to drop the troop level there," Matt said, reading Lee's mind. "But now he's keeping it the same level until he ends his term. The situation is deteriorating in many parts of the country. ISIS and al-Qaida are on the rise.

Lots of Afghans leaving the country. But we have a commitment to the Afghan people."

They were all silent for a long moment.

"What about that coffee?" Margo asked, but Matt said he had to get back to work. Lee said he'd have another cup, and Margo stepped to the kitchen to make a fresh pot.

"How is Luke?" Lee asked, a bit trepidatiously.

"How is Luke," Matt repeated. He paused a few beats, as if deciding on an answer. "Well, he's pitching in with the harvesting, and that's good. He understands what has to be done." He paused again. "I think he's maturing. You know, taking more responsibility around the place now that Mark is gone."

Lee wasn't sure how to ask. "What about all that . . . you know . . . stuff in his room?"

"Oh that's all gone," Matt said. "We had a come-to-Jesus talk about it. He cleaned up his act."

Lee wasn't sure what that meant. "Well," he said, "I just hope that's true. I haven't forgotten how he pointed that rifle at me."

"Unloaded musket. But he wouldn't do that now. He's over all that." He looked away. "Anyway, I have to get back. Nice to meet you," he said to Margo, who had put the hydrangeas in a clear vase and set them on the counter between the living room and kitchen.

"They're spectacular," she said, nodding her head at them. "Thank you so much, Matt. Good luck with the hemp."

"I'll drop that CBD cream by," Matt said. "Maybe the old man will give it a try. For his aches and pains."

After Matt left, with Spot trotting behind, Margo said, "So that's one of the famous Dunlap lads." Lee had told her all about them: the Confederate flag; the flat tires; the musket incident; Luke's white supremacy room; Matt giving Marcus the reefer. "Despite all that, there's something sweet about him," Margo mused. "But that brother! That's disturbing. Do you think Luke has really straightened up?"

Lee gave this a beat. "Matt's not the first person to be in denial about a relative. But I suspect once a white supremacist, always a white supremacist."

"I don't envy Matt having that responsibility."

"No," Lee said, scratching Smoky behind his ears. "It's got to be quite a load."

"THE problem with the world," Lee commented a few weeks later as they took their morning constitutional to the ravine with Smoky, "is that other people are in it."

"Oh God," Margo said. "The old curmudgeon raises his hoary head. You're talking about my family, right?"

"Well, only your younger daughter," Lee said.

Margo called her daughters every Sunday to check in, inquire about the grandchildren, and sometimes get a few words with them. There were two daughters, and regarding their mother's extended visit in South Carolina, they took opposite positions, naturally; they always had. There was Meredith, age forty-one ("I had her when I was twenty-eight," Margo explained, "when I didn't know what I was doing"), a GP married to an ophthalmologist, with two children. She was entirely supportive; all she cared about was that Margo was happy. Then there was Jane, age thirty-three, a divorced therapist with seven-year-old twin girls, an agitated ball of anxiety about what her mother was doing—and what this . . . this . . . old man who lived in a trailer—was up to.

"I think Jane'll come around when she meets you."

Lee stopped in the middle of the road. "She's coming here?"

Margo laughed. "We're going there."

"We . . . are . . . going . . . there."

"Will you, please? For me?"

"Have we met?" Lee said, starting to walk again. "I don't think I've made your acquaintance."

She swatted him lightly on the arm. "It will just be for a weekend. Not that long. Three days. We'll fly to Minneapolis in October, before it gets too cold there. You've always wanted to fly. Let the family meet you. So they'll see you're not holding me for ransom."

"How much do you think I could get for you?"

"Not enough."

"I hear Minneapolis is really nice in the spring," Lee said. "Summer even better."

Margo looped her arm through his, pulling him against her. "You'll come around," she said.

I T was a beautiful September morning, too early for the trees in Blue Ridge to have turned, except a few wild dogwoods scattered in the woods. Birds were performing a symphony all around them: chickadees chika-dee-dee-dee-ing, mockingbirds' tweets, trills, whistles, melodic riffs, and scolds, cardinals' high whistles as if flirting with pretty girls, and a large brown thrasher, rooting around at the edge of the forest, showed off in double phrases an impressive soprano repertory. Overhead two redtail hawks floated lazily on invisible currents. The temperature was mid-seventies; it was going to be a bright, blue day.

They had come to the ravine. The first time Lee showed it to Margo, he'd explained that not many cars came down this pot-holed, old asphalt road posted "Dead End" unless they wanted to unload an old oven, mattress, tires, or a body. To which Margo had replied, "That's nice. Saves polluting the air with cremation fumes."

Now they stood at the edge of the unofficial dump, peering down into the wide, deep crevice blanketed in a green vine with leaves covering everything like a living quilt. "They say if you drive an old junker off the bank into the ravine," Lee said, "by the next morning you won't be able to find it."

Kudzu had completely encased the trees that grew in the base of the ravine, shrink-wrapping them from bottom to top, long tendrils hanging down like leafy ropes. Kudzu completely obscured the mysterious shapes below—boulders, fallen trees, old appliances, maybe cars— rounding them into green sculptures, creating a fantastical landscape.

"It's almost pretty except that it's like something out of a science fiction movie," Margo said. "Creepy!"

"Kudzu's known as 'mile a minute.' It can grow at a rate of a foot per day. 'The vine that ate the South.' It's nearly impossible to eradicate."

"I wonder what all it's hiding."

Smoky began barking excitedly somewhere off in the distance. "Sounds like he's down in the ravine," Lee said. He whistled and called, but Smoky kept up the fierce barking. "He must have treed something. Maybe a possum. It's not like him not to come. Smoke, come! Come, Smoky!" he called and whistled again.

Across from them, a human figure began rising out of the bottom of the ravine. He was stumbling his way through the kudzu as if it were deep green snow. Smoky was trailing him at a close distance, still barking aggressively, sinking down into the vine cover and struggling for footing. Lee couldn't make sense of what he was seeing. No one would be in the ravine, not if he could help it. Margo grabbed his arm. "Who is that? Is he hurt?"

They stared as the figure clawed and grappled his way forward through the dense foliage, vines restraining his feet here and there as if to entrap him. Smoky was losing his footing as the leaves gave way beneath him, fighting to keep upright.

"That's Luke!" Lee exclaimed. "Luke Dunlap."

They watched as Luke fell and righted himself numerous times as he came toward them. "Luke!" Lee called, "up here, son. We'll help you up!"

Finally Luke arrived below them at the bottom of the ravine wall. He began climbing up the steep kudzu-covered bank, grasping vines and handfuls of leaves to pull himself up. Smoky had stopped barking as he fought his way up the wall too, foaming at the mouth, exhausted but not ready to relinquish his enemy.

"Smoky wants to protect us!" Margo exclaimed.

Lee knelt on the side of the bank. When Luke got close enough, he reached down and pulled him up by one skinny arm onto the asphalt. Luke sank back on his haunches, breathing so hard Lee was afraid he'd have a heart attack. His normally pale face was frighteningly red.

"Lee!" Margo had grasped hold of Smoky by the collar as he struggled to mount the top. "Help me, Lee!" Lee pulled Smoky up and lifted him under his front legs to get him onto the road. "Good boy!" Lee praised, "Good dog." Panting hard, white froth at his mouth, Smoky kept his eyes pinned on Luke. Margo kept her hand on his collar.

"God, Luke!" Lee said, turning to him. "Are you okay?"

Luke was still squatting on the asphalt, breathing jaggedly. He was wearing a filthy white T-shirt, cut-off jeans, and heavy-duty combat boots. His scrawny bare legs were scratched and bleeding, and there were more serious scratches on his arms and sweating face. He didn't look at Margo and Lee.

"Are you all right?" Margo asked. "Should we go get the car?"

"What happened?" Lee asked. He couldn't imagine how Luke had gotten so deep into the ravine.

Luke's breathing was beginning to calm, though he still took deep gulps of air. He hadn't acknowledged Lee and Margo.

"What were you doing down there?" Lee asked.

Now Luke turned a smirking face to him. "Training."

"Training for what?"

"For what's coming."

"What? What's coming?" Lee asked.

But Luke didn't respond. He got shakily to his feet and started limping off toward the woods to the left of the turnaround. Lee took over holding onto Smoky, who was straining to get loose.

They watched in silence as Luke disappeared into the forest.

CHAPTER TWENTY-THREE

WHEN THEY GOT home, they agreed that Lee should go talk to Matt about what they'd seen.

"I'm not sure what to say," Lee said. "If I ask if he's dangerous, Matt will say no."

"Do you think he's dangerous?"

Lee was sitting in the La-Z-Boy, drinking a glass of cold water. He got up and went to look out the window, half expecting to see Luke at the edge of the woods beyond the backyard. Hadn't Matt said he kept a tight leash on the boy? What was he doing thrashing around in the ravine, a crazy place to be if ever there was one. It was strange how he didn't acknowledge them. And what the hell was "coming"? Well, he'd better go talk to Matt.

But *was* Luke dangerous? There were plenty of not-quite-right people in the world, but they weren't dangerous. Luke had meant to scare him when he pointed that old, unloaded musket at him, and he'd accomplished that. But was it just putting a trespasser in his place or a real threat? The words he had spoken still burned in Lee's memory: "You're that nigger-lover that lives on our road."

"Maybe we should notify the police," Margo said. "Have them come talk to him."

"What would we say? He was in the ravine. He didn't threaten us. I doubt that's something they'd be interested in investigating. And I don't think making your bedroom a shrine to white supremacy is a crime, though it should be."

"I feel sorry for Matt. And for Luke, too. Living out here in the boondocks, apparently no friends, nothing to do but work for his brother. That's no life for a young man. No wonder he's crawling around in a ravine!"

"Well, one thing for sure. We don't really know him. I'll go talk to Matt and maybe Luke if I can. That should be interesting." He grimaced.

LATE that afternoon, Lee paid a visit to the Dunlap place. Per usual, he was greeted with a reception of yapping, barking, black-and-white mongrels, including five new puppies, black and white and yes, spotted. Poor old Spot had birthed yet another litter, the puppies trying to get at her sagging tits. She snapped at them, warning them off, while she made her way to Lee, wagging her bedraggled tail. "Hi old girl," he said, patting her stupid head. Maybe he should offer to have her spayed. But he didn't want to get any further into the Dunlaps' business. He threw the Milk Bones as far away from him as he could, and the mutts scrambled to snap them up, trampling the pups in the process, distracted enough for him to make his way to the porch. He knocked on the door. After a few minutes, when there was no answer, he used his fist. No answer.

At least Lyle's black Jeep wasn't there. But the pickup truck was in the yard, as was the tow truck, along with the derelict cars the Dunlaps were supposedly "repairing." There was an old, sunburned Miata he hadn't seen before. The spool table was empty of beer cans, and in the place where the McBees' Dodge had been under the pecan tree, there was now an Impala, its hood crushed from a head-on collision. The leaves of the pecan tree were beginning to yellow, parachuting to earth. Occasionally a pecan hit the car with a loud "bonk."

Maybe Matt and Luke were around back, clearing the hemp field for next spring's planting. He assumed they'd gotten the harvest in. He hoped he would find Matt alone. It would be hard, not to mention awkward, to ask about Luke if he was there. He thought about all the white supremacy stuff he'd seen in his room. Matt said he'd taken care of that, along with the Confederate flag and the musket. But what was inside Luke, what festered there? Who was Luke, and what moved him? From what Lee knew, white supremacists were driven by hate and anger they imbibed from the internet, filling them with racist and antisemitic loathing. But how far gone was Luke? Or was he playing at it, the way he played Confederate soldier and Tarzan of the Ravine?

According to news stories, those who knew Dylann Roof didn't suspect the racist hate that burned inside him. Or if they did, they kept it to themselves. But Luke was no Dylann Roof, Lee was pretty sure of that. Still, how did you really know? And what was he referring to that was coming?

He came around the side of the house and saw Matt culti-vating the barren field on a small apple-green tractor, churn-ing up the red-orange soil. All the hemp stalks were gone; the harvest was over. Matt was in his country farmer clothes, overalls, plaid shirt, straw hat; no corncob pipe. Lee studied him for a few minutes; he had a face out of the Depression, gaunt, angular, and starkly handsome. He looked around, relieved that Luke was not there. He turned to look at the second-story windows, half expecting to see a rifle pointed at him. Get a grip, he admonished himself.

"Matt! Matt!" he yelled over the tractor. When Matt turned to see who was calling, pleasure animated his face. He gave a hearty wave and turned off the engine, which coughed and belched black smoke a couple of times. He started toward Lee through the furrows in his mud-caked work boots, calling "Wendy, come see who's here!"

Surprised, Lee looked around just as the large wood door to the shed slid open and a woman in jeans and a faded blue work shirt with the sleeves rolled to her elbows stepped out. She was probably in her early forties, strong looking, like she belonged on a farm. Her dark hair was pulled back in a bushy ponytail that protruded through the back hole of a Braves baseball cap. Tilting her head, she looked at Matt questioningly as she joined them, and when Matt said, "This is Lee, the neighbor I've told you about," she smiled a deep-dimpled smile and offered her hand, giving Lee's a firm shake.

"This is Wendy MacDonald. When I was looking for help with the harvest," Matt explained, "Wendy signed on."

"Fool that I am. I was raised on a farm. I thought I'd escaped until Matt lassoed me with cheap wages and those brown eyes I couldn't resist."

"Blue eyes," Matt said, laughing. "Blue!"

"Let me see," Wendy said, pulling him to her by the front of his shirt.

"You can see why I hired her," Matt said with a grin, an expression Lee hadn't seen on him before. He took off his straw hat, ran his fingers through his long hair. "Let me wash up a bit, and I'll meet y'all out front. Grab some cold ones, Hon," and he disappeared into the house.

Wendy and Lee raised their eyebrows at each other. "Matt looks happy," Lee said.

"He's a good guy," Wendy said as he followed her around to the front of the house. "I haven't met many like him in these parts. I'll just be a minute. Make yourself at home over there." She indicated the spool table in the yard. "Oops, I forgot the linen table cloth! Oh well, we'll make do."

She went up the steps and in the front door. Lee took his old seat at the table, a wood dining room chair with half the cane back broken out. That must be Wendy's Miata. It looked rode hard and put up wet, he thought. She seemed like a nice girl . . . woman. Margo was training him to be more politically correct. He was musing on how glad he was that Matt had a girlfriend when they came out the front door. Matt was carrying three beers. Wendy had a round tray with cheddar cheese slices, Ritz crackers in a bowl, a bag of potato chips, and a carton of onion dip. They were making his visit into an occasion. Lee was touched. But he reminded himself of why he had come. He would have to get to that.

They all popped their tops and clicked their beer cans in a toast; the beer tasted unusually refreshing to Lee. This visit had made him anxious, but now he relaxed into the moment more. Matt filled him in a little on Wendy, how she worked as a bartender in Travelers Rest, that's how they met, how she grew up in Asheville, was divorced. "And glad of it," she piped up.

"What do you hear from Mark?" Lee asked. He helped himself to a piece of cheese and a cracker.

"Not much. He's still in basic training. They run 'em

ragged. I wouldn't be surprised if he doesn't become a long-hauler. He likes discipline and orders."

"Unlike Matt," Wendy said, cocking her head. Lee liked her. She seemed right for Matt. A lot of joshing. No bullshit.

"How did the harvest go?"

"That little green tractor?" Matt said. "We did well enough that I bought it at a farm auction over in Dacusville—1967 John Deere 110, $600. Hadn't been cranked in four years but the engine still turns just fine. Should make next year a lot easier. I learned a lot."

"I'm really glad to hear it worked out."

"How's Margo?" Matt asked. "I still owe her some CBD cream. And gummies for you. Ready for another one?" and he tilted his own beer up to finish the last swallow.

"No, I'm good," Lee said.

"You?" he asked Wendy, but she said she was good too.

There was no putting it off any longer. "One reason I stopped by," Lee said, wading in, "is to ask about Luke."

Matt was silent for moment. "We'll do that then," he said. "Fire away."

"Is he here?"

"He moved out. Couple of weeks ago. He's living with some dudes he knew in high school. Over in Tigerville."

Lee was surprised. "Margo and I saw him down at the ravine this morning. I mean, in the ravine. Down *in* it."

"Yeah," Matt said. "Weird. But that's Luke."

"He said he was in training. He didn't say for what." He watched for Matt's reaction, but when he didn't respond, he tried, "I'm not sure it's safe in the ravine." He sounded like a hand-wringing old lady. And Luke tromping around in the ravine was not really what he had come to talk about.

"Bring me another one, Babe," Matt said, holding up his empty can to Wendy. "I need some reinforcement for the inquisition."

Wendy gave Lee a sympathetic look. "Don't mind him. Not his favorite subject." She headed into the house.

"I can't control his every move," Matt said. "He's twenty now. He did pretty well in high school, C+ B- average." He let this sink in. "I think he's okay. He's always been a loner. All through school. That's why I'm glad he's moved in with these dudes. It wasn't good for him living here, especially after Mark left."

Lee wasn't sure where to go next. "Are you sure Luke isn't . . . I don't know what word to use. Not quite right?"

"That's three words," Matt said. Wendy reappeared and set Matt's beer in front of him, along with one in front of Lee. She popped the top on her own. Matt tilted his can back and almost emptied it, his Adam's apple bouncing. Lee eyed his beer and thought, "Why not?" He needed reinforcement for the inquisition himself.

Matt burped. "'Cuse me. You mean crazy?" He paused and burped again. "He's weird, but he's not crazy. Didn't you ever play war when you were a kid?"

"Do you think he's dangerous?"

Matt was quick. "Do you?"

"I have no idea. That's why I'm asking you. My only experience with him was when he pointed that stupid Civil War rifle at me."

"You gotta drop that," Matt said. He explained to Wendy about the musket, how it wouldn't even fire, there weren't bullets for it, and how Matt sold it as punishment for a little trouble Luke got into regarding some tires. He gave Lee a look.

"Does he ever talk to you about his racism?"

"He wouldn't talk to me 'bout that 'cause he knows I wouldn't agree with him. Anyway, I got rid of all that shit in his room. I could show you. No fucking Robert E. Lee, no Confederate flag, no fucking swastika, no Rhodesian patches, all that crap he used to have. All gone. He has a stocking job at Walmart in TR—though I'm not sure how long that will last." Matt looked out toward the road. "He's twenty, Lee. I'm doing the best I can to let him grow up. I can't lock him in his room."

They stopped talking as a loud pickup truck came barreling up Hidden Valley Road from the county highway. "Buckle up. Here come the dudes," Matt commented. They watched in silence as a Ford F150, the formerly red body rusted to burnt-orange, puffing black smoke out the exhaust pipe, wheeled into the yard and chugged to a stop near their table.

"What year is that thing?"

"I'm guessing 1970-something," Matt said. He stood up. "Dudes! Whadup?"

Three boys, including Luke, got out, all either deaf or dumb or both, Lee couldn't tell, and stood with their hands thrust in their jean pockets. The dogs were going wild, barking and charging but not getting close. Luke kicked at one, clipping it on its side, and it went yelping under the porch. He had a large Band-Aid on his cheek and another on his forehead. Angry red scratches on his forearms looked as if he'd fought a wildcat. "Yo, Luke," Lee tried, but no response.

The other boys, the former high school friends he was living with apparently, were sturdier looking than Luke, who was slight, his face pallid under his bowl cut. One of the boys had a beer gut that hung like a water balloon over his belt; his pudgy cheeks had squeezed his eyes into slits.

The other was the proverbial skin-and-bones. As if they'd been typecast that way.

Matt introduced them to Lee and Wendy: Jimmy and Joey. "How's life over in the tin can?" he asked amiably. "They're renting a trailer over in the Happy Hills Trailer Park."

"I know the place. I live in a trailer too," Lee said, hoping for a friendly conversation bit but running out of gas when the boys expressed no interest, not that Lee could blame them.

"How 'bout a beer," Matt offered, and both boys nodded. "I wouldn't kick it out of bed," said the fat one.

"Luke?" Wendy asked.

"Got any Smirnoff Ice?"

"Have you ever known us to have Smirnoff anything in this house?" Matt asked. He got up and put his arm around Luke's thin shoulders. "Beer or Coke, buddy. You look pretty beat up. Who won?"

Luke ignored this, shrugging Matt's arm away.

"How's the construction job going, Jimmy? Must have made for a hot summer," Matt asked.

"Quit," Jimmy said.

"Okay," Matt said. "Well . . . anything else in the pipeline?"

"That Fiesta Mexican Grill in TR? I'm busing tables, washing dishes. Learning the trade. I get free tacos and burritos."

"That's good, Jimmy. Good. How 'bout you, Joey?"

"I might enroll in North Greenville. If they'll accept my ass. And if my stepdad will pay for it." He blushed bright red.

Wendy brought the boys' beers. They were all silent as they opened them and took long quaffs.

Lee studied Jimmy and Joey. They were the average ones, the ones who never stood out in school, who got barely passing grades, whose parents probably had their own troubles and could barely keep it together. He felt for them; life would be hard. They were clearly not the brightest bulbs, but then, Lee figured, not everyone could be if the IQ bell curve was going to work.

"Are those potato chips?" the fat one asked, even though they were in a Lay's bag.

"Help yourselves," Wendy said. "Onion dip too. Pull up a chair if you can find one with a seat."

Jimmy and Joey descended on the snacks.

"So," Matt said, "what brings you guys to this neck of the woods today?"

"Uh," said Joey, or was he Jimmy? "You got one of those things? Can we borrow it?"

"Now that's an intriguing question," Matt said. "I've got lots of things, so it depends on what particular thing you're after. You're going to have to be a little more specific, Jimmy."

"You know," he said. "That thing that you use when you take a big dump and it won't go down."

Lee suppressed a laugh.

"Plunger." It was Luke, standing a little off to the side.

"Oh. *That* 'thing.' You know where it is, Luke," Matt motioned for him to go in the house and get it.

Fatty and Skinny were cleaning up the remaining food like buzzards on roadkill. "Keep it," Matt said when Luke reappeared with the plunger. "I suspect this won't be the only time y'all will need it."

There was a pause in the "conversation." Lee was getting nervous. The boys would be leaving any minute. This might be the only time he'd have to get something out of Luke that might help him assess whether he was as "reformed" as Matt seemed to think.

Before he could formulate a question, Wendy said, "So, did you guys watch the debate last night?"

"What debate?" Joey asked.

"Trump and Clinton," Matt said. He nodded at Wendy. "She's an 'f' word."

"Fucker?" Jimmy guessed, the wrinkles in his beefy brow deepening.

"Trump's gonna be our next president," Luke suddenly spoke.

Lee, taken aback by his sudden pronouncement, or any pronouncement at all for that matter, said, "Wow, Luke, that's quite a prediction. What makes you think that?"

Luke's face turned redder than his scratches. "He's gonna make America great again."

"A lot of people certainly believe that," Lee said, keeping his voice neutral.

"It's highly unlikely," Matt said. "But then again, a lot of people despise Hillary Clinton. She wouldn't be my first choice. But Donald Trump?" shaking his head. "No way."

"Well Hillary has my vote," Wendy said. "Not only is Trump unqualified, he's a racist, misogynistic pig!"

"Don't mince words, my love," Matt said. "Speak your mind."

"People call Trump a racist, but . . . niggers are the real racists!" Luke said hotly.

"How is that?" Lee asked.

"Moving into neighborhoods where they're not wanted." Luke looked straight at Lee. "White neighborhoods."

"Folks are mad as hell, and they're not going to take it no more!" Joey said.

"You guys sound so angry. Is it really that bad?"

"Hell yes," Jimmy said. "All these immigrants coming into our country. They're bringing drugs. They're bringing crime. They're raping our women. Trump's gonna stop that."

"No one wants niggers and wetbacks and rapists moving into our neighborhoods," Luke said, scowling. "Especially out here in the country." He looked right at Lee again, then looked away. He was holding the plunger by the handle, and for a moment Lee thought he might strike him with it. That would be something, being struck by the bad end of a toilet plunger. But Luke turned and went over to the truck and got in. Jimmy and Joey followed like dogs. Before shutting the truck door, Joey called back, "Thanks for the beers and the thing."

Matt, Wendy, and Lee sat in silence as Luke fired up the Ford, which took a few protesting grinds of the ignition. Please don't let it break down here, Lee prayed. Just let them be gone. Finally on the fifth try, the truck started, and with a blast of black exhaust, it rumbled out of the yard and turned right on Hidden Valley Road.

"Maybe Luke is going to lead a tour of the ravine," Lee commented. He didn't like them driving by his place. "Well, that was interesting."

"They're harmless," Matt said. "Just got some growing up to do. The thing is, there're people all over the country who think like them. Especially out here. They're mad as hell and think Trump is their savior."

"What made you such a liberal out here in podunk?" Lee asked.

"I'm not a liberal. I'm a libertarian. But in the military, you meet all kinds. You get all points of view, whether you like it or not. You learn to think for yourself. Trump is a fake. A fraud. And he's pulling the wool over a lot of people's eyes."

"He'll never be elected," Wendy said. "Never in a hundred, never in a million . . ."

Just then they heard the rumble of the Ford truck coming back down Hidden Valley Road.

"Well, that was quick," Lee said. "I better get home and see if my trailer's on fire."

"Call me if you need a 'thing,'" Matt said. "Let me get you those gummies and cream."

Lee began helping Wendy clean up the empty bowls and beer cans. He couldn't stop himself. "Do you think Luke is dangerous?"

She paused and looked right at Lee. "Dangerous? Do I think he's going to go in a Black church and shoot up a Bible study group? I don't know him that well, but no. Luke's not capable of that. In my opinion. But do I think he's a troubled kid? Angry. Yes. Lost. Yes."

When Matt came back to the table, he handed over a plastic baggie with assorted colored gummies and a small tin of CBD cream. "Tell Margo to rub it on her thumb joints. I guarantee it'll help. And you try a few gummies, old man. They'll help you chill."

LEE started the walk home. He undid the plastic bag and ate one of the gummies, a red one, cherry maybe, and then a blue one. What flavor could that be, and how long before he could chill?

He was absorbed in his thoughts as he came in sight of his trailer. Not on fire.

But his mailbox and post were lying in the ditch, hit-and-run victims again.

"I HEARD something out by the road," Margo said when Lee went inside. "A loud bang, then a truck burning rubber as it sped away. And of course, Smoky was going bananas. I didn't want to go out and see until you got home. But I had a pretty good idea."

Lee leashed Smoky so he could go see too, and they went out to the road.

"That little shit!" Margo said.

"I'm going to call Matt. We might as well go back inside. Nothing to do here."

WHEN Matt and Wendy walked over, Matt didn't speak, just took in the victim with a grim look on his face. Wendy and Margo introduced themselves, but no one had much to say.

"So I guess this lets Sue Ellen off the hook," Lee said.

"Who's Sue Ellen?" Margo asked.

"Our erstwhile mail carrier who reads her cell phone while delivering the mail. Not entirely reliable," Lee said. "And falsely accused." He raised his eyebrows at Matt.

"I'm going to talk to him," Matt said. "I'm calling him when I get home."

"Good luck with that," Lee said. "What are you going to say? 'Don't ever do that again'?"

THE next morning, Matt and Wendy brought over another bag of instant cement, a posthole digger, a shovel, and a bubble level. Lee supplied his toolbox, a bucket of water, and indignation.

Matt lifted the intact four by four out of the ditch. The mailbox itself hadn't been decapitated from the post, and it appeared to be undamaged "except for its pride," Lee remarked. "Do you think Luke wishes it were me lying dead in the ditch?"

"Don't be a drama queen," Matt said, standing the post up and assessing it. "It's just his way of giving you the bird. If he was really as dangerous as you seem to think, we'd be kicking through the ashes of your trailer this morning." He ran his hand up and down the wood. "No cracks or damage. These things are tough. I told him to cut the crap. He's had his fun. Enough is enough."

"That must have made quite an impression," Lee said.

Matt just gave him a "Don't blame me!" look. He opened and closed the mailbox on top: "Good as new."

WEEKS passed with the mailbox standing its ground. No more visits or sightings of Luke.

IN time, he faded into the background, like a bad dream that is all but forgotten.

CHAPTER TWENTY-FOUR

FALL BROUGHT A welcome change in the weather, with daytime temps mostly in the seventies to low eighties and the sixties in the evenings: pleasant weather (except for an occasional scorcher). One afternoon Lee and Margo drove up to get apples at an orchard near Hendersonville: Honeycrisp, Mutsu, Gold Rush, Pink Lady, Granny Smith, and Arkansas Blacks. They definitely overdid it on apples, but Margo got to work making apple sauce, apple crisps, and Lee's favorite, apple cakes with a buttery, brown sugar glaze.

Early one morning before daybreak, the phone rang. Lee fumbled to find his cell phone on the bedside table in the dark, cursing being waked from a dreamless sleep by a wrong number. But it wasn't a wrong number. It was his brother Earl's son Jed. He had never gotten a call from either of Earl's sons. So in that instant, he knew.

Jed explained through a clotted voice that Earl had collapsed while having dinner at the Poinsett Club last night. The ambulance was there within minutes, and those guys performed CPR, as did the emergency room docs, but he was . . . Jed couldn't say the word. "Gone," Lee supplied himself, unbelieving and yet overtaken by a cold wind that blew through him, leaving no room for doubt. Earl was gone. Had there ever been a more definitive word? *Gone.* The last time Lee had seen him was maybe a week ago. He'd stopped by the Ford dealership to drop off apple cakes for Lyle and Earl.

Lyle had settled in nicely at the service department, and earlier that month, he had started courses in Greenville Tech's automotive program. With work, school, and Sarabeth, he was so busy that Lee hardly saw him. He'd had a few second thoughts about giving an apple cake to Earl, who looked even more porky than the last time he'd seen him. An apple cake full of butter and sugar was the last thing Earl needed. But Lee handed it over. Earl had always loved apple cake, one of the few things their mother had made.

T H E funeral was at First Baptist, and the large sanctuary was packed. Earl had been a popular, well-known member of the community and the church. Lee, Margo, Lyle, and Sarabeth sat with the family. Earl's sons were now middle-aged with graying hair, and there were four attractive teenage grandchildren, several of whom wept openly. Beth—she and Earl had celebrated their forty-eighth wedding anniversary last spring—was dignified and dry-eyed. She and Earl had had dinner a couple of times with Lee and Margo. Earl and Margo had taken to each other, predictably, and Beth had been friendly but reserved with the Northerner. She'd invited Margo to fill in at bridge club, but Margo didn't know how to play bridge, and they left it at that.

Sammy was there with what was left of the Lunch Bunch—Buster, Bobby, and Joey; they had all attended another funeral the previous week: Erskin, their tower of strength in high school, had finally passed. Sammy explained as they stood around after Erskin's funeral that he was now part of a clinical trial for melanoma; his had metastasized. He was taking what he described as drugs with names that looked like someone was drunk when they typed them. "They're called immune checkpoint inhibitors," he said, shaking his head in bemusement. "And I've started attending an alternative medicine class taught by this cool chick. I now have a mantra: 'I'm going to beat this motherfucker.' I say it thirty times a day."

Lee was touched that Marcus and Del came to the funeral; they were among a scattering of Blacks, perhaps customers over the years of Earl's or from other parts of Earl's gregarious life. The McBees were a handsome couple, both tall and athletic-looking, with Marcus looking sharp in a summer sport coat, and Del turned out in a burgundy crepe dress with a short, smart jacket.

A surprising number of people got up to reminiscence about Earl, and as befitted his memory, there was more laughter than tears. Lee ricocheted between both and was wrung out after the reception, having shaken so many hands, had so many hugs, and struggled to place so many people, most of whom he didn't know.

In the weeks that followed, it was hard for Lee to believe Earl was gone. He'd been a happy soul, happy with his family, his friends, his life. Himself. It was strange how they had come from the same parents and yet had been so different. Had they been close? They didn't do things together much, but they kept in touch; it was clear without being spoken that they would always be there for each other. Now, since they hadn't seen each other that often, sometimes Lee forgot that

Earl was dead. Unreachable. Unseeable. He'd pick up the phone to call him. And then it would strike him hard like a punch to the throat that Earl was gone. Never again.

EARL'S death didn't change Lee's day-to-day life much, but in another way it did. Earl had been seventy-two, three years younger than Lee. He'd avoided thinking about the twin bugaboos of infirmity and mortality pretty successfully up to now, but suddenly they were right in his face. If Earl, his younger brother, could die, so could he. Granted, he was in pretty good health (he thought). Doc had him on Atorvastatin for his cholesterol, he didn't eat much red meat, ate a lot of vegetables thanks to Margo, who was practically a vegetarian, had only eaten a small piece of apple cake (and then another and another). He and Margo walked a lot, but his knees and left hip ached. Doc had recommended cortisone shots, which Lee didn't want to fool with, and he wouldn't even hear about a hip replacement. You couldn't replace a *hip*, for Christ's sake!

And granted, his balance was not what it used to be. But why would it be at seventy-six?

That number, seventy-six when he allowed himself to think about it, ambushed him every time. It was like trying to fit pieces that didn't go together: himself; seventy-six. He hated how Doc's nurse always asked him at his physical if he'd fallen in the last year. No! Though in truth he had come close a couple of times. He had stumbled over a yellow curb at the grocery store (the yellow so faded it was almost nonexistent), and then by God he stumbled over the same curb again the next week. Both times kind people—a young lady in black tights and not a day over sixty and a toddler in his twenties with a ponytail and nose ring, who treated Lee as if he were ninety—had come rushing to his aid, righting him, embarrassing him—as if he were old! No!

"WE'RE old birds!" he exclaimed to Margo one evening after they sat down to a dinner of salmon broiled with mustard and brown sugar on top, brown rice, and kale. "I'm seventy-six years old! You're about to turn seventy!"

She looked at him kindly. "I know both those things," she said. "This is about Earl's death, isn't it." *Not a question.*

"No. Yes. Maybe."

"You're a good seventy-six," Margo said. "I'm taking good care of you."

He took this in. "But there are genes," he said. "There's cancer and Alzheimer's and having to pee four times a night. There's talk of arthritic bones and artificial joints. Age is relentless."

"And it will definitely win."

"How many years do you figure we have left?" He felt those old-man tears fill his eyes. "I don't want to lose you."

She laughed. "I'm not going anywhere. Except Minneapolis. And you're going too."

"But how many years!" he said. "Time flies. What do you think? Ten years? If that? It's the luck of the draw. And what if something happens to one of us before then? What if one of us gets some horrible disease or loses our mind, or . . ."

"Maybe we should get married," Margo said.

Lee was taken aback. When he recovered, he said, "Oh. I see. You're after my money. Also the trailer."

"No, I just want your body."

"What's left of it. Okay, tell me your reasons."

"Well, love aside . . ."

"Right. Love is the least of it!" He glanced at his plate. His salmon hadn't been touched and looked gelatinous.

"It actually is, in our case. Love is settled. We love each other. We don't need marriage for that. But there are other things—legal things. It might be good if something happens to one of us if we're recognized as husband and wife legally."

He got it. The light dawned. "I don't know the rules exactly, but a spouse would have different rights than someone you're just shacking up with, right? Visiting rights. Health care power of attorney."

"Hey, I love shacking up," Margo said. "Maybe marriage would spoil that."

"Probably," Lee said. "We'd run out of things to say to one another. But maybe, just maybe, it would make us better. Formalize our commitment. And your family might take what we are to each other more seriously. I don't know. I'd rather bow out, if it comes to that, knowing you're my wife. And think of the fortune you'd inherit. Not to mention the trailer."

"And Smoky. But I don't like any talk about you 'bowing out.'" She shook her head to dispel the thought. "I'm turning seventy in November, Lee. Seventy. It doesn't seem possible."

"Wait 'til you get to seventy-six," Lee said, "if you want to see something that doesn't seem possible. Getting to know this old person I'm becoming is like meeting a whole new person. Anyway, anything could happen to either one of us at any time. If we're married, we'd be . . . God, this memory! What's the word I'm looking for?"

"Married."

Lee stood up, his left hip protesting, and knelt in front of Margo on the hard floor beside her chair. Smoky, alerted that

here was something different, came over to Lee, and Lee told
him to sit. He gave him a reassuring head pat. He took both
of Margo's hands in his. She threw back her head and laughed
but then looked right into his misty eyes.

"Will you marry me, Margo Williamson?"

Her plucked eyebrows shot up. She gave it a few beats.
Then, "Oh all right, Lee Trammell. If you insist." She pulled
his head to her chest, embracing it, kissing the top of his balding head.

"No offense, but you're kinda smothering me. Is that
a 'yes'?"

She released his head. "It doesn't get any more 'yes'
than that."

"Good," he said. "Now could you give me a hand up?"

CHAPTER TWENTY-FIVE

THEIR TRIP TO Minneapolis to see Margo's family in early October, which Lee had, as Margo predicted, come around to, was upon them. The plan was to fly to the Twin Cities to give the family a chance to meet Lee, to see he was not a gold digger or psychopath, and that Margo was more or less in her right mind. During the time Margo had been in South Carolina, there had been a few heated phone calls with daughter Jane, tears on both sides, and some shouting. Even daughter Meredith was becoming concerned. Margo informed both "girls" that she was entitled to her own choices, was responsible for her own life, and if she made a mistake, well, it was her mistake. "But Mom," even supportive Meredith ventured, "he's so old! He's seventy-six years old!" To which Margo responded, "Well I'm almost seventy! All the more reason to make the best of the time we have. I can't wait for you to meet him." She confessed to Lee that her heart beat hard at the thought of "the tribe."

They'd made reservations for October 7. They'd fly to the Twin Cities on Friday, and that night there would be a family dinner. "Oh swell," Lee said. "Me against *nine* of them."

"Four of them are children under ten, and you'll just *love* Grandma Lois and Aunt Dot," Margo said, mysteriously bursting out laughing. "We'll announce our engagement."

"That sounds like fun!"

Margo wanted to visit a few of her old haunts and see her two best women friends. And there was the matter of her bungalow in Southwest Minneapolis, near Lake Harriet, which was standing empty. She planned to get more clothes and the things she wanted to bring to Blue Ridge for what she described as "the duration," to which Lee responded, "You make it sound like a prison sentence." She wanted to meet with a real estate agent she knew to start the process of putting the house on the market. Lee worried that she was having a nervous breakdown. Could she really want to marry an old man and move—permanently—to Blue Ridge, South Carolina? He might have to side with Jane on this.

THEY drove over to Lyle and Sarabeth's to leave Lee's car; he didn't want to come back to four more flat tires. He felt uneasy about leaving the trailer. He wondered if it was even wise to go away, leaving the place empty, but this trip was important to Margo. He'd asked Matt to check on the place every so often, and Matt said he'd keep a close eye on things. He hadn't seen or heard from Luke and assumed he was still living with Joey and Jimmy. Lee reasoned (with himself) that they couldn't put their lives on hold over the "Luke Situation," as he thought of it. He kept his misgivings to himself, not wanting to put a damper on the trip for Margo, who was excited.

Lyle took them to the airport, with Smoky along for the ride. He and Sarabeth were happy to be dog-sitting for the weekend, practice for when they had the baby, Lyle said, to which Margo just rolled her eyes. Lee felt a pang when he patted Smoky on his pointy head and read the question in his eyes: *You're not taking me?* Lee felt like backing out, for any number of reasons, but he got their carry-on suitcases out of the Jeep's cargo hold, a lump in his throat and anxiety giving him heartburn.

After they'd checked in and proceeded through security, all new to Lee, they sat in the waiting area at the gate to board their flight to Atlanta and then on to Minneapolis-St. Paul. Margo was absorbed in a novel by Elizabeth Strout: *My Name is Lucy Barton*, leaving Lee to ponder alone what a big step they were undertaking: Was it premature or unwise? Maybe they needed more time together before bringing in her family. They must wonder if she'd lost her mind, flying to rural South Carolina to see an old friend—who wasn't even a boyfriend let alone a lover back when—and then impulsively deciding to stay on, of all things. He hoped she hadn't revealed that he lived in a trailer. And maybe, being home, she'd change her mind. He glanced over at her beside him, relieved that she wasn't a brooder like him. At one point, she seemed to sense his thoughts and reached over and squeezed his hand.

EVERYTHING about flying was new to Lee and interesting, if a bit terrifying. Walking through the jetway, like the tunnel of no return, he was fascinated by how this flying thing was done but also apprehensive. As he stepped into the open mouth of the plane, he noted two pilots in the tiny cockpit, right there within arm's reach! Shouldn't they be doing something? Checking the gas tank, cleaning the tiny windshield? He followed Margo down the narrow aisle between rows of seats, banging his carry-on against people's arm rests ("Sorry! Excuse me! Oops!"), gallantly carrying over his shoulder Margo's large, red, soft-sided Baggallini bag stuffed with presents for the grandkids, as well as a bag of Arkansas Blacks—the tartest apples—which he worried was against the rules.

When he started to lift Margo's carry-on toward the overhead bin, a young woman leaped up. "Let me help with that." She might as well have added, "Grandpa." Without giving him time to protest, she hoisted Margo's suitcase effortlessly and then his as well into the overhead bin, flashing an athletic smile of strong white teeth. Margo insisted that Lee take the window seat; she sat in the middle and immediately commenced a conversation with the nun on the aisle seat, black habit and all. Was a nun on the plane a good sign or a bad omen? He distracted himself by looking out the window at the little men directing the plane out of the gate with all the nonchalance of helping a car back out of a driveway. The plane was full, and everyone immediately occupied themselves with their little worlds of tablets, books, the flight magazine, or headphones; some were already catching a nap. As far as Lee could tell, he was the only one who paid attention to the demonstration regarding seat belts and oxygen masks and studied the diagram of the plane in the seat pocket, ascertaining where the emergency exits were.

They taxied down the runway, passing by the terminal with its airside garden where he'd sat so many times as a young man, a grounded observer of others taking off, going somewhere. Now he was the one. The plane gained speed, and then with a frightful roar it lifted off, gained altitude, and banked so that a view of the Blue Ridge mountains to the northwest appeared in his window and then was gone as they climbed into the sky. The sky! He tried to identify what he was seeing below, which small town, which lake, but all he could recognize as they lifted higher was Glassy Mountain, clearly identifiable by its big round dome. Then they were among the clouds.

And now those clouds were piled below them. They were above the clouds! He might as well have been an astronaut. Fluffy pillows of pure white, huge, down below, and a never-before-felt sensation of speed he couldn't exactly feel but could see as they streamed above the clouds. He thought of Earl, and even though it was idiotic, he wondered if he was nearer to him up here in the sky. If there *was* a Heaven, that's where Earl was. Grief welled up, tightening his chest. Tears came to his eyes.

Margo turned back from the nun to see how he was doing. "Well?" she said, taking his hand.

"I love you," he said.

THEY took a taxi from the airport to their hotel, The Normandy Inn and Suites, in downtown Minneapolis. Lee had never been in such a big city, or any city for that matter, only Greenville, a little city or a large town. Margo wanted to show him some of downtown before they were due for dinner. They were going over to Meredith's for the long-dreaded family dinner that evening with the nine terrifying relatives.

They freshened up from the flight and then went out on Nicollet Mall. "What are those?" Lee asked of the glass walkways high above the city streets. Margo explained that they were skyways. "People don't have to go outside in the winter. They can go almost all over downtown without freezing." It was a beautiful crisp fall day, emphasis on "crisp," since this was Minnesota. Lee hadn't understood that fifty in Minnesota felt different from fifty in South Carolina. In an old sport coat left over from his library days, he was cold. "You can't even imagine what it's like in the winter," Margo said, looping her arm through his. "I've spent my last winter in Minneapolis. Some people don't mind the cold, but I froze from October through May!"

"It's a beautiful city," Lee said. "All glassy and blue. I wish we had longer here."

"We'll come back," Margo said, "once we get this visit out of the way."

MEREDITH, the family physician daughter, lived with her ophthalmologist husband Keith and their two children, Baily, a daughter who was ten going on fifteen, and Martin, aka Snapper, who was eight going on five, in a three-story house in Kenwood, one of Minneapolis's fine old historic neighborhoods near Lake of the Isles. The house, painted white with navy blue trim, had a rotunda porch in front and what had obviously been a fabulous perennial garden in the summer, now showing brown telltale signs of frost.

Keith answered the doorbell, and Lee took him in (as Keith took Lee in, in that first instant when strangers size each other up, pretending not to): a nice man, personable and professional, cordial while not being particularly warm (like Minnesota). Lee felt looked over, and no wonder. Surely the family wanted to know what Margo had pulled up on her line. Meredith, wearing an apron over a red dress and black Chinese slippers with red peonies embroidered on the toes, came running in from the kitchen, and she and Margo embraced mightily and long, including Meredith kissing

Margo's curly white hair again and again. "Mother!"

After shaking Lee's hand with a strong grip and giving him a kiss on the cheek, Meredith excused herself back to the kitchen—a savory smell of onions, bacon, and red wine was wafting through the entry hall—calling back over her shoulder, "*coq au vin!*" Keith ushered Lee and Margo into the living room, a chilly room (to Lee) with a rounded lead-glass window facing the porch. "Lois," Keith addressed an old lady who was looking Lee up and down, as if she were considering buying him, "this is Lee, Margo's . . ." He was at a loss for the word. "Lee, this is Margo's mother, Lois. And this is her sister, Dot. Everyone calls her Aunt Dot."

Lee went over to the Victorian rose-colored sofa where they were seated and paused there, uncertain whether to shake hands or what, so he simply did a little (ridiculous, he thought) bow, as if paying obeisance to royalty. Margo, in the meantime, descended on the two ancient ladies and was giving them hugs and kisses on their wrinkled cheeks. Keith offered drinks, and Margo requested white wine, so Lee did too. She cut her eyes at him, grinning, almost laughing out loud, and he could read her mind: "Buck up; you're doing fine."

"So you're the boyfriend," Aunt Dot was saying, eyeing him. "I had a boyfriend once that looked just like you. Handsome, shy, but boy howdy could he . . ."

Margo quickly cut her off. "How have you been, Dot?"

This opened the door to a litany of complaints, health scares, actual health problems and their treatments, and trashing of the assisted living facility where, she said, she was being held captive. Keith reappeared with a tray of glasses and a bottle of Chardonnay. Meanwhile Margo's mother was staring at Lee. "I understand you live in a trailer."

Lee's eyebrows shot up. Who had let that cat out the trailer door? He gave Margo a look, and guiltily she grimaced.

"May I call you Lois?"

"Of course. That is my name. Bug over, Dot. Come sit by me, Mr. Trammell."

"Lee," he said.

"And tell me . . ."

Saved by the bell. The doorbell chimed, and in came Jane and her seven-year-old twin girls, beautiful children, like something out of a Degas, Lee thought. They were wearing identical dresses with pink velvet bodices and voile skirts, ballerinas going to the dance. As soon as they saw Margo, they rushed her and gave her big identical hugs from either side, reminiscent of other twins he knew.

"And you must be Jane," Lee said, smiling as best he could. She was dressed in black slacks and a black long-sleeved top, as if she were attending a funeral. She took a long, penetrating look at Lee. "And you are certainly Lee," she said, and when he offered his hand, she took it and shook it in both of hers. He must not have appeared like the ogre she'd expected, nor was she the threat he'd feared, just a daughter who was concerned about her mother's welfare. This moment over, Jane fell into her mother's arms and cried hard for several minutes, with Margo patting her back. "Oh Mother. I'm so glad you're here! And I'm so—sorry! I've been such a bitch!"

Meredith called Baily and Snapper down from upstairs and they made their entrance: Baily, with sparkly eye shadow, must have snuck some of her mother's lipstick. Snapper was sucking his thumb, which seemed odd for an eight-year-old. But they were nice, polite children who embraced their grandmother. They were excused from having dinner with the adults and took their twin cousins into the den to have their own sup-per of ham and cheese sliders, potato chips, and video games.

Meredith and Jane, having survived meeting Lee, and vice versa, sat on either side of him at dinner, which started off painfully but moved with the help of more wine through guarded interest in getting to know him, to more wine, which led to affectionate, funny stories they told on their mother, then more wine, finally arriving at warm smiles and happy, relieved feelings all around over dessert. At that point, a loaded Keith rose to make a toast (Lee was glad tomorrow was Saturday; he wouldn't be operating on anyone's cata-racts): "To Lee! Welcome to the family!"

As the daughters exchanged startled looks (Lee fig-ured Keith would hear about this later), they all raised their glasses. Lee lifted his glass to the family of which he was now apparently a part and thanked them for their hospitality. "I'll look forward to more such evenings," he said, feeling a blush creep up to what was left of his hairline.

"THAT was quite an unexpected toast," Lee said as he flopped across the queen bed in their room back at the Normandy. "I'm not sure Jane and Meredith were quite ready to declare me family. Did I pass the smell test?"

"You were yourself: polite, gracious, modest, charming without realizing it, nonthreatening, apparently sane. You were interested in them, willing to share about our life, kind, always that. What else?"

"Handsome, debonair, a genius, a comedian . . ."

"True. And they're just so nice. Minnesota nice. They also knew they had no chance of interfering with me, so they came around to rooting for you."

"What became of announcing our engagement?" Lee asked.

"I forgot all about that! I was a little nervous. Maybe they'd had enough for one night."

"They're all wonderful," Lee said. "This can't be easy for them. They don't want to give you up to a yokel in South Carolina. They love you. And you them."

"I'm certainly blessed," Margo said, flopping down beside him. "Thank God that's over!"

She turned on her side to face him, her hand on his chest. "We're going to have to get a marriage license if we're really going to get married, you know."

"No, I didn't know. Or I guess I did, way back when Elaine and I got married. Ancient times. I remember a nasty tyranno-saurus blocking the entrance to the marriage license place."

"And I suppose you did battle and hit him in the snout with your sword."

"My sword's not that big."

"I know," she said. She snuggled in his arms, and in a short while she was snoring softly.

But Lee couldn't sleep. Things had gone better than he could have imagined. Margo's family were good people, Minnesota nice (as she had described them); they'd decided to come around to wanting for Margo what she herself wanted. He puzzled, not for the first time, that Margo could leave behind her home of almost fifty years, her daughters and grand-children, her son-in-law Keith, who was surely a stabilizing sup-port for them all, her friends, her house, the city she knew and loved—all to come live with him in a trailer in Blue Ridge!

He thought about his own little family: His mother. His father. Earl. What might his life have been like if his father had walked away from that mob? He would have come home that night, swooped Lee up and thrown him over his shoulder, calling him a sack of potatoes. Lee's innocent childish laughter, his delight, his love, his *need*, still echoed somewhere deep in his heart. And then his father was gone, leaving Lee adrift and alone. What a mess his own life had been! All those years of bewilderment, festering sorrow and yes, suppressed anger, had sapped the joy out of him. He hated his father for what he had done. He hated him for being part of a lynch mob. He hated him for how he had betrayed and abandoned the family he had made. His father's actions had poisoned his life.

ON Saturday morning they met with the friend who was a real estate agent, and Margo arranged to put her bungalow on the market. Lee was rather amazed at her, at what he thought of as her self-determination. She didn't seem sentimental about her old life in Minneapolis. She and Lee went through the house, a charming, rundown, three-bedroom cottage, and she reminisced, recalling memories and moments but without the tears he'd expected. She talked about Joe, fondly, shared stories of raising the girls there, and took the family photo album, along with some winter clothes and books she valued, all to be shipped to Blue Ridge. After the house sold, they would come back to Minneapolis before the closing and get whatever else Margo wanted.

She told Lee what the real estate agent expected the house would sell for: an enormous amount, shocking them both. She and Joe had bought the house forty years ago, and it was in the highly desirable lakes area where house prices had skyrocketed in recent years. "You'll have something to leave to the girls and grandkids," Lee said. But Margo said most of the money would be for them first. If and when they had to move out of the trailer, along with Lee's savings, they would be able to buy a nice place in Travelers Rest, nearer to amenities and medical care.

Margo was busy all weekend: On Saturday afternoon she walked around Lake of the Isles with Pamela, an old friend from decades of walks around the lakes, book clubs, yoga classes, readings, movies, and endless lunches. Saturday evening she had dinner at a Vietnamese restaurant with Meredith and told her that she and Lee were planning to marry. Meredith, perhaps expecting this, took it in stride. "I like him, Mother," Margo related to Lee. She said at first she didn't know what to make of all this. "But now that I've met him, I can see it. He's good for you—and you for him. You don't need my blessings—but you have them."

On Sunday she had brunch with Jane and told her the marriage plans. Unexpectedly, Jane was neither shocked nor critical of this news, Margo reported. "It would be easier to object if I didn't like him," Margo quoted her. "But he's so sweet. I wish I could find a man like that. Only not one who is seventy-six."

LATER that afternoon she walked around Lake Calhoun with Susan, another close friend of thirty years who was thrilled that Margo had found love. She promised to come to South Carolina to visit her, and Margo promised she'd be back—she'd return once a year, and they wouldn't lose touch.

That evening, as the sun was setting and the evening cooled with the distinct chill of fall, she and Lee walked around Lake Harriet, the lake closest to Margo's bungalow, the one she had circled, she said, "ten thousand times." They would be flying back to South Carolina in the morning. It was the only time he had seen Margo, no crier, cry. Though she said she knew it was true that she'd be back for visits, the enormity of all she was leaving and what she was about to do, for the rest of her life, caught up with her. She and Lee sat down on a bench, and Lee put his arm around her shoulder and held her as she wept, while walkers passing by kindly pretended not to notice.

CHAPTER TWENTY-SIX

THERE WAS NO way Smoky could adequately express his joy
at seeing "his people" when Lyle delivered Lee and Margo back
to his house after picking them up at the airport. When Lyle
opened the front door, out rushed Smoky, who clearly wished
he had arms with which to embrace Lee. He had to make do
with racing around in crazy circles, leaping onto Lee's chest,
almost knocking him over, more circles, more leaps, licks and
then he noticed Margo getting out of the front seat of Lyle's
Jeep, and he rushed over to her with "hugs and kisses."

"Were you a good boy? Did you miss us?"

A panting, open-mouthed, delirious yes and yes!

As he transferred Lee and Margo's carry-ons into the
Camry, Lyle talked about how much Earl was missed at the
Ford dealership.

"Especially by me," Lyle said, and for a moment Lee
thought Lyle might tear up.

"There was something special about him," Lee agreed,
feeling a lump in his own throat. "Everybody loved Earl."

"I'm glad I got to know him," Lyle said. "Thanks for kicking my ass about that, Lee."

"Well, you're the one who did it. I just kinda got your ass in the door, and you did the rest."

They didn't linger since Lyle had to get back to work. "That was sweet how Lyle thanked you," Margo said as they drove out of Chick Springs and headed back toward Blue Ridge on the Poinsett Highway. "It'll be good to get home. Feels like we've been gone a month!" After Lee agreed, they rode in silence.

They turned off the highway onto the county road. "Doesn't it seem like there're more Trump signs than when we left?" Every third house or trailer had a yard sign, some of them homemade and oversized: *Make America Great Again!—Trump 2016.* "It's not possible he could win, is it?"

"Anything is possible, I suppose," Lee said. "But I don't think so. No one really believes he will."

"Except all these people with yard signs."

They turned onto Hidden Valley Road. They were both silent. Lee realized he was holding his breath and reminded himself to breathe.

They passed the Dunlap place, but no one was around the spool table. Now that Mark was gone and Luke was living with Jimmy and Joey over in Pickens, it was a different place—kind of deserted looking. Matt's pickup was in the yard but not Wendy's Miata.

As they neared the trailer, Smoky in the backseat began whining, glued to a back passenger window. "He recognizes . . ." Lee started to say, but then he exclaimed, "What the—" He pulled in the driveway: Crude graffiti was spray-painted in black all over the trailer's cream-colored vinyl front. Speechless, he and Margo got out and stood in the drive. Lee could make out "*Nigger Lover* and *White Power!* in shaky distorted script, along with a couple of swastikas and abbreviations that meant nothing to him—*WPWW, 14,* and *100%.* The paint on the swastikas had run, making them look childish if they weren't so revolting.

"Luke," Margo said.

"He's not much of an artist." Lee let Smoky out of the car and began dialing his phone. Smoky ran sniffing all around the front of the house with his hackles raised.

"You're calling . . ."

"The sheriff and Matt Dunlap." He gave the person who answered the phone at the Travelers Rest Sheriff's Department his name, a description of the vandalism, and his address. "Look," he said to Margo. "The idiot trampled all our little boxwoods." Lee had planted them last spring and kept them watered religiously through the summer, proud of his landscaping attempt.

"You need to come over here right now," Lee said brusquely when Matt answered.

"I can't right now, Bro. I'm . . ." Matt started, but Lee cut him off.

"Now."

WHILE they waited for a deputy and Matt to arrive, they called Smoky in and wheeled their suitcases into the house. At least all was well inside. Margo told Lee she'd unpack while he went around to check out back. Someone had tried to pry open the backdoor but had been thwarted by the double locks. Everything seemed okay in the backyard—until Lee noticed something brown on top of the picnic table. Someone—he corrected in his mind—Luke Dunlap had taken a big dump on the table.

He heard a car pulling up out front and went around to meet the deputy as he was getting out of his squad car. He was in his forties, so not wet behind the ears, Lee thought, and introduced himself as Officer Cooper. Lee couldn't help noticing he had an unfortunate physical resemblance to Deputy Barney Fife in *The Andy Griffith Show*. Doing a commendable Don Knotts imitation, Office Cooper noticed the trailer. "I see the problem." They both stood looking at the graffiti without speaking.

"Nice trailer," Cooper said. He walked over to take a closer look at the siding. He ran a finger over some of the paint. "Still relatively fresh. Probably happened last night."

"Do you think it'll come off?"

"Maybe. You might see some ghost but not bad."

"Jesus H. Christ!" they heard as Matt strode into the yard. "Good God almighty!"

Lee made the introductions.

"What happened?"

"Give me your best guess, Matt."

Matt pressed his lips together. "I'm really sorry, Lee." A long silence. "I'll make it right."

"Where is he?"

"Do you two gentlemen mind letting me in on this conversation?"

Lee explained that the vandal was Matt's younger brother, Luke Dunlap. When Cooper asked why, Lee could barely contain himself: "Because he's a white supremacist! Home-grown. They live right down the road. Luke has this 'thing' about Blacks. He's angry at me for befriending some Blacks who were renting down the road. He drove them off with his stupid Rebel flag. He punctured their tires!"

"Is that right?" Cooper looked at Matt.

Matt just shrugged.

"Is he at your house now?"

"I don't know where he is," Matt said. "He moved out to live with some guys in Pickens. I don't see much of him."

"Has there been any other vandalism?"

"He keeps knocking down my mailbox!"

"Are you sure it's this Luke person?"

"Pretty sure. Yes, sure. Who else!"

Cooper turned to Matt. "What do you think?"

"Probably Luke. Just a stupid prank."

"Why is he targeting you?" Cooper turned back to Lee.

"I told you! Because he's a white supremacist! You should have seen his room—all this neo-Nazi and . . ." he sputtered to a stop. "Do you think we need security? An armed guard?"

"So you're friends with a Black family that lives near here?"

Lee threw his head back in exasperation. "I didn't even know them when they moved in. I loaned the fellow a wrench once. Then they moved out . . ." How could he possibly explain it all?

"Do you think Luke is dangerous?" Cooper to Matt.

"Hell no. He's a punk kid. These are punk pranks. Dangerous? No way."

"Call him."

"He doesn't have a phone."

"Call the friends he's living with."

Matt scanned through his phone's contact list. "Jimmy," he said when someone answered the phone with a hearty "Yo, bro!" He put the phone on speaker. "Is Luke there?"

"He moved out, dude. Still owes us dough."

"When was that?"

There was a lengthy silence. Then, "Yo, Joey! When did the varmint move out?"

"Who fucking wants to know?"

"Give me that," Cooper said and jerked the phone from Matt. Any resemblance to Barney Fife had disappeared. "This is Officer Cooper with the Travelers Rest Sheriff's Office. Do you know where I can find Luke Dunlap?"

"Luke Dunlap!" Jimmy's stunned voice came through the speaker phone. "No sir. That would be a no. Sir. And he owes us rent! Sir."

"When did he leave?"

"Not sure. A week or two ago. Maybe. I think."

"If he's gets in touch with you or you know where he is, call me. Cooper, TR Sheriff's Office. Do you understand?"

"Did he murder some dude?"

Cooper just shook his head, looking half-amused, half-irritated. "Not that I know of. I just want to talk to him about some graffiti. A misdemeanor. He could be fined up to $1,000. Thirty days in jail. If this is his first offense, that is."

"Wow."

When Cooper handed the phone back to Matt, Lee said, "There's something else. Follow me." He led Matt and the deputy around to the picnic table in back.

They were both silent as they took in Luke's "calling card."

"Nasty!" Cooper said, shaking his head. "I'm going to need some information from you," he said to Matt. "Do you have any idea where he is?"

"No idea. We haven't been in touch. I didn't even know he'd moved out."

"Where might he go?"

Matt shook his head. "Maybe to Parris Island to find his

other brother. Mark Dunlap. He's in basic training there. I'll try to reach him."

"You do that, Matt," Lee said and turned and went in the house.

"YOU'RE pretty angry at Matt," Margo said.

"Oh, did it show? Most people keep a mad dog chained in the yard."

"I suspect Child Protection would be out here PDQ if Matt chained Luke in the yard. And Luke's not really a criminal. If he were, he'd have burned the trailer down."

"That time may come. How do you feel about living here now?"

Margo came out of the kitchen, where she'd been peering into the refrigerator. "As for feeling safe, I do. We have Smoky. He'd let us know if someone is creeping around the place. I don't want to let adolescent-punk vandalism ruin what we have here. This is our home, Lee. We love it. We don't have to leave." She stood in front of Lee, who had deposited himself in the La-Z-Boy.

"Well, I don't want him to win by running us off."

"It's not a war," she said. "It's not even a contest if we refuse to play. And he may be long gone from here by now. I suspect he's a coward and didn't want to stick around for any consequences, either from Matt or the law. Or you."

"We don't know him, and we don't know what's in his head. For all we know, he's a psychopath."

"Well, let's see what Matt finds out. And what he has to say."

"Matt," Lee said derisively.

Margo sat down in Lee's lap. "Where do you want to go

for dinner?"

He repositioned her on his bony old legs. "How can you think of food?"

"I'm hungry. Yellow Ginger?"

"I like their pad prik," Lee said, brightening.

WHILE Margo was in the bathroom freshening up, Lee got the safe deposit box out of the bedroom closet. He was surprised that it wasn't locked. Then he remembered he'd forgotten to lock it when he shoved it back into the closet the night Marcus showed up out of the blue to ask about getting together with Sammy. His father's pistol lay on top of his papers, along with the small, heavy box of bullets.

Margo came into the bedroom as he was opening the cylinder. "You have a gun?"

"It was my father's. For protection driving cab. My mother forced it on me before she died. Sammy and I did some practice shooting when I first got it."

"Do you know how to use it?"

"Let's just say I could if I had to. Do you?"

"I've never held a gun in my life, Lee!"

"Here," Lee offered.

Margo held up her hands. "No thanks."

"No, I'm serious. I want you to know where it is and how to use it. There's not that much to shooting it. Aim and pull the trigger. Slowly."

"God! Are you sure you're not overreacting?" She took it gingerly in both hands.

"Good. That's right. Hold it with both hands when you shoot. Let your left hand help support and control your right."

"I'm never going to shoot this gun, Lee. Is it loaded?" Alarm in her voice.

"I'm loading it now. For the time being. Just in case. I'd feel better knowing we have some protection if we need it."

She handed it back to him. "I don't like it."

"Like has nothing to do with it. I want you to see how to load it. I learned all this from Sammy. See this little thing here? It's the cylinder release. You push it, and out comes the cylinder—where you put the bullets. See, this one holds five bullets. Five empty holes. I'm placing one bullet in each cylinder. Now I'm going to rotate the cylinder back into the gun. Hear it click into place?"

"Okay, I see. Now unload it."

"Well, for now, I'm going to leave the bullets in it. Because if a situation arises where we need it . . ."

". . . we won't have time to load it," Margo finished for him. "You're scaring me, Lee."

"I know. It's scaring me too. I don't mean to." He paused. "Maybe you're right. They say never keep a loaded gun in the house."

He clicked the release to open the cylinder again, but Margo said, "No. Let's leave it loaded. For now."

He looked at her and saw the worried expression on her face. "We're never going to need it, my love. It's just for peace of mind. For a little while. We're going to keep it in the top dresser drawer, under your underwear."

"Oh great. I'll probably blow my head off rooting around for a pair of panties. Why don't we just keep it in the safe deposit box?"

"Would take too long to get to it. If we need to get to it . . . quickly.

"This is giving me the creeps, Lee."

"I know. Me too."

THE next morning Matt showed up with Wendy, two fellows who had helped with the hemp harvest, and Joey and Jimmy. Matt to Lee: "I'm paying them big bucks." Wendy gave Lee a little wave but seemed subdued, probably because of what she was seeing. Matt explained he'd been to Home Depot as soon as it opened that morning and talked to the guys in the paint department about how to clean spray paint from a vinyl-sided trailer. "They actually knew— 'Like this is the first time this has come up,'" he quoted their scoffing. They sold him four spray bottles of Motsenbocker's *Lift Off*, a stack of abrasion pads, gloves, and safety goggles. Matt's crew carried two sixteen-packs of Brawny paper towels and a couple of coolers with ice and water bottles onto the lawn. It was a cloudless October day with temperatures in the mid-sixties. Inside the house, Smoky was barking and scratching the front door, so Margo brought him out on a leash and let him smell everyone and make friends.

"Were you able to get ahold of Mark?" Lee asked Matt.

"Mark hasn't heard from Luke since he left for basic," he said. "He'll let me know if he does. You got a hose around here?"

Lee led him around back to get the one attached to the back faucet. Matt turned it on full force and blasted the insult Luke had left off the picnic table. "That'll do for now," he said, unfastening the hose. "But I'll be replacing that table in a few days. Now you and Margo skedaddle. When you come back late this afternoon, it will be as if this never happened."

"But it did," Lee said grimly. "Don't forget that. And I think you'll agree about who did it."

"He's mad at you, apparently."

"Didn't you tell him I didn't even know the McBees when they moved in!"

Matt shrugged. "I don't remember. But apparently he thinks you're responsible. You did befriend them."

"For which he's destroying our peace!"

"Only if you let it. Now where do I attach the hose in front?"

Lee showed him the front faucet behind a trampled boxwood. Matt called his "troops" to come listen.

"I thought we was going to work," Joey or maybe Jimmy said.

"Oh, you'll be working. This job's gonna take a little elbow grease. Now gather around, kiddies, and here's how you do it." He donned rubber gloves, put on goggles—for any blow-back spray. "I'm gonna test a little area here." He sprayed on the *Lift Off* and then scrubbed like a dervish with paper towels, then the abrasion pad, then more spray, more pad, more paper towels, until the exclamation mark on *White Power* was just a faint memory.

"Okay!" he said. "Grab your stuff, and let's do this! See you later, guys," he said to Margo and Lee. "It's better if you don't watch. Like an operation."

LEE and Margo were silent as they backed out onto Hidden Valley Road.

"Well, that was something," Margo said as they started past the Dunlap place.

"Something all right. And now we have to 'kill' a few hours, banished from our own home. What are we supposed to do? Drive around all afternoon? And what about our naps!"

Margo laughed. "We could go to a movie."

"At 10:00 in the morning?"

"Okay, I have a better idea," Margo said. "Let's take care of getting our marriage license. We're going to need one if we're ever really going to get married. It'll take our minds off things. Then we can have a leisurely lunch downtown and make a grocery list. I cleaned out the refrig before we left. We're out of food."

"We are definitely going to get married," Lee said. "Let's go."

ACCORDING to Google, the Marriage License Division of the Probate Court was near downtown Greenville. It was located in a utilitarian one-story maze that housed all the city's government offices. Suite 5600 was in the Probate Court Annex. A woman in her mid-sixties, who looked as if she were living only for the day she could retire and never again darken the doors of the Probate Court Annex, perked up when she realized Lee and Margo were not lost, as so many were in the maze, but actually were there to apply for a marriage license. Old folks! Here was something different; most people applied for their license online. She smiled broadly when she understood that yes, they actually wanted to get married.

"Normally you should have an appointment to apply in person," she said, "but we're not that busy. I don't get that many senior citizens. By your ages, most people have given up!" She laughed heartily at her own joke, and Margo grinned, but Lee was feeling self-conscious and unexpectedly nervous. He was in no mood for the clerk's teasing. After all, this was a big step, one he had never imagined for himself again: marriage! She requested their drivers' licenses and social security cards and gave them the Marriage License Worksheet.

"A Marriage License Worksheet! Is it like the worksheets we had in junior high? What do they want to know?" Lee asked as they sat down on hard plastic chairs to fill it out. "How often do we have sex?"

"That's the first question," Margo said. "Plus how many ways."

"Is there any math?"

"Only a little algebra."

"Are you sure you want to do this?" he asked.

"Fill out the worksheet?"

"Get married."

"Getting cold feet?"

"My feet are fine." He held them out for her to see. He had on one gray sock and one blue one. "Oops. But I like us the way we are. Living in sin."

"And you're afraid marriage will change that."

He considered this. "It's just that it involves the government. A license. Look here," he indicated the worksheet: "They have a lot of rules here: 'There is a twenty-four-hour waiting period by law from the time and date the original application and certification are filed to the time the marriage license can be issued.' I just never thought about what was involved, legally. I guess it makes sense but . . ."

"We can just walk out. We don't have to get married. We're already married, in our own hearts."

"No," Lee shook his head. "I want us to have all the benefits of being married, legally. Like we talked about. I just didn't understand how much was involved."

"This is nothing," Margo scoffed. "Not after you've been the mother of two brides who wanted big church weddings and kick-ass receptions. The *drama*!"

AFTER they turned in their worksheet and paid the $45 filing fee, the clerk, smiling happily, as if she were the one getting married, finished explaining all the next steps: how the applications are processed according to the wedding date ("We don't have a wedding date . . ." Lee started, but Margo gave him a "shush" nudge) and a few other chores, including recording signed copies with the Probate Court and South Carolina DHEC, whatever that was, within fifteen days of the ceremony to properly record the marriage.

The clerk asked if they had a minister lined up. "We're not religious," Lee blurted, and Margo gave him another poke in the side.

"Well, if you're looking for a church home, I go to . . ."

"No," Lee cut her off. "But thanks. Getting married is turning me into a grouch," he

whispered to Margo.

"Make that more of a grouch," the clerk said cheerfully.

"Touché."

"Perhaps you'd like a copy of our notaries list."

"That would be very helpful," Margo said with a big smile. "Thank you."

WHEN Lee and Margo got home late that afternoon—after lunch and grocery shopping, plus a leisurely stroll through Walgreens, they braced themselves for what they might find. Matt was still there, digging up the crushed boxwoods, but the others had left. They parked in the driveway and got out to see how the trailer had fared.

"It's amazing, Matt," Margo said. "It looks almost brand new."

And it did indeed. Almost. Lee was pleased and surprised.

A casual observer wouldn't notice or suspect that the trailer had been defiled with racist graffiti.

But when he stepped across the ditch to the road to inspect the whole thing, Lee saw that the trailer had what appeared to be a shadow across it, as if a cloud were obscuring the sun.

CHAPTER TWENTY-SEVEN

AS PROMISED, MATT and Wendy showed up one day with a new picnic table, padded by old blankets in the cargo bed of the pickup. It was a 72" dark brown resin table with attached benches. Matt was proud of it, describing how easy it would be to keep clean, no rotting or maintenance. Lee had assumed Matt would replace it with another wood one, preferably Southern yellow pine. He couldn't imagine a picnic table that wasn't wood, real wood that would record the elements and develop a patina the way his old one had. But keeping his disappointment to himself, he thanked Matt profusely, hoping this replacement marked the end of Luke's nasty business.

As the weeks passed with no incidents, Lee began to relax more. It was tiring to keep up a constant vigil. Margo had returned to "normal" a lot quicker than he had. She encouraged Lee to return to their routines, including their constitutional with Smoky to the ravine and back every morning. The walk was no longer the innocent pleasure it had been before the trailer was attacked, as Lee thought of it, but the fall leaves were at their peak, and he didn't want to miss kicking through the red maple stars, bronze poplar mittens, and the spiky bell-shaped rust and yellow oak leaves on the road. He found the ravine still unsettling, with visions of Luke plowing through the kudzu like a madman. But Margo believed in "immersion therapy" in which he had to face his fears by staring into the ravine, which was pretty much as it had been before the Luke violation. There were a couple of "new" discarded items—a gas stove, a bulky ancient microwave, and a long orange carpet runner that had unfurled as it was heaved over the side. The kudzu, its leaves not yet killed by the first frost, was already at work.

"See," Margo said, looping her arm through his. "No monsters in the deep."

ONE day Matt walked over with Spot to give Lee some news: Mark had gotten a call from Luke. He was working at a crawfish farm in . . . Matt tried to get the name out, something like "Cal-ka-chew" Parish in Louisiana. "It's near Lake Charles. Mark says Luke likes the work, it's beautiful there, and he's growing some muscles," Matt reported.

"Well, that's good," Lee said, meaning good that Luke was several states away. He thought of the little crawfish in a nearby creek when he, along with Earl and their mother, had lived in Slater. The weird critters scooted backward, hiding under stones, impossible to grab. They were so tiny, there wouldn't even be a bite if you cooked one up. After that, Luke became one of those slippery crawfish scrabbling through his dreams, maddeningly elusive.

ONE Saturday evening Lee was surprised to get a call from Marcus. He hadn't seen the McBees since the end-of-summer party at Sarabeth and Lyle's. The school year was well underway, and everyone was busy, Del teaching at Eastside High, the boys in the fourth grade at AJ Whittenberg Elementary School, Marcus working at the car parts warehouse where he'd been hired after he was fired from Fisher's. All was well with them, according to Sarabeth, who had a round baby bump that could be mistaken for belly fat, except that Lyle couldn't keep his hands off it.

"I hope nothing's wrong!" Lee blurted after he greeted Marcus.

"Hell no, man!" Marcus said. "Ain't nothing bad. I just got somethin' I wanna run by you." He paused. "You're the closest thing I got to a daddy." He laughed his deep bass laugh, teasing with maybe a drop of truth in it.

Lee was a little taken aback. He was hardly daddy material. "Well, your sons think I'm their uncle. No wonder you're mixed up. So yes, let's get together. I want to catch up with you. But Marcus, you can't come out here. Remember how I told you Matt's white supremacist brother punctured your tires?"

There was a long silence—or at least it seemed long to Lee—and then "Fucker!" A big snort. "I don't remember you telling me that."

"You were drunk. But anyway, Luke spray-painted graffiti all over the trailer. I'll leave it to your imagination as to the content. So for now, it would be better if you don't come out here."

"You should of called me. That's some ass I woulda loved to kick. You best borrow my piece."

"Your piece?"

"My firearm, cowboy."

"Oh well. That won't be necessary—I have my father's gun. Anyway, Matt and some folks cleaned the trailer, it looks almost good as new, and there hasn't been any more trouble. According to Matt, Luke is in Louisiana torturing crawfish. But for now, it'd be better if I came into town."

"I'd like to torture his crawfish."

Lee was silent as he tried to picture this.

"Doesn't make no matter, bro," Marcus said. "I want you to come here anyway."

They agreed on 10:00 Sunday morning. Anything earlier was too early, in Lee's opinion; in fact, 10:00 was a little early. But Lee wanted to see Del and the boys before they left for church. Marcus explained they might have left by then. "She likes to get there early to socialize, help out while the boys are in Sunday School. Now that she's started back to church, she's gone whole hog!"

THE next morning, Lee was apprehensive about leaving Margo alone at the trailer. Now that he thought about it, she hadn't been alone in the trailer since the "attack." But were they going to go on forever fearing that Luke would show up—and do what? Shit on the new picnic table? It was a battle between reason and his instincts. Reason said Margo would be fine for a couple of hours on a Sunday morning; they had to get back to normalcy, whatever that was. But his instincts told him not to take any chances. She could come with him. But Marcus had something he wanted to talk to him about, not have a social visit. He could drop her off somewhere. The mall, which she hated? Maybe Sarabeth and Lyle's? But when he asked her how she'd feel about visiting them while he got together with Marcus, she looked at him ruefully. "You think I'm afraid to stay here by myself. I'm not. I've stayed here alone plenty, in case you've forgotten."

"But that was 'before.' I just want you to be safe. I'm going to put Matt's number on a Post-it note and leave it right here." He scribbled it out and taped it to the countertop. "Call him if you need to. He can be here in two minutes."

"If he runs."

"He would. He would. And do you remember where the gun is?"

"Geez, Lee. Under my size five cotton-crotch polka-dot blue Jockey undies in the top drawer. You're beginning to get on my nerves. I promise you. I'll be fine. And truth be told, I wouldn't mind a little time to myself around here. Since the 'artwork,' we've been glued together like peanut butter and jelly. Tell Marcus I send greetings."

"Well, okay. But keep your phone handy." He turned to Smoky, who was watching this conversation intently. "Take good care of Mama, Smoke."

Smoky made eye contact with Lee. "I will!" he said with his brown eyes. "You can count on me!"

Lee kissed Margo goodbye, listened for the click of the door lock, and backed the Camry out the driveway. Turning onto Hidden Valley Road, he checked as he passed the Dunlap house to see if Matt's pickup was in the yard; yes, good. He turned on the county road toward Greenville. It has to be all right, he told himself. He'd only be gone a couple of hours, if that. They couldn't let Luke have so much power over their lives. He cursed him under his breath for a mile or two. Had Luke known how much he would disrupt their sense of peace and safety?

Oh. Yeah. That was the point.

H E pulled up in front of the McBees' rental house in Nichol-town where he'd first confronted Marcus about hitting Del and accused him, falsely, of puncturing his own tires. He remembered how Marcus had made' him ice tea and how awful it was. He braced for Maybell as he went up the railless stairs. Marcus could surely ask the landlord to put a rail up, but then from the looks of the place, his landlord wasn't the type to concern himself with such niceties, even safety-related ones.

Bark, bark, bark. Marcus opened the door, and Maybell rushed out to lick the back of Lee's extended hand. She was such a pushover, all bark and hopefully no bite. Marcus, in gray sweatpants and a Clemson sweatshirt, big, strong, young, grasped Lee's hand, but instead of shaking it pulled him into a quick chest-bump, reminiscent of an Obama greeting he'd seen on TV, only in Obama's case, it was with Kevin Durant.

"Good to see you, man! Where you been keeping yo-self?"

Lee explained that he and Margo had taken a little trip to Minneapolis so he could meet her family. "And them me."

"Are those wedding bells I hear?"

Lee just smiled. Just then Del came rushing out from the back of the house, dressed for church in a red-and-black plaid suit, a black bowler hat with a matching plaid ribbon, and high heels that lifted her a couple of inches above Lee. "Uncle Lee," she exclaimed, giving him a big hug. "We been missing your ass!"

Just then the twins ran in shouting in unison, "Uncle Lee's ass! Uncle Lee's ass!" Lee gave them each a high five.

"Language," Del warned.

"But you said it!" Jackson argued.

"And you can too when you get to be my age." She turned to Lee. "I hate to rush off, Uncle Lee," she said, grinning. "But we're going to be late for church if we don't leave five minutes ago."

"Not even Jesus showing up could stop Del from going to church," Marcus remarked.

"Marcus's been singing in the choir," Del said, "but he asked for a pass today." She put on a pouty face as she gave him a peck on the cheek.

"We all have a cross to bear," Marcus teased and pulled her to him for a better kiss. She swatted him off.

After Del and the boys left, Lee said, "Seems like things are going pretty good with you and Del."

"Like they say in AA, one day at a time. And like the preacher says, 'If your wife ain't happy, you better find out why and do sumthin' about it.'"

"That's good preaching," Lee said. "I think that's in the Bible somewhere."

"W E gonna go for a little ride, Mr. Lee," Marcus announced. That epithet captured Marcus perfectly for Lee: how he could combine respect, satire, affection, and teasing all at once.

"Just call me Dad," Lee said, and Marcus snorted. They went through the yard to Marcus's Pontiac. When he fired it up, Lee congratulated him on finally getting the muffler fixed.

"I figured it was time. It fell off." Again the big laugh. "I didn't want no cop pulling me over at night."

"Amen to that. Where we going? You're not kidnapping me for ransom, are you?"

"I figure you're not worth forty years in jail."

It was a gray overcast fall day with rain in the forecast. "Might get a thunderstorm," Lee remarked, to which Marcus gave the usual refrain: "We need the rain." They wove through

Nicholtown and turned onto South Pleasantburg Drive. After a dozen or so right turns and too-many-to-count lefts, they pulled to a stop in front of an older red-brick house, circa 1970s, two stories, with a weedy front lawn and a "For Sale" sign in the yard. They parked on the curb in front beside a large maple with brilliant red leaves.

"What neighborhood is this?" Lee asked.

"Beats me." Marcus paused. "I might buy this house."

Lee rubbernecked around to look at it better. "Wow" was all he could come up with. Then, "How much?"

"$197,500. The real estate agent says it's a bargain. The owners moved to Georgia or some damn place and are hot to sell."

"Wow," Lee said again. "That sounds like a real estate agent. That's a lot of money, Marcus."

"Thanks, Daddy. I didn't know that." He reached over and punched Lee in the upper arm.

"Buying a house . . . That's a huge commitment. There are a lot of expenses to owning a house."

"Aww, I'm just pulling your dick, Daddy. I wouldn't buy this house—even if I could. Which I cain't. I just like to drive by houses for sale and think about the day I'll be able to buy me one. Don't you worry, Daddy Downer. I ain't gonna jump off no cliff." He was silent as they both stared out the car window at the house. "I grew up in rundown public hous-ing. Water stains on the walls, cracked linoleum. Paper-thin walls. Smelled like damn Lysol all the time. To this day, the smell of Lysol makes me sick to my stomach. I told Del never bring Lysol in the house!"

They sat in silence. Lee noticed how the cumulus clouds to the West were moving fast, darkening into an ominous gray. The approaching storm pushed the fresh scent of ozone through their half-open windows.

Then like a sudden squall himself, Marcus exclaimed, "I want my boys to have a real house! Like this one. I want to provide for them. Not like my old man. A total piece of shit! A total fucking drunk! And a mean one! The only time he came 'round was to ask Mama for money and slap her around. I wanted to stay in school! Go to college. It was just Mama and me. She got sick, and I had to drop out. Got me a job delivering for an office supply company downtown. And you know what that asshole did? He asked me for money! For liquor. A sixteen-year-old kid with five dollars in his pocket and a sick mama."

As if on cue, there was a loud thunder clap, and suddenly rain was coming down with frightening force, whipping the red leaves off the maple. There was wind, there was thunder, there was lightning. In a matter of minutes, water filled the street. It rushed around the car as if it sat in the middle of a creek. The windshield became a waterfall.

"We got us a storm," Marcus announced.

"Looks like it," Lee agreed.

"Can't do nothing but ride it out," Marcus said as the sky gods vented their fury. He turned the windshield wipers on high, but when they couldn't keep up with the deluge, he switched them off, as well as the car engine. "Might as well save a little gas."

"What did you want to talk to me about?" Lee asked.

"I haven't forgotten. Here is what: I got a call from my old boss, Mr. Snoddy. He always liked me. Said he wished he could of hired ten like me."

"So I've heard."

Marcus looked over at him. "Huh?" They were encased in the cave of the car, the rain hammering outside, but it was dry and even cozy inside.

"Del. She's proud of you."

"Sometimes." Marcus snorted, his response to a lot of things.

"Anyway," he resumed, "Mr. Snoddy—what a name!—called. Said the parts department's in a mess! That white guy who wanted my job! Insisted he could do it!"—here Marcus practically hooted with glee—"couldn't handle it, the fool, messed everything up, and now nobody can find doohickey, and customers are mad! Mad! Wants me to come back. For more money!"

"Wow," said Lee, feeling like a broken record, his head spinning.

"But . . ." Marcus looked over at him again with raised eyebrows, "he's got a condition."

Lee waited, determined not say "wow" again.

"Snoddy says I got to go to AA or some other counseling thing, he don't care. I just gotta go. On account of that incident out behind the building. Every week. That's the deal."

"I thought you'd been going to meetings with Sammy."

Marcus was peering at him with emotions Lee had trouble unpacking: He was obviously enjoying surprising Lee with this news, but behind that excited facade, anxiety was writ large.

"I did, for a while."

"But this is good news, isn't it? I mean, congratulations!" When Marcus didn't respond, Lee said, "It is good news, right? You've been to meetings before. You can go again, right?"

Marcus stared out the front window. The rain was

slowing, running out of gas. The front windshield was plastered with red leaves.

"So what's the problem?"

Marcus clenched his jaw. "I'm scared," he finally said so softly Lee wasn't sure he heard him.

"Scared? Of what?"

Marcus gripped the steering wheel. "Being no count. Just like my dad. Loving' the sauce…" His voice caught. "That job at Fisher's? I already lost it once."

A thousand responses ran through Lee's mind. The predictable things, the easy things, the encouraging things, the unhelpful things. How Marcus would have a lot of support… if anyone can do this, Marcus… you're stronger than you think… Those kinds of responses. But he didn't speak.

They sat in silence. "The rain's letting up," Lee finally said. They were silent, listening to the downpour play itself out until it was nothing more than a few exhausted drops. "I don't know if you've been in touch with Sammy lately," he said.

Marcus shook his head.

"The latest CAT scan showed two spots on his lungs."

Marcus looked over at Lee. His face squinched into a severe frown. "I'm real sorry to hear that. Real *real* sorry."

"Me too," Lee said. They were silent again, and then Lee said, "Looks like the rain is stopping. How would you like to drive out to Lake Hartwell and pay him a visit? I've been meaning to go. You got the time?"

Marcus turned the windshield wipers back on, scattering the red leaves. "Point the way."

THEY drove south on I-85 without speaking. Lee called Margo on his cell phone. She answered immediately and asked what was up. He explained he just wanted to check on her.

"I'm exactly the way I was when you left," she said. "Fine! I'm getting a lot done around here —like cleaning out our closet and moving some summer things into Lyle's closet. Are you still at Marcus's?"

He explained that they were on their way to Lake Hartwell to see Sammy.

"That's good," she said. "It gives me more time to whip this place into shape."

"It's so nice to be missed!" Lee said. He felt relieved and determined to stop being such a nervous ninny.

"I'VE never been to Lake Hartwell," Marcus remarked.

"Well, now you have."

"I have? Where's the lake?" They had taken the Clemson exit off I-85 South, and after driving a few miles through pleasant open land, they'd turned left on Sandy Springs Road and were now driving down a narrow road with rugged wooded hills on the left and a ravine on the right. Scattered randomly and spaced widely throughout the woods on both sides were trailers, rustic cabins, modest two-bedroom homes, and here and there an expensive-looking vacation house.

"So where's the lake?"

"Down that hillside somewhere. The lake's not all big open water. There are coves, creeks, fingers of the lake. And obviously no zoning."

"I'm gonna get me a Lake Harwell house!" Marcus announced, punching Lee again in the upper arm. He was going to have a bruise there. "You think many of my kind have places out here?"

"About as many as in Blue Ridge. But I hear Lake Hart-well has several state parks with camping, picnic tables, trails. I bet the boys would enjoy camping."

Marcus gave his trademark snort. "I can just imagine the great night's doze I'd get in a tent out here in Whiteville."

"This isn't a natural lake," Lee said. "It's manmade. They dammed the Savannah River, flooded a huge area. For hydro-power and recreation. There's a whole town underwater somewhere at the bottom of the lake. Andersonville."

"You telling me they flooded houses and stores and churches and folks' graves?" Marcus stared out the window, giving a low whistle.

They had come to a section of road that crossed between two large bodies of open blue water.

"This area was first inhabited by Cherokee Indians. They called it the Center of the World. It was, I guess, of their world."

"Indians always getting the shaft. Just like Black folk."

"I can't argue with that," Lee said.

They were lost. They had taken several wrong turns through residential neighborhoods, Marcus shaking his cell phone; his GPS was hopelessly confused, possibly having given up. They finally came to Ridgeland Road, which Lee thought he recognized. It dead-ended in a T. They decided to try right, until they came to what Lee thought was Sammy's road: Howell Point Drive. "That's the name!" Lee exclaimed. "We have arrived."

THEY went down a steep drive and pulled into a large open area suitable for five or six cars, though only one car was parked there: Sammy's red Corvette ZR1. The house was one-story, white, with two dormer windows on the low roof and an open porch across the front with two old-timey rockers. A large American flag was hoisted on one side of the porch.

Lee had called Sammy on the way out, and he'd said to come on, he was expecting them, even though he wasn't. Lee tooted the horn and was relieved when Sammy came out on the porch, looking the same as always except half his scalp was shaved and bandaged. He had lost a little weight, Lee noted. Sammy didn't appear sick, except for the scalping, and as for the spots on his lungs—they would have to learn more about that. He greeted them heartily, in his usual Sammy way. "Guys! Welcome to my piece of paradise!"

"What would a place like this run you?" Marcus asked, to Lee's embarrassment. Not that he wouldn't mind knowing himself, though he wouldn't have the balls to ask.

"I'll sell it to you cheap when I'm dead," Sammy replied, and Marcus looked stricken. "Don't look so grim, my friend. I'm just messing with ya. But don't start packing your shit yet. You wouldn't believe all the fun the cancer guys have in store for me. They don't give up without a fight. Now, how'd you like a tour? The $1.50 or the $5.00 one?"

Marcus, subdued, embarrassed no doubt, just nodded. They went around the house, which was set in a stand of tall hardwoods, and came out facing a pond of greenish water down a steep hill. "That's part of Three and Twenty Creek," Sammy said. "When I was looking for a place to buy, this one shouted my name. That's my runabout down there." He pointed to a small boat tied to a dock down the steep hill. "I can access open water in five minutes but back here, I get a ton of birds. Loons, wood ducks, herons . . ."

"Sure is a nice place," Marcus said, a bit sheepishly.

"Let me show you my man cave," Sammy said, leading

them through an access door into an unfinished storage room that resembled a private flea market, full of whatever might come in handy "someday." He opened an interior door into a large recreation room with a faux leather couch and two deep swivel armchairs, a high top bar with four stools, a 75" TV, an assortment of Clemson flags and banners tacked to the wall, and a gas fireplace with faux logs. "I have good friends and neighbors around Hartwell," Sammy said. "And we've had us some good times down here. In the winter we turn on the fireplace and tip a few. Of course mine is root beer." He raised his bushy white eyebrows, giving Marcus a significant look.

They went upstairs to an open living room/dining room combination, a large eat-in kitchen that opened onto a deck facing the creek, a master bedroom and bath with a walk-in laundry. There were two more small bedrooms with what Sammy called a Jack-and-Jill bath upstairs. Sammy really did have a great place, Lee noted. He'd been a successful plumber with his own business. "I bought when the buying was good," he told Marcus. "I paid about a fourth of what the place would go for today."

To which Marcus gave an appreciative whistle.

T H E Y sat down on the deck overlooking Three and Twenty Creek. The weather had cleared, but it brought a cold front with it, the feel of fall, and they kept their jackets on.

"Autumn is truly upon us," Sammy mused. He served them Coke in beer steins he had collected in "before" time and a bowl of microwave popcorn. He was bare-headed, while Lee and Marcus wore baseball caps. Lee worried Sammy would catch a chill out here in the elements, but he seemed undaunted.

"Time for 'the talk,'" Lee said after they had caught up for a while. "Tell us what's going on with your health, Sammy."

"How much time you got?"

"We got time, man," Marcus said. "We got all day."

"Well," Sammy said, looking out at the green pond. "Those spots they found on my lung on my last scan? They've grown. The lower lobe from four millimeters to six and the upper one from two millimeters to . . . I forget. Anyway, they say they're very small. Which is good. They could be any number of things—scar tissue, benign tumors, fairy dust—but they want to know. Turns out I really hit the jackpot having melanoma on my head. A whole city of lymph nodes and blood vessels up there—like Grand Central Station for cancer looking to catch the next train out to your lungs, your liver, your brain."

Lee and Marcus were silent.

"Come on, you guys. I don't feel sick. Just scared. I figure that's par for the course. Anyway—they want to 'go in.' Do a little slicing and dicing."

"To get rid of it?" Marcus said, his voice rising hopefully.

"It could be benign, didn't you say?" Lee added.

"Or it could be malignant." Sammy gave them a slow, sweet smile, as if understanding that he needed to bring the children along slowly.

"And then?" Lee asked.

"Oh you'd be amazed at all the tricks and treatments they got in their doctor bags," Sammy said. "They love clinical trials, probably sign me up for two or three. But enough about me. How you doing with your sobriety, Marcus my man? I miss you at meetings."

"I'm holding . . . But . . ."

"You're afraid of slipping." Sammy turned to look at

Marcus, and his face, so weathered and aged now that Lee really saw it, was a study in compassion. There was no other word for it.

Marcus nodded. "You got it, man."

They sat in silence for a bit. Then Lee said, "Tell Sammy about Mr. Snoddy."

"What a name!" Sammy said. "I remember you telling me about him. How he wished he could hire ten of you."

Marcus and Lee exchanged a look.

"He wants me to come back. To Fisher's. For more money. To run the parts department." Marcus paused, as if waiting for the congratulations that didn't come.

"And you're afraid you'll blow it," Sammy said. "You'll go off the rails."

Marcus nodded.

"Do you believe in God?" Sammy asked.

Lee had never known Sammy to talk religion or God. But maybe cancer had made a convert of him.

"I guess," Marcus said uncertainly, as if trying for the right answer.

"I don't know that I do," Sammy said. "But I've listened to a lot of guys in AA who do. Believe. And it kept them sober, some of them. I've been feeling it a lot more now that I'm down here in the . . . What's the word," he turned to Lee.

"Foxhole."

"Yeah. I've felt something that might be God. Or something divine, let's just say. Sometimes I pray. Not asking to be healed. Just to . . . commune. Not to feel alone. To ask for guidance. And strength." He paused for a long moment. "You could try that too, Marcus. I'm just saying."

IT was time to go. Sammy walked Lee and Marcus out to Marcus's car. There were hugs, man hugs, Marcus joked, but Lee noticed he held on to Sammy the longest and hardest. Tears glazed his eyes. "Thank you, man," he said, his voice clotted. "For . . . everything."

"Anytime."

"Margo and I are getting married, Sammy," Lee said. "I hope you'll come to the wedding. Be my best man—like always."

"Aww shucks, Lee. I was hoping for flower girl."

LEE and Marcus drove out the narrow dirt road to the main asphalt road. They were silent until they got to a stop sign, and Lee wasn't sure whether to turn right or left. Marcus put his address in the GPS on his phone, which had recovered its mind, and after a few twists and turns they were on the straight shot of I-85 back into Greenville.

"Congratulations," Marcus said after they had driven a few miles.

Lee looked over at him. "For?"

"Getting married, man. Best thing I ever did."

"Thanks. I believe that'll hold true for me too." Lee was silent for a moment and then said, "You know how you told me about your father, Marcus? In front of that house you're never going to buy—which I'm relieved about."

"Thanks, Dad."

"Well, now I want to tell you about my father."

"Your dad?" Marcus glanced over at him with raised eyebrows. "Okay then. Shoot."

"My daddy disappeared when I was six. I never saw him again. He killed himself."

"Say what?"

"I'd loved him, and then he beat me. When I was six. I hated him after that."

"You say he killed hisself?"

"He was part of a lynch mob that snatched a Black man out of the Pickens jail. They thought he'd killed a white cabbie."

"Man!"

"They took him out to the woods and beat and stabbed a confession out of him. Then finished him off with a shotgun." Lee was silent. "My father committed suicide after that."

"That's dark, man!"

"For a lot of my life, I lived that darkness."

They rode in silence until they took the Mills Avenue exit into Greenville.

"Your daddy lynched a Black man!" Marcus exclaimed. "That's dark all right, man!"

"I'll say," Lee agreed. "Real dark."

Marcus looked over at him. "But you're not your dad, Lee. I can testify to that."

"And neither are you, Marcus. Neither are you."

CHAPTER TWENTY-EIGHT

THEY WERE HAVING a party.

The invitations, gala Hallmark "Please Come!" cards, decorated with colorful balloons, had been mailed to their friends and family, who were now gathered at the trailer on this chilly early November evening. The recipients were invited to celebrate Margo's seventieth birthday. No presents allowed, just your presence! But Lee and Margo had an ulterior motive for this party: in addition to celebrating Margo's birthday, they were going to get married. At the party. Surprise!

THEY hadn't really thought about who could marry them. All they really knew was that they wanted to get married, and they wanted to do it as a surprise at Margo's birthday party. It wasn't as if they didn't know about weddings. But they didn't know the playbook for this kind of wedding.

They'd looked over the list of notaries the clerk had given them when they applied for their marriage license. There were several who had websites, so Margo got out her iPad.

The Marriage Notary advertised "A Stand-up Celebration."

"As opposed to a lying down one," Lee said.

Margo hit him with the list. "Here's one: 'Ask me about a $100 flat fee. Flexible and accommodating; open to any kind of service—religious or secular; formal or casual; LGBTQ welcome.'"

"That's nice, not to mention amazing," Lee mused. "Two years ago gay marriages were illegal in South Carolina."

"Here's another one. 'Just make it legal. Sign your papers in our strategically-enhanced Butterfly Garden. Also finger-printing service.'"

Lee slipped down on the couch, extending his legs out straight and tilting his head back on the scrunched-down back cushion. "Wake me when it's over."

"Here's one in Greer. Maybe she'd be willing to come up to Blue Ridge for a strategically- enhanced fee."

The next day Margo called the notary, Peggy Sue Johnson-Reid. The date of course was easy: Margo's birthdate: November 5, luckily a Saturday night. The Presidential election was coming up on November 8. Lee was glad they could have the wedding and party before the election; he didn't believe for one moment that Trump would be elected, but the proliferation of "Make American Great Again" signs in the Upstate made him nervous. Margo left a message on voicemail, and Peggy Sue called back that night . . . out all day marrying people, Lee speculated. Margo, feeling unexpectedly nervous, explained the plan, the birthday party, the surprise wedding. "That sounds wonderful!" Peggy Sue said. Then, all business, "I normally charge $100 if you're within ten miles of a 29607 address."

"We're not in town," Margo said. "We live in Blue Ridge; it takes about thirty minutes to get here. Will that be a problem?"

There was a long pause. "Will it be during the day or at night?"

By now Margo was determined that Peggy Sue had to marry them. She liked the sound of her voice and how she had said "wonderful!" They negotiated the price, $150.00, but Peggy Sue expressed some concern about driving up to Blue Ridge at night. "I know it's asking a lot," Margo said, "but I feel it has to be you!"

Peggy Sue laughed and said she would get her husband to bring her. She explained that she was into weddings; she had had four herself. It was not that she was just a notary who performed marriage ceremonies as a job. She was a love-promoter. She believed in love. "I do too," Margo said happily. "I'm in love." She had found the right person to marry them. Peggy asked if they were writing their own vows or if they'd like her to send a couple of standard ones.

"We'll do our own," Margo said decisively. She said she'd mail Peggy Sue directions. "We'll see you on the 5th around 6:30 then. We'll plan on the ceremony a little after that. It won't take long, and you won't be out late."

"That's so thoughtful," Peggy Sue said agreeably. "And if you have any questions or requests, call me. Otherwise, see you in early November."

"S O you're writing our marriage vows," Lee said when Margo hung up the phone.

"No, *we're* writing our vows," Margo said. "It'll be fun. And meaningful."

"Can this marriage be saved?" Lee said theatrically. "I'm not much of a writer, you know. Can't we just get some standard ones off the internet?"

Margo rolled her eyes. "Of course there will be the usual vows, the 'do you take' stuff, the have and hold, for better or worse, for richer, poorer, *etcetera* 'til death do us part."

"I do," Lee said. "I'll just be nervous to say so in public."

"You'll be among friends and family," Margo said. "Oh this'll be fun!

ON November 5, at 6:40, they heard a car pull into the driveway at the trailer. Peggy Sue and her husband knocked on the trailer door. At first Smoky set to barking, but as soon as Lee opened the door, he began sniffing them excitedly. Wow, what a bouquet! Peggy Sue explained that they loved dogs: they had three, a cockapoo, a Schnauzer, and a wiener dog. Peggy Sue's husband, who was a small, black-haired man with a pencil mustache, knelt down and ruffled Smoky's nape, and Smoky licked his face. The guests, already gathered, grew quiet at the sight of unexpected strangers. A Keith Jarrett record, *Facing You*, played in the background.

Peggy Sue was a big woman, dressed prettily in a pink suit, with eyelash extensions and dark hair growing out from her last blonde dye job. She had a big smile, and she and Margo embraced like long-lost friends.

"Everybody," Lee said, "let me introduce you to our friends, Peggy Sue and . . ."

"Hugo," the husband rescued. The guests—Sarabeth and Del (Jackson and James were at a sleepover) were sitting on the couch sipping ginger ale, Joey and Buster from the Lunch Bunch, along with Lyle, had pulled out chairs from the dining table and were drinking beers. Sammy and Marcus were catching up in the kitchen over Diet Cokes. All were a little mystified that they had never heard of these friends, but they greeted Peggy Sue and Hugo heartily, lifting their drinks toward them in welcome. Peggy Sue in her pink suit stepped to the end of the living room and faced the group: "May I have your attention please?" A surprised hush fell over the guests.

"I suppose you're wondering why I've gathered you all together here tonight," she began, grinning at the very little joke. Sammy called out, "And I bet you're gonna tell us!" The others, in good spirits and wondering what was going on, laughed.

"I am indeed," said Peggy Sue, who was apparently accustomed to commanding a crowd, even a small one like this. She motioned Margo and Lee to join her. They stood on either side of her, Margo in an ivory dress with lace sleeves, Lee in a navy Perry Como style cardigan sweater. Lee was sweating on his forehead, feeling a little weak in the knees. "I know you know you've been invited here tonight to celebrate a special seventieth birthday. So here's to Margo: Happy happy birthday, Margo!"

The group, still mystified but in good spirits, lifted their glasses and sang a spirited Happy Birthday song, with Marcus in his deepest voice adding "And many more!" Everyone clapped, and Lyle raised his glass: "Margo, the secret to staying young is to live honestly, eat slowly, and lie about your age! To Margo!"

"To Margo!" people cheered.

"I think I can do that last one," Margo said.

"Birthday kiss, birthday kiss," Del started up a chant, and Lee, feeling shy and happy, stepped over to take Margo in his arms and kiss her on the lips. When he released her, the crowd applauded, Lee blushing as Margo said "again!"

After the second kiss to applause, Peggy Sue called out, "Order in the courtroom! We have other business."

"Oh my God!" Sarabeth exclaimed. "She's here to marry them!"

There was a moment of stunned silence as the guests caught on. Lyle called out, "Dang! The old man is tying the knot!"

"Hurrah!" several people cheered.

Peggy Sue told Lee and Margo to stand facing each other before her. The group quieted, and Peggy Sue began:

"Family and friends of Margo and Lee, welcome and thank you for being here on this important occasion. We are gathered together to celebrate the very special love between Margo and Lee, by joining them in marriage."

(Old-man tears filled Lee's eyes.)

"There will be no dearly beloved, no betrothed, and no ancient rhyme of the married. For this day, the day of Margo and Lee's wedding, is about love."

There was a hush in the room. Lee and Margo were looking into each other's eyes.

"Someone once wrote, 'If love is not all, then it is nothing. If love is all, then it is everything.' Love isn't just a word, it's an action. Love isn't something you say, it's something you do. We're gathered here today because Margo and Lee have decided they love each other so much"—she paused slightly—"that they want to get the government involved."

Laughter.

"It's time to exchange your vows."

With shaking hands and voice, Margo read from a note card, pausing between each line to look Lee in the eyes: "Lee Trammell, you are the light of my life. You are my dream come true. You're my best friend and one true love. I get to laugh with you and cry with you. I get to care for you and share my life with you. I will love you 'til my dying day and beyond."

Now Lee, tears blinding him, wiped his eyes with his handkerchief and took several deep breaths. He wondered if he could get through this. He took out his card. "Margo, you are my one true love, and I will love you forever . . ." at which point Lyle called out "Make that *ad infinitum!*" Lee looked startled and then he grinned. "Right, Lyle. Margo, I will love you *ad infinitum!* I never dreamed you'd come to Blue Ridge and claim me. Thank you for that." Now his voice faltered, and Peggy Sue reached over and patted him on the arm, giving him time to collect himself. "Margo, there is no one better than you. I love you with my whole heart. You've loved me with a love I'd never experienced before and didn't even know existed. Thank you." He paused. "I will try to earn that love every day, to support you in all things, and to remember to put the toilet seat down." Laughter. "Amen, brother," Sammy called out.

"Please repeat after me," Peggy Sue intoned.

"Margo, do you take Lee to be your partner in marriage, to live together in matrimony, to love, honor, comfort and keep, in sickness and in health, for as long as you both shall live?"

"I do."

"Lee, do you take Margo to be your partner in marriage, to live together in matrimony, to love, honor, comfort and keep, in sickness and in health, for as long as you both shall live?"

"I do."

"By the authority vested in me, and in accordance with the laws of the state of South Carolina, it is my honor to now pronounce that you are married to each other. You may now kiss to seal your vows."

Lee took Margo in his arms and kissed her, and Smoky went nuts, barking and rushing up to them to try to get in on the action. Their friends clapped and came forward to congratulate them, hugs and pats on the back all around.

MARGO had invited Peggy Sue and Hugo to stay for dinner, but they declined, saying they needed to get back to let the dogs out. Margo wrote the check with a generous tip, and she and Lee walked them out to their car. Margo told them she and Lee couldn't be more pleased with how things had gone, and she and Peggy Sue embraced. "You made it through," Hugo said to Lee, patting him on the back. Lee waited for the familiar "old man," but instead Hugo said, "I just hope you'll be as happy as Peggy Sue and I are."

Lee helped Hugo back out of the drive, and he and Margo stood on the blacktop of Hidden Valley Road and watched as they drove away in the dark toward the county highway.

"Do you think they'll get lost?" Margo asked.

"Yes," Lee said, putting his arms around her and drawing her close. "But like the rest of us, they'll find their way home."

"That's kind of profound," Margo said, snuggling against his chest. It was a chilly night. The trailer's front porch light cast a small semicircle in the darkness.

"Marriage has turned me into a philosopher."

"Uh oh, "Margo said. "But maybe we should go in. I forget how dark it can get out here."

"Well, at least Halloween is over," Lee said, holding her tighter, "so there aren't any goblins and ghosts in the forest." But something about the dark woods made him uneasy. He wished he had brought Smoky out, but he was too interested in what was going on in the kitchen, hoping to get anything that dropped on the floor. He was glad he'd asked Marcus and Del to drive out with Lyle and Sarabeth. He still didn't want a McBee car in the yard.

"Are there any stars?" Margo asked, tilting back her head.

Lee looked up too. But it was still too early for the whole starry show. That would come later that night.

NOW it was time for a feast. Margo had told people not to bring anything, but of course, no one listened to that. Del brought baked potatoes with all the toppings, Sammy chips and salsa, Joey store-bought potato salad and slaw, and Buster watermelon chunks; Margo had made a big pan of lasagna. Sarabeth brought a bakery birthday cake with "Happy 70th Birthday, Margo!" written in pink script on a white cake with green icing. Marcus brought chicken wings and spareribs pre-cooked long and slow in the oven to finish on the grill.

Marcus pronounced himself a grill master, and the men stood around to supervise under the back porch light. Lee had bought a Charbroil grill when Lyle first came to live with him; he had imagined them cooking steaks in the backyard, but somehow that never happened. After Lyle moved out, what was the point of grilling for one? Plus Lee was afraid of the grill. The *whoosh* when he pushed the starter button sounded like a small explosion.

"When's the last time you cooked on this thing?" Marcus asked, lifting the lid.

"Let's see," Lee said. "What year is this?"

"Don't mind him," Lyle said. "I checked it out. I got a new propane tank, and I cleaned the grates with fatback. This puppy fired up like it was about to take off at the Indy 500."

"Okay," Marcus commanded. "Stand back! I'm turning the thing on!"

Lee hopped back a few steps.

Whoosh!

"Jesus," Sammy exclaimed.

"I see what you mean," Marcus said.

"Is it safe?" Lee asked.

"That's just the way it starts," Marcus said, adjusting the knobs. "See? It's calmed down."

"Thank God."

Del, Margo, and Sarabeth brought out chips and salsa and trays of chicken wings and ribs and set them on the picnic table. Smoky followed close behind. He was very interested in chicken and meat.

"I'll do the wings first," Marcus was telling Del, "and then the ribs will take . . ."

Suddenly Smoky began growling, a low guttural sound that stopped all conversation. All heads turned toward the dog, who was staring at the backwoods, his hackles raised, lips drawn back to reveal sharp fangs.

Lee, shocked, yelled, "Smoky, no!" But before he could get to him, Smoky was racing toward the back of the yard. There, a small figure dressed in black, the hoodie of his sweatshirt pulled over his head, had emerged from the forest, carrying an assault rifle.

THEY say when you're about to die your life flashes before your eyes. Lee had heard this, but now he found it wasn't true. What was true was how much knowledge could flash through your mind in the nanosecond before a trigger is pulled and none of it is about the past. He knew immediately the easy stuff: that this figure was Luke, that the first killed would be Marcus, then Lee and the other men, then Del, Margo, and Sarabeth. You couldn't call it "thinking" because thinking was so slow, and this knowledge was instantaneous, like the tail of a comet streaming eons of knowledge in its gaseous streak. It carried with it Jackson and James, orphans now, and Sarabeth and Lyle's parentless child, and what so many others have felt when confronted with an assault rifle: disbelief, horror, and most of all the anguished cry: *Why?*

"NO!" Lee was screaming and running toward Luke, who had stepped into the yard, and was raising the rifle. "No! Stop! Luke, don't!"

The others behind him at the grill had frozen. Not believing. Not able to. "Get down!" Lee was screaming back at them, and just then Smoky leaped to clamp his teeth on Luke's forearm, throwing off his aim. A shot went wild, and Smoky and Luke were wrestling, Luke yelling in pain, cursing, trying to fling Smoky off his arm. "Luke, don't! Luke, drop the gun!" Lee was screaming, but before he could reach them, Smoky was flung to the ground, the *rattatat* of the assault rifle, Smoky's sharp yelp of pain, Lee's "Noooo!" and then Smoky lay still as the bullets pummeled him on the ground.

Luke turned the rifle toward Lee, who stopped ten feet short of him, hands in the air. "Luke, don't do this!" A shot rang out. Surprise bloomed on Luke's face. He took a step or two toward Lee, the rifle dropping from his hands, and then, like a tree falling, he went face first to the ground.

Lee's knees gave out. He sank to the grass, burying his face in his hands, harsh sounds erupting from his mouth.

After a few minutes or an eternity, he felt a hand on his shoulder. He looked up into Matt's stark face.

"You! You shot him!"

"I did."

Lee didn't trust his legs to stand up. They were weight-less, useless.

Finally, with Matt's firm arm around his shoulders, he got shakily to his feet. He turned and looked back.

There the faces of his family and friends were spotlighted under the back porch light, as if on a stage surrounded by darkness. And in another of those nanoseconds of blinding knowledge, Lee understood how they all had almost died by hate-filled, meaningless bursts of gunfire— as so many have and so many will.

HE turned then and walked over to where Smoky's body lay on the ground. He knelt down and buried his face in the black fur. "Good boy," he cried. "Good good boy. Good dog."

CHAPTER TWENTY-NINE

ALL THE POLICE cars with their red and blue flashing lights had gone, the ambulance with Luke's body, police officers who had taken statements from them all, the coroner, all gone. Officer Cooper had interviewed Matt for over an hour, and he would have to go to the station tomorrow, but Cooper didn't expect him to be charged. Someone had covered Smoky's body with a blanket, and the woods were silent again.

Lee and Marcus were sitting across from Matt at the picnic table. Above them, the starry night was fading; the sky was just brightening in the East. The others had finally been allowed to go home and Margo was inside. She'd told Lee she wanted to take a shower, to try to wash away what had happened that night.

It was chilly, but none of the men wore a jacket. Every now and then, a violent shiver ran through Lee.

Matt looked across the table, meeting Lee's eyes in that direct way he had. His blue eyes were rimmed in red.

"The gun cabinet . . . The glass was broken, and . . ." He stopped, and they sat in silence. "Maybe all the military training or just—I knew. I got my MK12. I hadn't shot it since Iraq. But I always kept it ready. I ran through the empty field and came up through the woods behind your trailer. I heard the gunfire."

"When he shot Smoky."

Matt nodded. "I came up behind him. There was no time to hesitate." He paused. "I'm a good shot."

They sat in silence for a timeless time. Still the sun rose until it was daybreak.

"He was my brother," Matt said. "But I had to kill him."

"You had to, man," Marcus said softly. "You had to."

"I'm sorry about your dog," Matt said. "I'm sorry." He paused. "About everything."

Lee nodded. "Let me ask you something, Matt. Why do you have all those guns?"

Matt shook his head. "I don't know." Another silence. "I've just always loved guns. Part of our culture, I guess."

"He could have killed us all," Lee said. "He almost did."

Matt had no words.

CODA

WITHIN the month, Lee and Margo moved to Travelers Rest, first to a rental apartment, and then when Margo's house in Minneapolis sold, they bought a two-bedroom brick house in a cul-de-sac a couple of miles from town. It had a nice yard, and the neighbors were friendly and welcoming.

They lived in TR for several years, until Lee, passing eighty, developed congestive heart failure. They moved to an assisted living facility in Greenville, where they were nearer to Lyle and Sarabeth. At age eighty-four, Lee's heart gave out. A few years later, Margo moved to the skilled care section of the facility. As her needs increased and the bright light of her mind dimmed, her daughters moved her to a nursing home in Minneapolis. Her room had a view of a lake, and in her last winter, she sat in her wheelchair at the window, watching snow blanket the world below.

DEL'S wish came true: Lyle and Sarabeth had twins, weighing in at just under five pounds each, a boy and a girl. They named the boy Lyle Lee Trammell and called him Skip. The little girl they named Deborah Anne and called her Debby. They made a point of telling the kids about Lee and his wonder dog Smoky, leaving out the bad part of the story until they were young adults. Lyle received an automotive technology associate's degree in applied science from Greenville Technical College and was hired by Century BMW as an automotive technician, responsible for vehicle repair and oversight of the apprentice technicians. Sarabeth left her job as a paralegal to stay home when the kids were little, but when they started school, she went to law school. She a became a partner at the firm where she'd been a paralegal. She and Lyle were a constant support for Lee and Margo through their various transitions and challenges.

MARCUS and Del remained Lee and Margo's devoted friends, helping them with moves at various points and visiting Margo after she was alone, the same as family. They were like an aunt and uncle to Skip and Debby. Marcus maintained his sobriety, becoming a church deacon and singing in the choir. With Lyle's encouragement, he went to Greenville Tech for automotive technology and worked his way up to the title of equipment engineer specialist at BMW. Del continued with her teaching career, a popular, tough, and influential person in many teenage students' lives. Jackson graduated from Claflin University in Orangeburg, and James graduated from Allen in Columbia. James followed in his mother's footsteps and became an elementary school teacher. Jackson found his place in commercial real estate. Marcus and Del celebrated their thirtieth wedding anniversary in 2035.

SAMMY became Patient Number 1782 in 2017 in a clinical trial for the newest immunotherapy cocktail. He'd feared his age would be against him but was found to be an excellent and enthusiastic candidate. He received a twenty-seven-page document explaining his treatment plan and all the possible side effects; because the drugs hadn't been tried on humans, he was warned they might discover some new problems. At the end of the first year of the trial, his scans were cancer-free. Lee and Marcus visited often, and when the cancer returned aggressively, they stood watch at the hospital where he died in 2022. He left his lake house to Marcus and Del.

MATT sold the farm and moved to Santa Barbara County with Wendy where he grew cannabis with a legal permit in a greenhouse formerly used for orchids. He and Lee kept in touch for a couple of years, then silence.

LEE'S trailer and his two acres of land, including the forest in back, were cleared a few years after Lee sold them. Someone built a three-story, five-bedroom white plantation-style house with columns and a circular driveway in front on the property with a pool in back.

THE Dunlap farmhouse was demolished, and all the old cars, out-buildings and junk were removed. A subdivision of single-family homes, Blue Ridge Acres, was built on the land.

THE abandoned concrete block house the McBees had rented was vandalized and used for target practice. The roof eventually caved in, and the remaining shell became home to forest creatures who took up residence there.

IT wasn't long before no one remembered the previous residents of Hidden Valley Road.

ACKNOWLEDGEMENTS

EIGHT OR SO years ago when I first began doing research for my novel that became *The Empty Cell*, a friend arranged for me to meet with the Lunch Bunch, a group of Black men, Sterling High School graduates, 1956, who got together once a month at The Golden Corral for lunch. They were willing to tell me about what it was like growing up in the Jim Crow South. One of those men, Samuel D. Miller, was particularly loquacious, entertaining, and eager to talk about his upbringing, his life experiences as a Black man in Greenville, his present life, and his faith. We began to have lunch every so often at the Red Lobster, and over fried shrimp, we became good friends.

It's hard for me to imagine how I could have written *Hidden Valley Road* without Sam's stories, knowledge, and generosity (also big laugh). He's not in the novel, not one of the characters, but in a way he's all through it. (Maybe he would dispute that!) I want to thank him for being my friend, putting up with me, and for always helping me when I asked him things I wanted to know. Thank you, Sammy. You have enriched my life so much!

I also want to thank Tanesse Campbell for sharing her life stories with me. One of the reasons I wanted to move back to the South (from Minneapolis) was because I missed Black people; I wanted to have some Black friends. Tanesse filled the bill! She's warm, funny, and smart. I love her great stories and her. Thank you, Tanesse!

There are other people whom I want to acknowledge. These are those kind souls who read the book in earlier drafts. I've discerned that it's not that much fun to read a novel-in-progress (or even just parts of it) by someone who is not a *New York Times* best-selling author; in fact, it's a chore. So thank you, reader friends, for your generosity and feedback!

Thank you, Furman Professor Scott Henderson, for your in-depth review and pages of thoughtful, perceptive observations and suggestions! Invaluable! You're invaluable! Thank you, Ginger Alden, for always being a supporter and for your engaged, intelligent notes. Peyton Evans, editor unparalleled, thank you for your pithy comments and for pointing out the pink in the sunrise in the cover photograph! Thank you, Nancy Black Dillard, for stepping out of your comfort zone to read an early draft and give me honest feedback; Jesse Dillard, thank you! You gave me a real boost when you said the characters, places, and descriptions were so real and personal to you; Joan Cochran, thank you for your warm, supportive comments (and friendship); Pat Michelsen and Carolyn Bishop—thank you for pitching in and trying to set me straight about Lake Hartwell; Linda Robertson, friend of my youth, writer in your own right, cheerleader, thanks for your inspiration and *joie de vivre* through thick and thin— love you dearly. Betty, beloved sister, you have shown me your courage and character through a tough year. Thanks too to the librarians who took time to talk to me about their jobs: Joyce Rogers; and Karen Allen and Jimmy Smith of the Greenville County Library System.

I don't have adequate words to thank the people who brought the manuscript to fruition and into the world: They are the best! Proofreader and copyeditor Amanda Capps, your generous support, your tireless commitment to excellence, your advice, your engagement in the project, your wonderful self: Thank you for everything! And Alan Dino Hebel and Ian Koviak at *the*BookDesigners, you're wonderful at what you do: making books beautiful. I'd write another book just to get to work with you again. Thank you for your patience, kindness, and professionalism; they mean the world to me.

And now and forever: Thank you, Jeff, for never saying no (well, almost never . . .) and for your unwavering love.

ABOUT THE AUTHOR

Paulette Bates Alden is the author of two collections of autobiographical short stories: *Feeding the Eagles* and *Unforgettable*, along with a memoir, *Crossing the Moon*, and three novels: *The Answer to Your Question*, which won the Kindle Book Review's 2013 Best Indie Book Award in the suspense category; *The Empty Cell* (2020), which traces four characters whose lives are upended by the lynching of a young Black man in 1947; and *Hidden Valley Road*.

A former Stegner Fellow at Stanford University, she taught courses in fiction and memoir writing for many years at the University of Minnesota, where she received a Distinguished Teaching Award. She was a Jones Lecturer in Creative Writing at Stanford and a Benedict Distinguished Visiting Professor in creative writing at Carleton College. She taught many writing workshops at the Split Rock Arts Program and the Key West Literary Seminar. She now lives in Greenville, South Carolina, where she was born and raised.

If you enjoyed *Hidden Valley Road*, please post a review on Amazon and Goodreads and help pass the word by posting the link on Facebook. Thanks!

For more information, visit **www.paulettealden.com**